DESERT DREAMS

◆ ◆ ◆

BY

LONNIE BARNARD

Copyright © 2019 Lonnie Barnard

All Rights Reserved.

No part of this book may be used or reproduced by any means, graphic, electronic, or mechanical, including photocopying, recording, taping, or by any information storage retrieval system without the written permission of the publisher except in the case of brief quotations embodied in critical articles and reviews.

ISBN # 9781699227220 (Print)

CREDITS

I first would like to thank my wife, Vicky. Writers can get a little OCD and so neglect other important things. I wrote this in three months while working among all the ministry things I do. So, thank you sweetie, your patience makes this all possible.

Second, I would like to thank Edie Bakker for the hard work of editing. She did this out of love for our common bond and struggles of serving Jesus.

Third, I would like to thank Bethany Miller for her art work on the cover. Our friendship and connections in the Lord's work led to an amazing revelation, which I will discuss in the postscript.

Fourth, I would like to thank my daughter Stephanie Atkinson who started me on this whole writing journey some years ago by encouraging me often to pursue it.

There are many others also to thank and they shall remain nameless except God in Heaven knows.

Lastly, I do thank my Lord in Heaven who gifts, inspires, and fills me with His vision.

FORWARD

    This book represents a lifetime of considering why our churches have lost their impact. This discovery process prompted the writing of this book. Now with any look at effective Christianity, the Bible is our go to resource. I believe Jesus modeled the most effective teaching methods ever and that teaching has always been very hands on.

    What I mean by that is, that he trained his apostles as he walked down the roads teaching and immediately putting those teachings into hands-on demonstrations. We do well to learn from that. My challenge was to find ways to communicate this without being so confrontational with traditional church, that the methodology put churches on the defensive rather than consider the practices being taught.

    For this reason, I chose to weave the Biblical concepts into a fictional story. But the principals do apply and as you will see in the postscript, I believe are anointed. These concepts would be in vain if my readers do not look for ways to implement in their own churches and lives. For this reason, I would like to point you to my blog site (https://lonniebarnard.wordpress.com) where I will present opportunities to serve. This will be a continuing effort as it will be updated from time to time. As of now, I am still deciding on how to effectively donate and use whatever the proceeds are to places and people in need. Thank you for reading in advance and remember you will not have finished until you read the postscript.

Lonnie Barnard

CHAPTER 1.

I could see the lights of Tucson quickly fading in my rearview mirror. Slowly the mountains interrupted my view, and the lights disappeared completely in the morning mist. Finally, the sun shone brightly over the horizon of the mountaintops. We were all in. The journey had begun. I suppose it was appropriate that our journey pointed us toward Hermosillo, Mexico. Even though it was only five hours away it was an entirely different world, a city of mud huts with tin roofs, poor people barely eking out a living surviving on the barest of necessities.

All this began as I sat with my deacons in early morning prayer before our Sunday morning service.

From where I was seated my eyes looked up as James Miller prayed. I caught a glow as the sun began to just peek over the eastern horizon. That's when it hit me. I was made for much more than this. I had never been willing to settle for anything less than God's best, but there I sat, just watching the sun rise. There had to be more than this to life, so why was I settling. I bowed my head and silently prayed to God. *Whatever it takes, I am willing, just show me the way.*

As I preached that morning, I did so with a sense of tremendous relief. Two thousand people listened, and it was a rousing service. They must have sensed something had changed. I could hardly wait to get home and share the new vision God gave me, with Laura and our two boys. As we finished our lunch it was Laura who first spoke up.

"Billy what is up with you? I noticed a certain smile on your face as you first got up to preach and it hasn't left you yet.

5

What is going on?" she asked.

"I want us to pray this through first, but I think God wants me to resign at Grace Church," I replied.

"And that's why your smiling? Billy that doesn't make sense!" she remarked.

"Well Laura let me explain, at least what I know."

"OK, go ahead." She looked at me cautiously.

"You know how I'm always complaining how our people seem to be halfway Christians."

"Yeah."

"Well I made the same complaint to God. OK? He told me that if I would go all in, He would answer my question."

"How does that connect with you resigning as pastor?"

"Well you see, God's not happy with our church either."

"Now Billy how could that be," She looked surprised. "It was only ten years ago that we started this church with fifteen people. There were over two thousand there this morning."

"Laura, I don't think God defines success as numbers. I think He's more interested in quality."

"Hmm, you might be right," she said thoughtfully.

"That's just one point. I think I have a whole lot to learn and I think what He told me means that if we will go all in, He will show us what His plan really looks like," I said.

"OK, this 'all in' thing, what do you think that means?"

"I'm not really sure, yet, but you know your dad's friend, Jorge?"

"Yea."

"I keep seeing him in the vision."

"Well Billy, you know he lives in Hermosillo."

"Yeah, I know, but I keep seeing us in his house there, and then I see us on his big ranch south of there."

"Is there more to what you've seen?"

"Yeah, I see myself alone in the desert there. I think God wants to meet me there."

"Wow! Bobby? Bryan? did you hear all that? Laura announced incredulously.

Bobby and Brian, my two sons' faces brightened up immediately. "Yes mam! Let's go to Mexico! We're ready!" They both exclaimed.

"Hmm, I guess all them Spanish lessons might have been part of God's plan." Bobby, the eldest, said. "Well, at least maybe they won't go to waste!"

"Hold on family, there's a lot of praying to do. There's a lot of planning. We're not just going to jump into something. I think we should start by setting aside thirty minutes every evening to pray, and then at breakfast every morning we should report on what God is telling each of us.

CHAPTER 2.

Each day after our evening meal we prayed with the boys. All of us prayed for God to show us His will. In the morning we discussed what He had shown us in answer to those prayers.

The boys were all in for the trip, but for them it was more about the adventure. Laura and I were fearful of the great risk we could be facing, but despite the risk, it became clear that God was definitely compelling us to move in this new direction.

I summoned the courage and made an announcement to our church. After several meetings, I agreed to a one-year sabbatical. Our next six months were filled with the task of selling and disposing of most of our worldly goods including our furniture, one car, and our house. When we had everything boiled down to what we could carry in our Suburban, the journey began. On Monday morning at 5:30, January 4th, we pointed our trusty vehicle toward Hermosillo. All the arrangements were made. Jorge was expecting us in the afternoon.

Soon we came to the border crossing at Nogales and they inspected and checked our passports. We were on our way.

As we moved south of Nogales, the sun began to rise strangely to my left. The Saguaro cactus became visible and Laura looked at me.

"We are really doing this, aren't we Billy?" She said.

"Yes, we are, and we have no plans, at least not our own, just a destination."

"That's what God wants," she said.

"Yes dear, I believe that with all my heart." I glanced behind me. Both boys were sound asleep. I looked at Laura and said, "Why don't we use this next four hours to review our time at Grace Church? I think it would help us get some perspective on what plans God has for our future."

"Billy - our future - that's your department," she responded, "but I do have plenty of questions."

"OK go." I replied.

"Where did this sense of dissatisfaction come from at Grace Church?" Laura asked.

"Well it's much more than Grace Church. It's churches throughout America, at least the ones I know about. We have lost our children. We have lost our generation. Our communities are filled with crime and violence. Our government is corrupt. But when you really think about it, it is the church's responsibility to lead and promote righteousness in our world. There's no way around it. It's our fault. It's the churches fault. And if we're failing, why do we insist on doing things the same way? We have got to do something different. We've been doing our own thing."

I paused for a bit to let that sink in. Then I asked her, "Do we believe God has the answers? Because if he does, then why aren't we asking him what's wrong, instead of adding new programs, and on and on?"

"So, let me get this straight Billy," she said. "You think that at some point the church stopped listening to God and started developing their own plan?"

"Exactly Laura.

"Think about it, Laura. If we were doing church right, do you think our children, I'm talking about Christians, would feel it necessary to be deciding sexual preference at 13 years old? No way! Look at the homeless problem or drug addiction. How well are we doing with these problems? Marijuana legalization, have we gone insane? I believe it has always been the church's responsibility to counter the direction of culture. The problem is that the church itself looks like the world, instead of offering the choices that Jesus taught us in order to make a completely new world!

"The straw that broke the camel's back for me, was all

those hours I spent counseling people that seemed to have no intention of making changes that the Bible teaches are necessary, in order to solve their problems. In those last months at Grace Church I developed a strong sense that nobody really heard what I was saying. One thing for sure is that most Christians have no intention of obeying God's word, and sadly, they shake their heads and wonder why we're in such a mess.

"Then the worst part of it dawned on me. I was just like them, a hearer of the Word, not a doer. No more! Never again! If turning this around needs to start with me, I'm all in!"

"Me too! I'm with you Billy. I'm all in too!" Laura announced.

As the conversation continued, I looked out the window. "Have we been talking that long? I think I can see the tall buildings in Hermosillo." I said. "Let's pray before we get there, Laura."

"Do we have to close our eyes, Dad?" Bryan asked, wanting to join in.

"No son. Of course not. We just need to focus our mind on the Lord."

I prayed, "Here we are Jesus, just like you told us. May our newfound obedience open the doors of your plan to make a real difference in the little part of the world you have given us. Amen."

CHAPTER 3.

As Highway 15 made its way into Hermosillo, memories came rushing back to my mind. This was not our first trip there. The Catedral de la Asuncion came into view. To me, it served as a monument of Catholicism in Mexico. Most Americans would be startled at the stark contrast in Mexico between Evangelical Christianity and the Catholic church. This made me think about how far Christianity has drifted from that first church in Jerusalem. The Catholics in this region managed to blend their form of Christianity with the ancient religion of the native Yaqui Indians. There were little enclaves of evangelicals in Hermosillo who were often attacked and persecuted by the local Catholics.

We passed by the old dump grounds and you could see thousands of makeshift shanties where almost half the population lived. It used to be worse, but a semblance of prosperity had come to Hermosillo since Ford had built the stamp plant. We made our way through town past the state Capitol and as we reached the southern outskirts, we could see Jorge's fine home on the side of a hill overlooking the whole city. I opened the code on the electric gate, and as we pulled in the driveway, there was Jorge with an entourage standing in the yard. We entered the house and smelled food being prepared for us. Right away, we were escorted to a patio dining area and seated.

"Billy how was your trip?" Jorge asked immediately.

"Uneventful except for the scenery. I love the beauty of the desert, especially at this time of year when the rain has brought it into bloom." I said.

"Let's pray," said Jorge, "Now we shall eat. There will be time to talk later. I can see your boys are hungry."

"Yes sir, we are!" Bryan and Bobby exclaimed. Jorge bowed his head and we all held hands.

"Thank you, Senor, for the safe journey of my friend Billy and his family. Bless this food which you have provided and bless them as they seek to walk with you."

Hermosillo is famous for its giant flour tortillas which they call Sabaquera. We were not disappointed when they brought a plate of them to our table. Usually they come with toritos, but instead; peppers (guerro), shrimp, crab, onions (sautéed), potatoes, several kinds of cheese and traditional sauces were laid out. Each person was to place whatever they wanted on the Sabaquera. This was lunch. A choice of fruit juices was brought to quench our thirst and wash away some of burn of the peppers.

"Everyone get enough to eat?" asked Jorge, when most of the food was gone.

"Yeah!" replied the boys in unison.

"Boys, if you would like to go with my friend Juan," Jorge said, "he wants to give you a tour of the desert south of here. He will teach you the names of some the plants, and if you're lucky you may get to see some of the wildlife.

"Billy and Laura, I think we should have a serious discussion right away about God's plans for you."

"That works for us," we both smiled.

We all got up from the table. Laura and I followed Jorge into the living room and made ourselves comfortable.

"So, Billy," began Jorge. "I understand you resigned your church. You've sold pretty much everything you own, called me, and set all this up. So, what is all this about?"

"Jorge, I think this trip is about seeking God's answers to some questions which have plagued me for years," I said.

"Such as?"

"Well Jorge, I think all this started with my counseling sessions at church. I was trying to help parents deal with sons and daughters making choices of sexual preference at ages when those choices shouldn't even be on the table. And then I was working with all the issues of drug and alcohol addiction in sixteen-year-old kids. On top of that, even ten-year-old kids seemed to be ruling their families. It kind of boils down to this. Christianity in the public forum, in schools, the military and on and on, no longer seems to be a force.

"You name it," I went on. "In government, education, families, communities and everywhere, the church had become a safe place, a sanctuary for those trying to maintain some levels of morality. But now we are losing ground in leaps and bounds. The church, Christianity seems to be dying. We have to do something. I just don't know what. I think the good news is that I don't have to know. I know the One who does.

"Maybe that's why we're failing. We keep trying to come up with our own answers." I paused, and then asked rhetorically, "Why would we do that? Do we think we're that smart? Our own efforts are marked by failure.

"It is foolish to have ever taken that road. If we know the Creator of the universe, who knows everything, why wouldn't we just go to Him?"

Jorge just sat there listening intently. "I plan to make my way into the desert and take time alone, just me and God." I said. "I want to pray and wait and then pray and wait some more. Like Moses, I'm not coming out of the mountains until I have some answers."

"Sounds like a plan, my friend." Jorge nodded supportively. "When do you want to head for the ranch?"

"The sooner the better."

"Then we'll leave tomorrow," he nodded. "Do you have supplies?"

"No, but I have a list," I said.

"I'll send Juan to pick them up when he returns with the boys," he suggested.

"Perfect! Thank you so much!"

"So, Laura and the boys are going to stay at the ranch house with me and my wife?" Jorge asked.

"Yes sir, if that's okay with you and Maria."

"We'll take good care of them. You won't have nothing to worry about."

"I know that. That's one of the reasons we came here."

CHAPTER 4.

Laura and the boys took several things out of the suburban and Jorge's wife, Maria, showed them to their rooms. Meanwhile Jorge and I sat out on the patio.

"Jorge, how long does it take to get to the ranch?" I asked him.

"It takes around an hour and a half."

"Good then we will have time to do one more thing before we leave tomorrow."

"What's that?"

"Laura and I would like to visit the barrio where the poor people live," I suggested.

"Are you sure you're ready for that?" Jorge looked surprised.

"I think so."

"You know that's a pretty ugly side of Mexican culture," he said, matter of factly.

"Yeah I know. That's why we want to go there. As Americans, I think we fail to understand the poverty of much of the world. I think that etching a view of it in my mind would help me see the heart of Jesus before I begin my desert journey," I explained.

"Well, I think we can make that happen. I know you've seen the old bus sitting out back. We use that to feed the children lunch each day. Juan, or I, or whoever we have available, take that bus each day to the poorest barrio, feed the children, and teach a bible class for them."

"They don't go to school?" I asked surprised.

"Very few do. That is part of my church's program. We are

teaching them to read and write."

"Perfect, we would like to go with you. What time would we get back?"

"Around three. Make sure Juan has your stuff for your desert sabbatical ready in the morning, and as soon as we get back, we will head to the ranch," Jorge suggested.

"Sounds like a plan."

That night Jorge gathered me, Laura, Bobby and Bryan around him and prayed for us all.

"You know where your sleeping, right?" he checked.

"Yes sir!" we replied.

"If you need anything Maria is right next to you. Holler and she will help you. Goodnight all!" He rose up to head to his room.

"Goodnight Jorge!"

Laura and I prayed and read scripture with our boys, tucked them in and walked to our room next door to theirs. A thermos of coffee and two cups waited on a small table at the foot of the bed. Laura and I sat on the straight back chairs surrounding it. I poured us each a cup and we prayed again together. Laura prayed first.

"Lord I know the troubled heart of my husband. I know he sees the scenes of this troubled world with your eyes. Show him your plan for how we are to do our part, your will, for having Kingdom impact. Bless our boys. Help us to be the best parents we can. Help us to teach them that your plans for us will become a part of who you are raising them to be. Lord, bless the work of your hands as you shape us into your family. Teach us to share the love you have for the poor and the lost of this world. Amen."

Then I prayed. "Lord you know my heart and it's heaviness, you know because you gave it to me. Now teach me how to make a real difference. I want your plans not mine, your family not mine, your church not mine. I repent for the times I've tried to do your will with my plans. I seek your voice. I seek your instructions. Not my will but your will. Amen.

We sat silently sipping our coffee which by now was getting cool. "Laura, you heard my prayer. You know my heart." I said. "Sometimes I'm overwhelmed looking at our two boys, and the world we will be asking them to live in with all the evil they will have to deal with. It forces me to get really honest with myself.

"The world our parents grew up in was not too bad. Neither was the world we grew up in. But the world our sons face is evil. We must be honest. We are failing. The church is failing. We need a great spiritual awakening if we are to turn this around. But all of this is beyond us. We need a miracle from God himself."

"Billy," she asked solemnly, "Do you think there is another revival left before God brings all of this to an end?"

"Laura, I don't think it works like that?"

"What do you mean Billy?"

"I don't think God sits in Heaven wringing His hands saying woe is me, I don't know what to do. I believe that when God gave Adam dominion over the earth, He gave him the responsibility to run it. I do understand that the task was far bigger than Adam, but in those days, He gave Adam the evening walks for instruction. It is when Adam lost those walks through his sin and rebellion, that Adam lost his ability to care for things properly. For us though, and every Christian, that walk is restored in Jesus. When Heaven becomes a reality, it will be because all the believers have made the choice to walk with God, and to do things His way. Laura, that's what makes sense to me. I believe that believers can find a little bit of Heaven, right in the middle of this evil world if they are completely committed to a personal walk with Jesus. I think when the Holy Spirit came, He pointed us to relationship with Himself."

"Good thoughts Billy. Give me a kiss and let's go to bed."

"Sounds like a plan, Laura."

"Do you know how often you say that?"

"No. Why?" I asked.

"Let's change it to 'sounds like God's plan.'"

"Deal!" I agreed.

We climbed into bed and Laura said, "Love you!" as she pulled the covers up to her neck.

"Love you too. Goodnight!" I lay in the dark and heard the soft screech of an owl in the distance, and further off, the faint howl of a pack of coyotes. This was the new beginning I had come for.

CHAPTER 5.

Morning greeted me bright and early, at least that's what I thought. I made my way to the kitchen, and on the counter, I found a fresh pot of coffee and a large bowl of fruit. Seeing the bowls and silverware sitting there, I realized I was not the first one to get up. I dished out some banana, papaya, and pineapple pieces, poured a cup of coffee, and made my way to the dining room table.

As I sat there enjoying the morning with my Bible opened to Acts, I heard music that I would have never expected to hear on this remote hillside on the outskirts of Hermosillo. I remembered the song, La Cucaracha, from my boyhood and the sound of it seemed to be coming from a truck that was pulled up to the front gate.

I made my way to the shade on the front porch. As I sat there sipping my coffee and munching my fruit, I could see that Juan had met the truck and they were loading large metal containers from the truck to the back of the bus.

Not one to sit idly by with curiosity gnawing at me, I went to the bus. I saw that a number of coolers were already loaded and that an assortment of open cooking burners was neatly stashed on shelving in front of the coolers. That made sense, because it turned out that the bottles, they were loading were butane for connecting to the burners. As I made my way through the bus, I saw that there were rows of bookshelves filled with children's books, and boxes filled with clothes and shoes. It was obvious that a lot of effort and planning went into this daily ministry. My head was spinning with ideas for my church back home.

I heard the voice of Jorge calling from the barn near the bus, so I went over to it. There I discovered tons of clothes and a row of freezers.

"Billy," Jorge said, "This is my calling. We serve the children of Hermosillo. Once a year we also travel to Durango and Guadalajara to help children there. We wish we could do more, but we depend on our church here and churches in southern Arizona for resources and there is never enough." As he talked, he kept on working. "Laura's dad and I became friends when I built the Ford plant. I did construction for many years. The great blessing that God gave me with the Ford contract allowed me to prosper. That's when I bought the ranch and built this fine house. Now I give back. I serve every day. I wake up to do what I can to help my people and to lead them to Jesus. Jesus lives in Heaven with his Father but His heart lives in Jorge Maldonado."

"Jorge, I have not even begun my journey into the desert to meet with Jesus, but he is already teaching me his ways. I am embarrassed that I have been so blind," I said.

"Remember this Billy. Jesus lived in the streets. He lived among the people, the poor, the down and out, and sinners. Jesus wept because he could see the pain in their faces. His heart was with the orphans and those who had so little, who had no one else to care for them. Wait till we get to the barrio. You will see."

I turned my head and walked away so Jorge would not see the tears streaming down my face. Then my eyes met Laura and my two boys seated on the porch eating their breakfast. I could not help but be overwhelmed by the great contrast I was hearing between the prosperity of Americans and this other world, so close by, and yet in many ways so very far away.

I could barely make out the logo of the Tufesa bus company on Jorge's bus as they finished loading it for our day mission trip. It somehow seemed appropriate that this bus which had once transported day laborers into Tucson would now be bringing hope to the next generation, who cast a wishful eye toward the land of prosperity to the north.

At ten that morning Jorge and all his workers got on the bus. This morning, they were joined by the Pearce family. As soon as we arrived, the workers began unloading and preparing all the food. Those butane bottles began to sing with the fires cooking. The aroma of food wafted across the shanties. At times the good smell almost drowned out the stench of the dirty ground the inhabitants sat on. At the sight of the bus the crowd began to gather. Old women and old men took their places at tables and chairs that were flying into order from the luggage container beneath the bus. Those people who were able bodied, helped in organizing the event.

After the meal, the children found the soccer (futbal) balls and games and laughter surrounded us. Dirty faces and ragged clothes were magically transformed into sounds of joy like I remembered from my boyhood when I, too, had been free to play with my friends in the streets. As I looked around me, I could see all the trappings of poverty, but somehow the laughter caused it all to strangely vanish.

Our adventure was wrapping up, but first Jorge asked me to share a Gospel message for all the people gathered there. Altogether there must have been over two thousand people present. It was easy to share with them, and Jorge translated. My heart shouted with compassion affecting every word I said. It was not my compassion, but a pouring out of the new heart that Jesus was giving me.

Over 50 children and 42 adults had their first meeting with Jesus that day as he saved their souls. They were as saved as any American had ever been, in the comfort and finery of our church in Tucson. The best thing for me, though, was the new heart the preacher preached with that day. *Thank you, Lord! You're so good, all the time!*

CHAPTER 6.

While returning to Jorge's house, I sat alone towards the back of the bus. I wanted to take time to reflect on the event like I always did when I preached in Tucson. While there was chatter all around me, I was alone, just me and Jesus, discussing the days service. I thought about things that had been done and said, and about how I could do better. My alone time in the back of the bus was usual for me, but my conversation with God was far different.

The events of the day had given me a completely new picture. I was seeing things far bigger than anything Jesus and I had talked about in the past. I had been failing to see the primary goals the Bible had outlined, which were to lead people to Jesus and teach them to become his disciples. This was about relationships, strong bonds and deep friendships. I began to see that until there are such bonds, people don't care what you have to say. I could see this in the children's faces as they crawled into Jorge and Juan's laps. They were teachable because they knew these men loved them.

As soon as we arrived, my gear was loaded into a trailer which Juan hitched to Jorge's Rubicon. Jorge had told me how rugged the trip would be and that the Suburban would need to stay in Hermosillo. Jorge and I climbed into the front seats with Laura and the boys sitting in the rear. I had a lot I wanted to discuss with Jorge and the hour and a half trip would be the perfect opportunity.

"Jorge tell me how you got started doing the ministry at the dump," I asked.

"It started like this," Jorge explained. "Every time I would drive by there, God would prick my heart. Sometimes I would drive slow enough that I could see the faces of the children. It started with me taking a group to try and teach them how to read. I knew that without some education, there was no hope. They were destined to be locked into poverty just like their grandfathers before them. Somebody had to break the cycle.

"As we were finishing the Ford plant, I tried to hire competent workers. We needed people who could read and write. Of course, it was about that time that my financial resources were reaching a point where I could actually do something about it and so I did. It had only been a few years earlier that Laura's Dad had led me to Christ. Every time I came to Tucson, he would drop whatever he was doing to teach me the Bible and mentor me. In between he sent me a lot of study materials through email and the mail service. Did you see all those books in my den on my bookshelves?" he asked.

"Yes sir," I nodded.

"Nearly every one of them was sent by Laura's dad. I read all of them. You remember all those old children's Sunday school books you shipped here?"

"Yes."

"Every one of them was used to teach the children how to read, and all about Jesus."

"Jorge that was probably ten years ago," I said.

"Yes Billy. It was. Since we started the classes, we have led over twelve hundred to Christ, mostly children. Some have begun training to become missionaries and pastors. A few are already ministering."

"Did you hear that Laura?" I asked, looking towards Laura in the back.

"Billy, I knew much of that already," she replied as we drove on.

"How come you didn't tell me?"

"I tried, Honey. You were too busy doing the work of the church."

"Boy you got that right! I was too busy doing the work of

the church instead of the work of God. Thanks Jorge, I needed to hear all that.'

We had been heading east on Mexico 20. At Mazatlán we turned north toward Nacon. Just north of Nacon we turned onto a gravel road back to the east and started our ascent. Jorge said it was only about thirty miles to the ranch headquarters, but it would take at least an hour. We drove past a lake, then a school. Jorge looked at me and said, "Do you like the school?"

"It's nice," I said.

"That's another one of our projects," he said. "We noticed that no matter how much effort we put into the children; we were still fighting the battle of the culture of Hermosillo's downside. When we bought the ranch, we did so as a ministry. We brought families out from the barrio, trained some to run the ranch, and trained others as Christian educators. We built the school as an in-depth discipleship program starting at childhood. The ranch workers' children are also being trained this way. We even bring orphans out to the house to be trained."

"How many children go to the school?"

"Almost 200, and most live on the ranch. Children of the local folks also get free education."

As Jorge was finishing his story, we crested a high peak and dropped into a beautiful little valley where I could see our home for the next few months.

'It's gorgeous, Jorge!" I exclaimed, looking out the window.

"Yes, it is, Billy."

"A good place for God to train boys and girls to be world changers. Thank you, Jorge. Thank you, God, for making men like Jorge. Amen."

CHAPTER 7.

The air in the mountain high valley was fresh and cool and I rolled down my window. The compound below held about 8 or 10 buildings at first glance nestled among trees instead of just cactus. One, in the center, was larger and seemed to be a meeting place or a chapel. There was a lake on the property, and fields, and I could hear a couple of cows lowing softly.

"Dinner could be ready any time, Billy. But I am thinking, we have a couple of hours before dark. We could take the Jeep for a drive and I could show you a little of the beauty of the ranch," Jorge said slowing down to a stop.

"What do you think Laura?" I turned to face her.

"The boys and I would love that!" she replied. "Let's go!".

We started up the gravel road and climbed higher and higher until my ears started to pop. It was genuinely cool in the evening up there.

"Dad look!" exclaimed Bryan. A deer, a mule deer buck, ran across the road in front of us.

"Billy, I want you to know when I bought the ranch the deer population had almost been extinguished," Jorge explained. "We have taken care of them. Every year a biologist surveys the ranch and sets a harvest number. Hopefully as we climb, you'll see the bighorns which are now thriving. There are puma, or as you call them mountain lions, too. There are ocelots, bobcats, desert cottontails, many jackrabbits, and even a few rare small Coues deer."

We climbed through the oak brush which gave way to pine trees and after a short while we emerged above the tree line altogether. Jorge suddenly stopped the jeep and pulled out two sets of binoculars, handing them to Laura and me.

"There straight up, above those large boulders are six desert bighorns! Look at the papa! He is magnificent! You see them? Jorge asked.

"I've got them. Do you see them, Laura? Just to the left of the largest boulder."

"Yes, I can see them now," she said with awe in her voice.

"Mom! Dad! Can we use the binoculars? We can see them, but we want to see them close."

"Here," I handed them my binoculars and they quickly focused up on the steep cliffs.

"Oh Mom, Dad! He is so pretty!"

"All a part of God's creation boys," I said. "And God put us here to take care of them along with all the other things."

"Billy, that's part of our philosophy. We call it holistic. God gave Adam authority over all of His creation. We blew it, but one day we'll get it right."

We all enjoyed the silence for a minute and then Jorge continued, "This is what I love about this place. You can't see any slums here. You won't see any signs of sin here. This is what Heaven will look like."

"Amen, Jorge!" I responded. "It's time for us to turn around and head back." Light was fading fast. "We don't want to be navigating these roads after dark. Laura? Boys? Was that cool or what?"

"That was awesome," they all said at once.

When we arrived back at the ranch the yard was lit up. Five men sat in chairs on the porch playing instruments. A saxophone, a guitar, a bass, an accordion, and a snare drum belted out a welcome as families danced in the front yard.

"Bienvenidos!" yelled everyone. As we entered the house a good-sized crowd followed. A large dining hall was in front of us. Everyone seemed to know where their seat was. We wandered toward the front where a table for six awaited us. As we took our seats, Jorge slid the chair out for Laura, which kind of embarrassed me, but mainly reminded me of the courtesy

I should have been showing. Jorge then introduced us to Armando, his main man on the ranch. We took our seats, but Jorge remained standing. He reached for his Bible which had been placed on the table next to his place. He opened it to Acts 2 and read the passage where the church gathered for the first time and the Holy Spirit came upon them. Then he repeated the phrase, "and they were all in one accord," in English and Spanish. All repeated after him and said, "Amen." Then Laura and our two boys understood and also repeated the phrase and said "Amen." Jorge said, "Bless this food and bless us, your church, Amen." With that, food was brought out and we had our evening meal.

    I was mesmerized as I looked around at all the smiling faces and heard laughter throughout the room. I could see peace in the faces of my family. I silently thought, *Jesus we can have a little of heaven right here on earth. We just have to learn the faith of obedience.*

CHAPTER 8.

As I prepared my plate my mind seemed to be jumping all over the place. I noticed the dining room seemed to be grouped into large family units. Conversation and laughter filled the room. Quickly my eyes shifted to the abundance of food set before me.

The meat for the evening was roasted goat carefully sliced into bite sized portions and topped with a sauce I wasn't familiar with, but it obviously consisted of a mixture of tomato sauce and cheese, and it was spiced with fresh peppers. The vegetables were an assortment of squash, potatoes and fresh pintos. The tortillas didn't look familiar to me. Jorge could see the look on my face as I took my first bite.

"Billy, what do you think? Tasty?"

"Might take a little getting used to," I said, awkwardly.

"They are made of flour ground up from mesquite beans, very healthy," he explained.

"Do you remember the word I used to describe our approach to teaching?" Jorge asked.

"Holistic?"

"Yes. That is our approach to all we do. All the food you are eating was raised right here on the ranch. Even the cabrito came from the south pasture.

"I know you don't understand all the conversation going on around you so let me explain. They are discussing their work for tomorrow, plans for the children, family plans, and the weekly mission trips they make back into Hermosillo. The food is organic and our work is organic too," he said smiling. "Everyone here has a job to do. Everyone is either doing their own job or helping someone else to prepare for their job. The children learn a strong work ethic. They are expected to achieve excellence. They work side by side with adults.

"The worst sin in our community is a failure to get along with others. We are a team. We depend on each other, not just for food, clothing and shelter, but to lead everyone in Hermosillo to Christ. That is the mission of the whole community. When each team makes their weekly trip into Hermosillo, they are preceded by the testimony of the team before them. What the lost in Hermosillo see when we arrive, is a community that prospers, that loves one another, and that will allow no one to go hungry. But most of all, our community doesn't want anyone to go to Hell. We all work to lead families into the good and eternal place of Heaven."

A child passed by Jorge and he patted him on the back. "We must show them something that is attractive to them," Jorge continued. The testimony of this community and of our lifestyle go to Hermosillo long before our words. Through our testimony we have become the living word just like Jesus taught us to be."

"Jorge, how did you come up with all this?" I asked, incredulous.

"The idea came as I prayed and read my Bible. There were things I noticed that the church was not doing. We were teaching God's word in the sterile environment of a classroom. Jesus taught in the streets of His homeland. Our church buildings became a liability. Our people were no longer doing hands on action. Bible teaching had become just the gathering of knowledge, instead of also the wisdom of doing."

Jorge continued his long and interesting explanation of the ranch's philosophy. "When our children sit in the classroom it is mainly to get them to sit still long enough to learn to read and work out math problems. Such fundamentals are just tools that facilitate what they really need to know. We focus on families. Through them, the children learn morality, the proper roles of husbands and wives, how to pray, and the importance of Bible study." He paused. "But we do not want our children to become attached to the sheltered environment they live in here. We want to train them to be missionaries. We know that in order to do this they need to have well established morals and a value system that enables them to evangelize the real world without being snatched into its culture."

"Jorge, I am blown away by what you are doing here," I said. The scope of the project was almost overwhelming.

"Not me, Billy. This shows how God can use a willing heart. I am just a servant of Jesus."

"Well anyway, I think I need to delay my wilderness time a few days and get a careful look at what you are doing here," I decided.

"That's fine with me, Billy. You're welcome here as long as you like," Jorge invited. "Pray this through and do the will of God."

I turned and looked carefully at Laura. "Laura, you don't mind me hanging around with you and the kids a few days?"

"Billy, I think we are looking at a living breathing Bible. This compound is living just like John, Peter, Andrew, Thomas and all the disciples. I think we should take advantage of it and learn all we can," she agreed.

"Pray with me," I said to Laura and Jorge. "Lord I can see it is your will for me to understand what you are doing here. You are showing me how you want to use me to lead my family as well as a new mission to take back to my home in Tucson. Is this your plan?"

"Yes, my son." I heard a strong voice in my heart. I paused for a minute to be sure I was hearing from God and not just my own heart.

"Amen, then!" I said out loud. "It's settled, Jorge. I have no timeline. I just want to know and do God's will."

"Good then! I will teach you all that we are doing here," said Jorge.

CHAPTER 9.

After we had finished dinner Jorge looked at me and said, "You know, what we are doing here came with a lot of planning. You haven't met all of them, but tomorrow morning is our planning meeting. Each week I meet with leaders in every area of our ministry. Tomorrow is the executive meeting. If you are willing, I'd like you to join us."

"I would love to," I replied eagerly.

"We start with a prayer session and early morning Bible study," Jorge explained. "Then after breakfast we meet. It all starts at six am, are you up for that?"

"I'll be there."

Laura and I settled into our new rooms and read scripture with the boys. We prayed over them and put them to bed. I told Laura about the early morning meeting, so we turned in early. I had trouble going to sleep with all the information I was processing. Then I talked to my Lord and He gently led me into a wonderful night's sleep.

By five thirty, I was in the kitchen. Maria was already there, and coffee was made. As I sat silently talking to God and sipping on my coffee, Jorge slipped into the room. Each of his board members made their way to the little dining room off to one side of the kitchen. Each one had a Bible in his hand. Jorge read Acts 7, about Steven's sermon, and finished as Steven was stoned while the man who would soon be the apostle Paul, held their coats. As he closed his Bible, he reminded each man of the seriousness of the task God had set before them. Each prayed, and as Jorge closed, breakfast was brought into the room. You could see by the faces of these men, how much they loved each other, and how seriously they took their work.

From there we moved into a large office with a conference table in one corner. Five of us took seats at the table, with Jorge setting at the head and me setting to his right. Jorge introduced me to each of four leaders with a brief description of their specific roles.

"Jose is my financial man. He not only takes care of our daily expenses but organizes fund raising, manages investment and endowment accounts, and prepares the budget for our daily operation as well as for future planning and projects.

"Armando is in charge of Ranch management. He not only oversees farming and animal husbandry, but works with our spiritual leader, Adolfo, to manage our school and training for its daily operational needs. More on that as we tour the daily operations of the ranch.

"Adolfo, who is our spiritual leader, is key to all we do. He carefully makes sure that everything we do is built around God's plan for a spiritual outcome. He holds services at the school, and on Sunday he turns the school into a Church for all of us.

"Finally, there is Benito. He is a mechanical engineer but also has significant architectural training. Along with classes where he teaches our up and coming whiz kids, he coordinates construction here. He also helps me run my construction company in Hermosillo and is instrumental in business development in the city. Currently we are building another car parts plant in Hermosillo."

With that introduction, the meeting began with each leader giving a report on their part of the operation. A financial report was placed before each member. Each board member then passed out their own report for their specific area of leadership.

The main business for the week, was the progress on the plant and the warehouse being built. With both projects a little behind schedule, Benito made an appeal for more workers. It was decided that ten men could be spared from the ranch operation to do construction for thirty days. With that Jorge handed out his plan for future projects which included a manufacturing plant in Hermosillo for crafts products to be sold in the U.S. and Europe. He next brought up an upcoming City-wide revival they had been planning for the "Futbol" stadium in Hermosillo. They prayed once more, and the meeting was adjourned.

After the meeting, Jorge said, "Meet me in front of the house in thirty minutes. I know you would like to see your family before we take the tour. We will be gone all day, so Maria has prepared us sack lunches."

I went and spoke with the boys and Laura for a few minutes. Maria had plans to take them to the school and they were going to sit in on some of the classes. Thirty minutes later I met Jorge and Armando at the Jeep and we began our tour of the ranch.

CHAPTER 10.

Jorge, Armando and I climbed into the Jeep. Our first stop was only a quarter mile down the road. We pulled up in front of a large metal building. Burned across the entrance on a large barn wood plank, was the word "IMAGINACION." It wasn't hard to translate. "This is where our think tank is located," Jorge said.

As we walked through the front door we immediately turned to our left and entered a cluttered room filled with computers, white boards and blueprints hanging from the walls. Workstations were scattered in each corner. "This is where we dream," Jorge said. I noticed a prayer altar over against the back wall. There was a geometrical print on the floor of the room but it was worn off in front of the alter.

"Here we dream. We think of ideas for jobs, ideas for products, ideas for innovation, and any other ideas that support the vision we have which is, 'The Kingdom of God is at hand.' All ideas are prayed over, carefully studied, and if God is in them, implemented right here. We'll talk about some of our ideas later as we drive but let me take you to the shop in the back before we leave here."

In the shop, was an overhead crane system. "Billy, we do maintenance on all our equipment back here. Keeping our own equipment maintained is high priority. We have parts for our bulldozer, our tractors, as well as parts for pumps and generators. Our off-grid power system includes wind turbines, solar generators, water pumps, and much more, all of which are taken care of here. Notice the essential parts and equipment on the high shelves! However, our favorite part of the shop is the equipment which includes lathes, benders, welders and a mill.

We have all kinds of raw materials for fabricating whatever we need for building prototypes or our dream projects.

"We have a new family soon to arrive. David and his wife, Julie, and their daughter will be here next week. He is an MIT graduate, a master electrical engineer, with a significant understanding of computer hardware and software. He came to us with these skills all because he could see what we were doing with the children. Julie is a math teacher with an extensive knowledge of the Bible. We have a workstation ready over in that corner for him to start putting some his ideas into reality. David found us because one of the children who came from the barrio got a full ride academic scholarship to MIT last year.

We walked a hundred yards down a gravel drive and came to a food processing building. There, workers were sorting through vegetables that came from fields you could see below. A few were set aside for meals, but most were cleaned and prepped for a canning operation which took place along the back wall. Pressure cookers were heating up on large commercial stoves ready for great big jars waiting on a long work bench.

People from a smaller warehouse to the rear collected the jars when they were full and cool, and stocked them on shelves. "Billy, all the food we carry to the barrio is raised right here. Let's walk on."

Next door was a butcher shop. Two goats and a hog were being skinned and dressed in a shed with a floor drain. Inside the shop itself, carcasses were being sliced into usable portions. Some of the meat was placed in a cooler and the rest was placed in a walk-in freezer. "Most of our meat is cured by smoking," Jorge explained as he opened a door to a smoke house. I peered in to see meat hanging from racks as the smoke swirled around it. "Operating the freezer uses a lot of electricity so we smoke as much meat as we can. Occasionally one of the cooks will come down to pick a ham and cure it with salt or sugar. We are constantly looking at how we do things to minimize costs. We have a responsibility to use every peso well.

"Follow me next door," Jorge requested, as we walked out

the front door to a building which was smaller. "There's no one here today so it's a good time to show you this." In the building there was an assortment of laboratory equipment. "We have several volunteers who drive down from the university in Tucson," he continued. "They regularly test our food and process holistic medicine from the many types of plants we have here on the ranch. We also test our composted fertilizer, water and sewer system for potential health problems. Operating a community like this comes with a lot of responsibility. We are blessed with a lot of expertise in our staff and with volunteers."

"I was thinking what a great plan you have here, but I had no idea it required so much work," I remarked.

"Billy, it was all in God's plan, and anytime, anywhere we have a need, He sends someone to take care of that need. As a matter of fact, lest I forget," Jorge paused and looked up. 'Thank you, Lord! You are wonderful and amazing, Amen!"

CHAPTER 11.

After lunch, we all loaded into the Jeep again and Armando drove. We went a few hundred yards down the road. Suddenly Armando skidded the Jeep to a stop. "Do you smell that?" he asked.

Jorge answered from the back seat. "I know what that is, or should I say 'whom'! Guys, I know that aroma. It's one of the sweetest on earth, like Gardenia's, maybe." He continued, "I don't know why, but what I do know is, every time he shows up, that's the aroma I smell."

"Who Jorge?" I asked.

"I don't know his name. I just call him 'Mercury.'"

"Who are you talking about? Why does 'he' smell so sweet?" I asked again in wonder.

"Because when he shows up, he always brings a message from Jesus."

"Roll down the windows," Armando said. "There has to be a gardenia bush nearby."

"Armando and Billy, all I can smell outside is that creosote bush next to the truck," Jorge said.

"Me too," I agreed.

"I am telling you, the smell is in here with us, Billy! It's in the seat next to me! I am telling you he's here!"

"Mercury?" I asked, looking at the back seat next to Jorge. But I saw no one there.

"Yes! Bow your head and close your eyes. He has something to tell us." Jorge said.

"Billy," said a kind but majestic voice out loud.

"Yes," I answered.

"This is my man Jorge, he is chosen," the voice said. It seemed to be speaking to me. "He is highly esteemed in God's Kingdom. I am giving him words for you. Listen to Him."

"Billy, Jorge, let's pray!" Armando said, somewhat shaken.

I was taken aback by it all too, but I felt a strange sense of peace. "Jesus thank you for teaching me. Thank you for revealing your plan!" I prayed.

Jorge also prayed. "Help me to give Billy understanding in this plan from you. Amen." Then he added, "Mercury, will you show Billy a sign?" Suddenly a great wind came and deposited all the leaves of the creosote bush in our laps.

"Wow, was that an angel? Hallelujah!" I exclaimed.

"Glory to God!" Jorge added.

"Does that happen often, Jorge?" I asked.

"Not like that, but Jesus does speak to me every day. That was for your benefit, Billy. I believe Mercury is an angel. Jesus wanted you to know how real He is, and how important what we are doing is! That's why He sent him. There is a plan, a big plan going on here, and Billy you're right in the middle of it!"

"I've been in the ministry a long time Jorge. Why now?"

"I think, Billy, it's because you are all in. At least that's how it was for me," Jorge said.

"What am I doing different than I have before?" I asked.

"You sold everything! Jesus became number one, your heart's desire."

"You never sold everything, Jorge?"

"That's not how it works Billy. All that He has given me has been His for a long time. For me it was my work, my business that I had to give up," Jorge said.

"But you still have it Jorge."

"No, I don't Billy. It all belongs to Him,' he said.

"What about you Armando?" I asked.

"I've never had much, but for a long time now, whatever I do have had belongs to Him. Mainly that just me and my family,' said Armando.

"I think I get it," I said thoughtfully. The smell of Gardenias left the Jeep. "So, Jorge, what did he tell you to say to me?" I asked.

"Not much, Jorge replied. He just said to show you what we are doing, and that he would show you what to do with that information."

"You've were already been doing that, Jorge." I pointed out.

"I know, but you were not taking it seriously enough. Billy, your trip alone with God in the desert began as the sight of Tucson faded in your rear-view mirror. I know. He did that for me over ten years ago. Everything you now see, started on that day. It is all far beyond my wildest dreams and I think my journey is far from over. Knowing how God works, it seems as though his plan for you is also a new door for me too."

"Why does God hold back from most men, Jorge?"

"Two things," Jorge explained. "He has to be able to trust them, for His power is great, and His works are mighty. Secondly, He only uses men who can handle that much power with great humility as they give him the glory."

Armando eased the Jeep on up the side of a hill. We rounded a bluff that had blocked our view. Suddenly, I could see a beautiful mountain lake in the upper end of the valley that stretched below us.

"Billy this lake is key to our farming operations. You might notice that our farming season is nearly over. We are harvesting the last of what has been a very good season. We've already had a first frost, and the flurry of activity you saw in the food warehouse was preparation for next year. Every seven years we let the fields lay fallow to replenish the nutrients of the soil. That's what gives us our abundance. For seven years compost piles are built up to make the soil healthy for future years. All this is biblical." Jorge was in thought for a moment. It's ironic how this is almost a physical representation of the spiritual preparation we do with our children and the wisdom we use. The lighter workload in the seventh years enables us to use all the workers to accelerate training and revival during that time.

"It's all about renewal. We are human. We have to make sure we take care of our own spiritual health, otherwise we will become useless to those we want to reach," concluded Jorge.

"Are those compost piles next to the fields below?" I asked, seeing mounds of black dirt along the edges.

"Yes Billy. We place them next to the fields to minimize effort as we work them into the soil."

"I notice the river runs between the fields, is there a reason?"

"Yes. As soon as the fields are harvested, we flood them with water from the lake. It is rich in minerals from volcanic rock. The water trickles down from the mountains above."

"I see that you built the house next to the lake," I observed.

"Yes. The water from the lake is filtered for drinking, laundry and domestic use," said Jorge.

"What is the dark pool below the fields?" I asked curiously.

"That is our septic catch pool. After careful preparation, it is recycled for fertilizer. It works out very well because the mountain soil tends to be quite alkaline. The organic material added, achieves the proper PH."

We made our way toward the upper end of the lake and I could see that it was lined with what appeared to be fruit orchards. "Do you raise your own fruit too, Jorge?" I asked, amazed.

"Yes, we raise apples and pears and an assortment of nut trees. Planting them near the lake makes it easy to irrigate them when we hit the dry season of spring and early summer. Usually by the end of July, the rainy season comes and replenishes our water sources."

We crossed a timber bridge and turned right, alongside a stream. Above the orchards, I could see barns and corrals. Several horses had their heads buried in feed troughs along the fence. Fences stretched up into the hills.

"Billy this is our livestock headquarters," Jorge said. "The vaqueros are already in the pastures that extend up and over the mountains. There are tack rooms, and even a little blacksmith shop inside the barn.

"A goat pasture lies to the south, but you might find goats anywhere on the ranch and often on neighboring properties, unfortunately. We brand the goats when we can, but often the kids are unmarked, and some are wilder than the bighorns. We gave up on keeping all our fences goat proof. It took more work than it was worth. With the poverty that surrounds us, it is almost like leaving a little grain for the gleaners," Jorge laughed.

Armando drove the jeep out into one of the main pastures, and you could see vaqueros working cattle just like they did a hundred years ago. Once again, an abundance of wildlife made its presence known. The road slowed the jeep down to less than five miles-an-hour, so we hardly scared the deer, hawks, and jackrabbits away. It was easy to see why the vaqueros preferred to ride horses.

We pulled over to rest under a grove of pine trees. "Billy, by the time we get back to the house you will have seen about ten thousand acres, said Jorge. "The ranch includes another thirty-two thousand acres. As of now the only access to that back country is on horseback or ATV. Our plan is to establish four other communities like our headquarters. Water is available, and sites are already planned. As God provides the funds we will build, but right now we must train folks to lead. We are doing that every day. I believe as soon as we have trained enough staff, God will send the money. I am so very thankful for what He has already done, but I believe there is much more to come.

"If I do my job properly, I must train a successor. I believe God has chosen a man named Juan for that, but it will take time to prepare him. Billy and Armando, will you pray with me about that?" We bowed our heads.

"Lord thank you for all you give me. Empower me with your words to pass it on to the next generation, Jorge prayed simply. "Amen."

"Jorge, I want to know more about how all this vision came to you," I said.

"Are you sure you want to know the details Billy? It might be painful."

"I don't care how painful it is Jorge, I need to know," I insisted.

"Are we ready to go?" Jorge asked, seeming to put me off for the time being.

"Yes sir," Armando and I both replied.

Jorge looked at me seriously. "Then I'll tell you as Armando drives us back."

CHAPTER 12.

As we rode along, my mind tossed around those words," it might be painful." "Jorge what did you mean by 'painful'?" I finally asked.

"Well, God showed me the correct answer to that question in a Sunday morning service at your church in Tucson. It was not from any positive realization, but from questioning what I was seeing.

"Remember, it had only been a couple of years since Laura's dad had led me to Christ. I was baptized in your church by you. There were only about fifty people in the congregation back then. We had to drag out a horse trough to baptize me in.

"Then two years later while Laura's dad was helping me with the details of the Ford contract, I stayed there for an extended time. I was so excited to be able to attend your church again for a few months. I was glad that I could finally start learning how a church functions, as I was planning on starting a church in Hermosillo.

"But one Sunday morning I sat there watching as you introduced the high school graduates from that year. The last girl that you called up was very noticeably pregnant. Each graduate had received some applause but when she came up there was a standing ovation. I have to admit I was very confused. It was certainly admirable that she had persevered through hardship, but it seemed to me that the others were really bigger heroes. Then I thought, *I wonder if these people who are honoring her would be willing to watch her baby as she attended college. Would she be able to be the kind of mother her baby deserved?* Maybe, but doubtful.

Then I thought about the children in the dump in Hermosillo. Many of them had been abandoned because a young mother couldn't afford them. Who would take care of them? What you don't know is, that I too was raised in the dump until I was twelve. Then a local carpenter took me into his home and gave me a new life. In a similar way a different carpenter who died on the cross for me two thousand years ago to give me eternal life.

"When the young lady was applauded for a bad decision, it sent me mixed messages. I lay in bed that night thinking all this through and I wondered if any of the other young ladies that were honored that morning had also gotten pregnant but covered it up with an abortion. Certainly, many in the High School already bore a lot of emotional scars. We couldn't turn our heads from the boys either. Weren't they just as guilty? I thought a lot about the girl's situation. Would the father of the baby marry her? Would he get a job and support his baby? Would he even be in her life? I suddenly had so many questions, but no answers. Such thoughts plagued my mind. I needed answers.

"It was no different in Hermosillo. In fact, it was worse. The problem was Tucson had the church. It had many churches but was that really making a difference in young lives? Or was the applause that morning the church's vain attempt at doing good. If it was, it wasn't working." Jorge was silent for a while and seemed to be deep in thought.

"Billy, what happened to that girl? Where is she now and how's her baby? Did they get married?"

"As far as I know, she's living with her parents." I had to think about it for a minute. "As for the boy, she wasn't sure which one he was."

"No DNA test Billy?" Jorge asked. "Why shouldn't the father at least have to support his child?"

"The truth is Jorge, the one she thinks is the father has been in and out of drug treatment centers and is probably living on the streets, if he's alive," I responded.

"That's the problem, Billy. We have lost that generation. It is full of aimless, pointless lives, fueled by despair and hopelessness. We have to take them back. We have to restore the years the locusts have eaten.

"I returned home and began my journey," Jorge continued. "God laid a call on me that day, but I wasn't prepared. Juan took over the Ford plant. I became friends with the Mayor of Hermosillo who owned this ranch. It was primitive back then and I would drive out here with my camping gear and a load of books. I read the greats, C S Lewis, Francis Schaeffer, John Bunyan, Martin Luther, but mostly I read my Bible. I practically memorized the life of Jesus as well as the birth of the church in Acts. While I learned, this vision began to unfold.

"I could see how far we had drifted from those early days of the church. Sometimes I would spend weeks in the mountains, alone, just me and God. I realized that those early Christians became a community and the whole idea of what I call 'holistic' began to unfold. They ate together. They learned together. They prayed together. They loved each other. Whatever problems came up they solved together. They learned how to forgive and be patient with each other. They had the threat of arrest and execution hanging over their heads, so they had to rely on each other. The Jews hated them. The Romans hated them. The Greeks hated them. All they had was each other. But that was God's plan, and so they prospered." Jorge began getting excited.

"The great love they had for each other was something the world had never seen. When the world saw what was happening, they saw something many wanted. The testimony of the believers became the wheels of the Gospel. Billy, we don't have to figure this out. The pattern is well established. We only have to go back and learn from what God has already given us."

"Amen Jorge, Amen!" I agreed, starting to catch his vision. "What really blows me away, Jorge, is that with no formal training and not much experience, you could teach me so much! Jorge, I think I have become way too tied up in the traditions of what I grew up with, in the church. All that has blinded me from reading my Bible for what it actually says. I've been using it to validate the traditions of men that have become so entrenched in my thinking."

I felt humbled. "Pray for me, Jorge," I said.

"I will right now," Jorge responded. "Jesus my Lord, my savior, and teacher of my spirit. Open the eyes of Billy that he might see your glory and be engulfed in your will. Show him your plans for him and his family. Amen."

CHAPTER 13.

We wound our way down the mountains back to the high desert. The plant life changed from the pines of the misty mountains, to oaks, and then to dry scrub and cacti. I began to see the plants as a visual illustration of our lives. I would have liked to have stayed in the lushness and safety of the high mountain pines, but I had to return to the dry places. The Saguaro cactus, Prickly Pear, Agave, and Mesquite trees, all had their beauty when seen from a distance but when you looked at them up close, they were full of thorns. The Cholla, or jumping cactus, was a nasty plant full of thorns, but when it bloomed it turned the desert floor white.

Looking at the thorny cacti, and the beauty that came out if them, led me into a somewhat mystical and deep reverie.

Men also have thorns, just like cacti, I thought. All the thorns came into the world with sin. The thorns are the consequences of sin. God gradually shapes us and prunes us and removes the thorns of our lives. One day when he has finished with us, He will remove all of our pain and defenses. He will remove the thorns from the cacti, too. But for now, the thorns have a reason. They protect the plants from animals who would eat them. The thorns in our lives, the consequences of sin and our reactions to sin, also have a reason. They lead us to God. God gives men protection, in the form of love. This process of love, or grace, can be painful as it tears away the bad effects of sin. Few people would see that the consequences of sin could be a good thing, but it leads us to God.

Sin, itself, brings death. God allowed sin, which in itself, leads to death, to lead us instead to Himself who is our only real protection from sin. Thus, even sin can indirectly lead us to God. When men understand that God himself, our creator, is our only true protection against sin and its consequences, the thorns; they will no longer be necessary. All of us build walls of protection around us for self-preservation. These walls can cause pain. These same walls can cause us to embrace the love of God, as we search for a way out of our pain. When we find God, it is called salvation.

Also, when we get involved with the lost world, we pick up the pain of others. We take on their thorns. But we grow through pain when we have God on our side.

Someday there will be a world where no thorns will exist because there will be no more sin. The thorns of the desert will be gone when sin is gone. Heaven, and one day this earth, as it takes on its final state, will be just like the Garden of Eden in Adam's day.

Jorge was thinking about thorns too. "Billy, have you ever noticed that the nastiest thorns on a mesquite tree are on the new growth?" he mentioned, breaking our silence.

"Hmm, you're right," I agreed.

"The most tender succulent growth has long hard nasty thorns," Jorge said. "That's like our children. They are most vulnerable to the consequences of sin. They need our protection, so that's where the church must focus," Jorge paused for a moment.

"Let's go back to that pregnant girl that walked across the stage but this time we'll make it personal."

"OK Jorge." I was listening intently.

"You know that years before I married Maria, I lost my first wife and daughter," Jorge said.

"Yes," I said.

"Do you know how?"

"No, I don't." I said.

"In those days I had started my construction company but was really struggling to land contracts. Then I met a man, we'll call Pedro. He was connected, you know, the underworld.

He was the owner of a group that smuggled illegals into the US. He also smuggled drugs into Tucson and Phoenix.

"I began helping him by slipping drugs in on the truck that I used to haul building materials across the border. I had the necessary permits and a man from Tucson driving for me. My boss, Laura's dad Joe, didn't know I was doing this because I was paying a man in his warehouse to hide them among the supplies. It was a man who went to your church, but I am not going to mention any names.

"Joe found out, fired the man, and called me into his office. I broke down and that was the day he led me to Christ. Of course, I had to break ties to Pedro. As you know, that usually doesn't go well. One day, on a trip to Durango, my family and I were ambushed. I lost my wife and daughter that day. I returned to Hermosillo, but I could not even attend the funeral for my wife and daughter.

"I wished I had died that day, but God had a plan for me. In my grief He comforted me. I began to return to visit the dump. Each time I would bring food and books to teach the children. The grief began to subside. As I watched the little girls, they became my daughters. I knew that my wife and daughter were in Heaven and I was driven to see that the wives and daughters of others would be able to know the Jesus that had brought me through all of this.

"A few months later I woke up one morning and there was a million dollars in hundred-dollar bills in a sack next to my bed. A note from the bag said, 'Feed the children.' I know the money probably came from Pedro but there was no way to connect it with him. I prayed about it for several weeks because I struggled with using what I knew to be illegal money to do God's work. But God gave me peace, and I went about putting the money to good use.

"In my mind's eye, when I see the girl walking across the stage, I see the face of my daughter. It always raises the question; how can we raise our children to be Godly? How do we teach them the sanctity of marriage and the sacredness of sex in marriage? How do we train them to be true ambassadors for Christ? How do we protect them from the ravages of the culture that makes sin so easy and yet so deadly?

"As I carry the shame of the death of my wife and daughter, I can only strive to rescue the next generation from the same fate with the love that comes through Jesus. Billy, I pray that you can learn this kind of redemption without having to pass through the fire of pain that I have to live with."

"Thank you, Jorge. And thank you Jesus for the fiery furnace we call life," I said solemnly. "May the fire in your heart, burn in my soul to do your will. Amen."

CHAPTER 14.

As we descended into the valley, I could see the ranch headquarters again. Lights were beginning to sparkle in the windows and I thought it was a beautiful site. Jorge had one more thing he wanted to tell me about before dinner. "Meet me in my room," he said. "I want to show you something."

"As soon as I see my wife and boys and clean up a little, I'll be there,' I said.

I entered Jorge's room and could see that he had a YouTube video pulled up on the flat screen above his desk. The title was "James Dobson's Interview with Ted Bundy." He hit play, and what followed was a death row interview with Ted shortly before his execution. It seems Ted had become a Christian and would let no one else do the interview because he believed he had some important things to say. In this video, Ted told his story of how he was raised by good parents in a Christian home.

At around ten he found some explicit magazines and that led to an addiction to pornography. That had led to fantasy, and as a young man he committed his first rape. Every time he raped, it left him only temporarily satisfied, and each time required more and more violence in order to satisfy. That violence led to the murders of the young women. While in prison, Ted Bundy gave his life to Jesus Christ. As a believer he came to understand the dangers of pornography and how it had led to his horrendous acts. His last act in life was a warning for other men of the danger.

"Billy, what do you think?" Jorge asked.

"It's hard to imagine that something that doesn't really seem all that harmful, could carry Ted to those depths of depravity," I replied.

"That's why I wanted you to see the video," said Jorge. "Ten years ago, when I first saw it, my eyes were opened to the seriousness of our problem. Sin is progressive. Sin without repentance provides Satan with a wedge by which he will pull us deeper and deeper into our own depravity. This is the birthplace of perversion.

"Did you know that statistics show that it's likely that over half the men in your church are struggling with these issues? Problems like this are subtly piercing the minds of our children on TV, on the internet, on Instagram, and every other media outlet imaginable. It is in the culture of public schools, the culture of our youth, you name it. We are in spiritual warfare. We have to see that. We must address these things. Christians have turned their heads long enough. How can we talk about the horrors of the Holocaust when over fifty million babies have died at the hands of legalized abortion? When you get an honest look at how things are, it's pretty overwhelming.

"I spent a lot of time praying and a lot of time studying when I realized all of this, but mainly I just started doing what I could. The more I trusted God in what I was doing the more doors He opened for me to do even more. I read all of Chuck Colson's books. What an impactful man. To think how God could use the craziness of Watergate and prison time to shape him." Jorge paused.

"Billy, I have something to tell you."

"What is that, Jorge?" I asked.

"I have been praying to our Creator to send me someone to embrace all that He has taught me and take it back to share with the United States. Are you that man?" asked Jorge.

"Maybe," I replied, somewhat overwhelmed at the thought. "I don't know yet, but I am certainly looking at what you are doing and understanding the revolutionary nature of it! I'm just not sure how God wants to use me in this, and how to implement it in my own church."

"Billy, the secret to all this is, you don't have to know.

Faith is knowing that He will lead you each step of the way. Faith is one day at a time. If we don't do things that way, we tend to run ahead and do them on our own. Not only that, but we might start to think we're really something, when it is all Him."

This left me with much to ponder. I turned toward the dining room and said. "Let's go to dinner. The smell is making me hungry."

"Let's go," Jorge said.

CHAPTER 15.

It was no secret that dinner was almost ready. "What's cooking Jorge?" I asked.

"I'll let that be a surprise for you."

I went in the house and caught up with Laura and the kids.

"I've got a surprise for you tonight," she said. "I've been helping in the kitchen. I wanted to learn one of Maria's secret recipes."

"For what?" I asked curiously.

"You'll see."

I turned to the boys and gave them each a hug. "Bryan, Bobby, do you know?"

"Yeah, but we're not telling," Bryan said for them both.

"Okay. You can't keep the secret for long. Let's have dinner! Wash your hands Billy. You too, Bryan."

As we entered the dining room there was a buffet set out along the back wall. I couldn't help myself, so I started lifting warmer lids and searching out the source of the aroma. First there were all these buns, not like American hot dog buns but larger and they smelled delicious. You could tell they had been fried in bacon drippings. Then the dogs; giant sausages, spicy with peppers, and oozing with cheese. There were bowls with an avocado sauce. With that, I got it! We were having authentic Sonoran hot dogs, but these were not like the ones you see from the street vendors. They were extravagant.

"What do you think, Billy," asked Jorge. "Laura told me these were your favorite."

"Yeah, they look wonderful!" I exclaimed. "I see all the veggies, Jorge. With these sausages I can flourish in my own creative element! No two are just alike!"

"Let's gather up and pray," said Jorge. "I'm hungry!"

"Me too!"

Over two hundred people gathered in the dining room and they all seemed like family. What a blessing for a man who had lost a precious wife and daughter. God knows how to wipe away tears.

"Billy would you do the honors? I'll translate."

"Lord," I began. "Thank you for the bounty of food but thank you most for the bounty of new-found friends. Amen."

After dinner we did our evening Bible study with Billy and Bobby. We then prayed with them and put them to bed. Laura and I climbed into our bed, very tired after the busy day. "Laura, tell me how was the school," I said as I pulled the covers up.

"It was amazing! Phenomenal! but I had rather show you," she said enthusiastically.

"I had kind of thought about beginning my wilderness journey tomorrow, but I suppose it can wait,"

"Billy, it should. You are not going to believe the things they are doing at the school. You won't believe them without seeing them."

"Let's call it a day," I replied. We shut the light off, said a quick prayer, and fell fast asleep.

The next morning after breakfast, a group of parents, the younger children, and all the teachers, loaded on to two school buses. We were accompanied by Adolfo.

"Where are the older kids, Adolfo?" I asked.

"They all have chores to do," he replied. "They will be here in an hour or so."

"Why so many parents?

"If we are to teach children, we must also train their parents. The parents are expected to help their own children and teach them manners. Many of the parents have little or no education, themselves. Often, we are working hard, trying to keep them up with of their own kids. They are also expected to model spiritual leadership in their families. We include the Bible in their reading lessons. You'll see when we get there." Adolfo explained.

"That's right, Billy," added Laura. "The first class I want to sit in on is the parenting class."

"Sounds like a plan Laura," I agreed.

As we entered the parents' class, we were very pleased at the courtesy and respect all the folks showed us. They were each gathered in groups of six. First, they discussed their particular issues, and then, one at a time prayed for each other. As they finished, a large screen lit up with a scripture reading for the day. The scripture was shown in Spanish with the English parallel directly to its right. The teacher helped with the English words, and briefly explained what they meant. In their groups, the more advanced helped others with difficulties.

There were four people who went from group to group. These turned out to be people who had completed their training. Adolfo explained that each day volunteers came from the community to help the others. He also explained that this was highest priority, so any workers from around the ranch were free to volunteer time at the school at any time. The school teachers also spent time with each of the families, ensuring that all was going well.

Discipline was important, and misbehavior was not tolerated.

"Do you spank the children?" I asked.

"Sometimes, but rarely do we need to. It is part of our holistic approach that there are always plenty chores to do to correct any misbehavior. The children learn our non-tolerance policy very fast, and they become our best teachers of discipline. When a couple of kids have chopped wood for a few days with the blisters to prove it, they spread the word. The culture of good behavior takes hold in a hurry. Anyone who does misbehave, also has to go home and face mamma and daddy," Adolfo explained. We stepped into the bright sunlight.

"Before we go to the elementary classes, I want to show

you some of the testing we do," Adolfo said. "When each child enters our program, they are tested. We look for what methods will best suit each individual child for learning. For example, some are visual learners, others audible learners, and others are doers. They are hands on learners. Often the type of learners they are, will shape the proper career choices for them. What we know for sure is, that understanding a child's learning style, helps us find the best ways to teach him. One of my jobs is to build a teaching model for each child. The teachers get to know each child well and are expected to stay with their group of children throughout their elementary years.

"Occasionally we may have to shift teachers because of personality clashes but most teachers will stay with one group of children for six years. If a teacher has problems adjusting to the children's needs or their spiritual issues, they are invited to go back to Hermosillo. The truth is, if the teachers don't love their students, they will never make it here. We continually re-evaluate how we do things and are always looking to improve. The teachers' relationships with each other often promote innovative and creative ideas so we meet with them frequently. We have used ideas from James Dobson, Kevin Leman and other top ranked Christians in the field, to develop our methods of teaching.

"Billy," Adolfo said.

"Yes."

"Let's take a quick tour of our classes." Adolfo then led us to visual classroom where stacks of books, whiteboards, and a video projector graced the room. The children were clustered in groups when we arrived. Each group read their assigned book. As they were wrapping up, the teacher handed a question sheet for each child to answer questions about the reading assignment. After that, we moved to the auditory room. There children read out loud and questions were asked and answered out loud. For the hands-on learners, each time a paragraph was read, there was a puzzle piece to be placed in its proper spot matching that part of the story. I guess the part that surprised me most

Lonnie Barnard

was how the kids worked so well together.
    It was time for us to move on because the Secondary kids had, arrived and we wanted to see their classes.

CHAPTER 16.

"Before we go to the secondary classrooms I want to drop by the office and show you our evaluation system, Alfonso said. We wandered over to a small building with a lot of files and papers scattered on desks. It was all very busy but neat.

"Sit right here beside me so you can see the computer screen," he motioned. I'll pull up a couple of names, so you can see how we do this. Alfonso turned on the computer and typed in a password. "Here, Alfredo Munoz. He's fifteen years old and has completed most of his academics. He spends his afternoons in our machine and welding shop. You might ask, how he got here! Alfredo is one of our hands-on learners. After extensive evaluation, it was determined that Alfredo's gifts were in trade related fields. He has artistic ability, and likely will be involved in some sort of manufacturing, or production related field. After his evaluation was complete, we met with him and his guardians and prayed with them. We asked for guidance, and with his direction, determined his future course of studies.

"Notice that I said 'guardians' instead of parents. Like Alfredo, many of the children are orphans when they come here, and they are assigned to families. Whatever their skill set may be, we encourage them to seek spiritual guidance before making any decisions. Often, the skills we discover open doors for them. They may even take these skills into a missionary oriented service. Many skills will get them into foreign countries to share the Gospel.

"Next let's look at Pedro Garcia. He is one of our top academic students. He excels in math and science but is also a hands-on kid. He spends an hour each day in our machine shop like Alfredo, but with a different angle. He will graduate this year, though he is only sixteen years old. All our programs are goal oriented so students that excel can graduate early. He plans to major in mechanical engineering and is likely to receive a scholarship to Arizona State University.

"Look. Here is Marcia De La Rosa. She is a musician of supreme talent. She plays the violin and guitar but is also great at the piano and organ, as well as any other keyboard instrument. She has written several of the praise songs we use on Sundays. She is only fifteen and already has an offer from Julliard."

"Alfonso, it seems you have some very gifted students." That seems unusual considering most of them came from the Barrio at the dump!' I blurted out.

"Billy, we don't see it that way. We think that Christianity and a good discipleship program should produce students that achieve at a very high level. If we set our hearts on the things of God, why wouldn't He supernaturally empower us to produce true world changers! Why shouldn't Christians be the hardest working, most dependable people in the world! The bottom line is, when a person sees a Christian, he should see someone he would really want to be like.

"Everything we are trying to do is to give these kids the best opportunity we can at showing the world just how attractive it is to be like Jesus. We want to produce the smartest, kindest, most loving, most giving, hardest working kids in the world. God is interested in making us the best we can be. That's our goal. Each time I watch the next group graduate, I wonder how many they will lead to Christ?"

Alfonso got up from his chair and changed the subject. "How much do you know about Philosophy?"

"A little."

"Then we'll go to that class next, although we call it 'apologetics.' Philosophy is just part of what they are learning."

We entered a room where the students were in a deep discussion about Niche. Felecia was presenting her opposition to Niche's "God is dead" scenario from, "Thus spake Zarathustra".

She said, "Niche did not come to his conclusions because he had carefully thought through and reasoned his case. He began from his own immoral perverse lifestyle, and then tried to find a philosophy that would justify it. Did you know that he spent the last years of his life in an asylum and likely died from syphilis?"

"Good Job Felecia!" I exclaimed. "Alfonso that's college level thinking!"

"That's the plan, Billy," he said.

"Let's go to our construction shop," Alfonso suggested next. "Billy, I want you to meet Julio, the teacher of these students. He used to work for Jorge's construction company, but as he got older, we put him here to teach. You know, it's easier on the back, especially as the kids can do the physical work for him. We try to introduce them to all phases of construction; foundations, framing, roofing, trim and carpentry. They even get introductions to plumbing, electrical and HVAC. After a couple of years, they are expected to narrow their choice down to a preferred trade, but some continue to learn more about all trades in order to prepare themselves for construction management. Students who plan on going into engineering or architecture are expected to get some hands-on experience here too," Alfonso explained.

"Although all our secondary students take Bible classes each year, they are also assigned study programs to follow at home. Our plan is for spiritual development to be primarily addressed in the family environment.

We moved outside again, and I looked up amazed at the deep blue sky. "Let's head back to the office," Alfonso said. "I want to show you how we assess development. This is how our students advance to their next level." Back inside the office, we sat down at the same desk. "Let's look at the screen again. We'll go back to Pedro Garcia's file. Notice as we look at his math development, how quickly he moved from basic arithmetic to algebra, through geometry, and is now completing calculus. Because each student is so carefully evaluated, they are set up with curriculum that is tailor-made. Our office group takes their evaluation and writes a program for the student personally. They progress at their own pace. Our teachers are very knowledgeable and spend a lot of time with each student, especially if they run into an impasse."

"Billy, do you see what I mean?" said Laura, who had been following along quietly the whole way. "This whole thing blows my mind, Billy!"

"I suppose the thing that makes all this work so well," Alfonso responded, "I mean a key factor besides the fact that we are following God's plan, is that our teachers only have about five hours of class time each day. We spend a lot of time evaluating our methods, assessing their effectiveness, and making necessary changes and improvements."

"Alfonso, can Laura and I pray for these kids?" I asked.

"Of course, you can, Billy. Let's walk to the front entry," Alfonso suggested.

"Laura, you first," I said.

'Lord," she prayed, "bless this work of your hands. Teach these young ladies to be the best they can be." Laura's heart was on the girls. "Make them the most wonderful mothers and best, most supportive wives of the men they will marry. Bless those you have chosen for other work and give them a special anointing for what you call them to do."

"God, anoint and bless the next generation of world changers you are training," I continued. "May they serve you with excellence and courage and bring your love to a lost and dying world. Amen."

CHAPTER 17.

That evening after dinner Laura, Bryan, Bobby and I slipped out onto the front porch. It had been a whirlwind of days and they filled my mind with thousands of thoughts. I could easily see that all the ideas God had brought into the heart of Jorge, had already had a phenomenal impact on the lives of this little community. True discipleship was reality in this place. It did not come without a lot of effort but mostly I could see that the hearts of the people were "all in," committed. I could also see that in this poverty-stricken country, a little hope could go a long way.

"How could we pull this off in an affluent country like the US?" I wondered aloud. "Laura what do you think?"

"I don't know Billy. We've been trying to get our church members to take a class or just to rethink the way they do parenting and haven't had much luck even with that. Here's what I do know Billy. Our God is wise enough. He is powerful enough to do it!" Laura said with conviction.

"I know that's true Laura, so the question is why doesn't He?" I asked.

"I think the problem is us. He wants to, but He waits on us to be all in. Billy, I think we are there, but remember, Jorge didn't do this by himself. Look at this community. God has built an entire community around His plan!" Laura said.

"Yeah, Laura. It makes me think, would we be wasting our time to go back?"

"Maybe, Billy. I don't know."

"I mean, Laura, if we could be more effective here why wouldn't we just stay?" I wondered.

"Billy, I think we need to remember that at least part of Jorge's effectiveness is his heart for his people. Our heart is for our own families, for our communities. I think before we leave, God will answer those questions. He's not going to leave us hanging." Laura's confidence was encouraging.

"Bobby and Bryan, are you checking out the stars?" I asked.

"Yeah, Dad. Are there more stars in Mexico than in Tucson?" asked Bryan.

"Well, it certainly seems like it, doesn't it, boys?"

"Sure does!" exclaimed Bobby.

"No. To answer your question look toward the mountains across the valley. We can't see anything. That's right guys, the mountains are totally dark. You know this situation illustrates God in a spiritual sense," I said.

"How's that?" they asked.

"The darker it seems around us, the brighter His light shines. He hung every one of those stars in its place. He named each one of them. They're all his creation," I said.

"Dad, our God must be really big!" Bobby exclaimed.

"That's right Bobby, bigger than we can even imagine."

"Then Dad, why doesn't he fix all this?" asked Bobby. "I mean sin and all the evil?"

"He is fixing it Bobby, but He doesn't wear a watch. Everything happens in His own time. He knows why. It's all in His plan, boys" I said.

"Laura." I turned to my wife enthusiastically.

"Yes sweetheart," she answered.

"I think that's our answer!" I exclaimed.

"What are you talking about, Billy?"

"He wants us to wait! He hears our prayers. He's already answering them. There are things that only He can do. When He gets them ready, He will share with us what He wants us to do."

"Billy, do you suppose that He's already at work in our church back home preparing the hearts of our friends? And if He intends for us to go back there, He will tell us what to do when the time comes?" she asked, getting excited.

"That's exactly what He's probably doing and that's His plan," I suddenly realized.

"We will go back to the church, ready to do what we've failed at for the last ten years, only it will all be different this time. Some days I need to remind myself of who God is. Looking at these stars reminds me just how small I am, and just how much I need Him."

Jorge and Maria came out onto the porch with us.

"Good evening folks! May we join you?" Jorge asked.

"Of course, you two are always welcome to be with us! I said.

"Looking at the stars, huh?" he asked.

"Yes, sir, and enjoying every minute of it!" I said. "Where have you been, Jorge? I was looking for you earlier."

"I was helping Maria and the others with the dishes," Jorge replied.

"You do that?" I asked, surprised.

"I think it is important to maintain a servant's heart," Jorge said. "If the others see that attitude, they will understand that they too must never outgrow the need to serve. Now here we are sitting on the porch gazing at the vastness of creation. If that doesn't humble you, nothing will!"

Maria snuggled up to Jorge. "When the weather's nice, we sit out here and pray," she said shyly.

"That's a good idea. We always pray with the boys each night. Tonight, we can do it here with our new family," I suggested.

That night, six believers in Jesus Christ prayed as God unveiled a few of the mysteries of His Kingdom and filled their hearts with faith that would lead them to serve and worship Him, the one true God.

CHAPTER 18.

"Billy, before you and Laura go to bed, I want to discuss something with you," Jorge stated.

"Jorge is now a good time?" I asked.

"Perfect, have a seat," he replied. "Laura, you're welcome to join us."

"I think I'll put the boys to bed," Laura replied, taking the boys by the hand and leading them inside.

"Fair enough!" said Jorge. "Billy, are you ready for your trip to meet with God?"

"I'm ready enough, but He hasn't moved me there yet."

"Good," said Jorge. "I'd like for you to take a trip to Hermosillo with me tomorrow if that's alright with you."

"I'm up for it. Where are we going?"

"To the Federal Prison there. I want to show you something," he said.

"Let me check with Laura, but I'm sure it will be okay," I replied.

"You'll need to be up at five."

"That's fine I'll be ready."

"Goodnight my friend," Jorge stood up to go in.

"Goodnight, Jorge."

I went inside to where Laura was lying awake in bed waiting for me. "Laura, if it's okay with you, Jorge has asked me to take a trip with him to Hermosillo tomorrow," I said.

"That's fine, where are you going?" she asked sleepily.

"To the Federal Prison," I said nonchalantly.

Laura looked up quickly, "Sounds dangerous!"

"Probably, but I trust Jorge," I assured her. "Let's pray!"

Laura was eager to pray first. "Lord, give Billy a soft heart, your heart, as you show him the great needs of the people you love, the people you teach us how to love. Bless the work of this ranch, the finest example of Christianity we have ever seen. Amen."

"Jesus, my Lord and Savior, protect my family as you unveil your plan for us," I prayed. "Teach my sons your ways and help us to be good stewards of the gifts you give us. Amen."

At 5:00 AM, Maria was up as usual, with a thermos filled with coffee. She had two sabaqueras, filled with eggs, bacon, cheese, chorizo and a dash of hot sauce prepared for us to take with us. We quickly got on the road to Hermosillo. I was grateful for sippy cups, made for children and mountain roads! Early in the morning, to my delight, I watched a puma dash across in front of us. I watched the sun as it slowly lit up the mountain tops across the valley. Saguaro, Cholla, Black Brush, and Lechugilla drifted past my window. Jackrabbits holding tight to the brush, seemed to be alert for mountain lions shopping for breakfast. As we crossed a dry ravine, Desert Willow and Tamarisk made their appearance. Soon an abundance of Cholla in full bloom gave a white backdrop to violet flowers of the desert Senna.

We pulled over to pour a second cup of coffee, and when I crawled back into the Jeep I was not pleased. I had picked up a couple of Cholla pods as passengers. Apparently, Jorge was quite familiar with the problem. He tossed me a pair of pliers to expedite their removal. My attempts at getting the pods off with my fingers, only resulted in a painful transfer, rather than removal.

"Billy, I'm not going to explain what we will see," Jorge said. "I don't think words can adequately describe it. What I do want to say though is, nothing I have ever seen has more impacted my sense of the miraculous. Most of what you have already seen, gave me a sense of awe. But when we started our partnership with Prison Fellowship and experienced the results you are about to see, I fully embraced the power of Jesus to transform the world."

We pulled up to the gates and guards approached the Jeep. Jorge pulled out an ID card, but from the conversation it seemed they knew him quite well. We drove down a narrow road to the headquarters building, and he pulled out the ID card again, this time swiping it through a keyless entry pad. Heavy magnetic locks opened with a loud clank, and we entered a secure area with two guards carrying AK 47s. These guards manually opened a second set of gates. The warden met us in the lobby and escorted us to his office.

"Louis, I want you to meet my friend Billy," Jorge said. The warden gave me a quick glance and turned back to Jorge.

"Jorge are you planning on going to the Christian section of the prison?" he asked.

"Yes, but later," Jorge replied. "I'd like Billy to get a tour of the regular prison section first."

"Okay," replied the warden sternly, "but you'll have to sign some waivers first and then I will furnish you two guards as escorts."

"Waivers? What's that Jorge?" I asked. They sounded ominous.

"They are waivers of responsibility from the government," Jorge explained to me. "Violence is a common occurrence."

"Have you ever had a problem?" I asked, trying not to sound nervous.

"Yes, but not anymore. They know who I am. That's a whole different story. I'll share it with you later."

We entered one of the wings of the main cell area. The first thing that hit me was the smell. A horrendous odor punched me in the nose as the door slammed shut behind us.

"Are you sure you're ready for this?" Jorge asked, as he handed me a face mask.

"I doubt it!" I said. "But I think I need to do this." The next thing that hit me was an uncanny sense of the presence of evil. The hair on the back of my neck stood up. I looked around at the graffiti. Guns, knife battles, and even naked females and sex acts, and of course profanity in Spanish as well as English, splattered across the walls.

"Much of the graffiti was written in excrement and blood," Jorge explained. It was then that I understood the source of the smell. "This prison was opened in 2012. It's the nicest one in the Mexican system, so you can only imagine what some of the others are like."

We walked toward the recreation yard, where basketball games, soccer games and workout sessions were all taking place at the same time. As we stood there watching, three separate fights broke out within ten minutes. The guards seemed helpless or oblivious to control the chaos. "Billy somebody dies in this yard almost on a daily basis," Jorge said. "Come on, I want to show you something else."

We made our way down a hallway and exited through another door which clicked shut loudly behind us, to a building across another yard. As we entered that building, fresh air and coolness hit me but the sense of evil prevailed. "This is where the Cartel prisoners stay," said Jorge. "They have TV's, kitchens, air conditioning, video games, a movie library and who knows what else. This building was built from donated funds, and you can only imagine where the funds came from."

The guards then led us down another hallway and out another locked door to arrive at another building. Immediately the sense of evil was replaced with peace and we saw a large group of men gathered in a dining room, seated at tables with open Bibles.

"Two years ago, there was a revival in this prison conducted by Prison Fellowship," explained Jorge. "These men are Christians. The man teaching them is from that first group of believers. Each week some of our men come here to teach. What do you think Billy?"

"Well the first thing I notice is the difference in the smell! This building is clean and the graffiti here is beautiful artwork. The atmosphere is one of order and peacefulness!" I exclaimed.

"Makes perfect sense doesn't it, Billy?"

"Yes, it does, but the contrast blows my mind."

"It should. This is the most visible example of the power of the resurrection I have ever seen. Each week ten of the men from the general prison population are invited to stay here for a week. Most never leave. They stay here because they too, become changed men. Isn't this what the world needs to see out of Christianity? Truly transformed lives. Miracles. That's what God does. These men will one day leave here as true disciples, men of God. They are the next generation of missionaries and evangelists."

"Amazing Jorge," I said with awe. "Just amazing!"

"Yeah, Jesus is like that."

"Amen."

CHAPTER 19.

On our way back from the prison we passed the dump barrio. I could see the bus there, and my mind drifted back to our time there. "Jorge, I am amazed at all the different things you're involved in," I said. "Where do you come up with all these ideas?"

"First, I don't really see them as my ideas, but God's," answered Jorge. "I don't think God gave them to me until my heart was ready."

"What do you mean by ready?"

"Those early days when I really began to walk with Him, were spent in prayer and Bible study." Jorge explained. "That's how I learned His ways, how He thinks, and how He works. I began to love others like He loves me and began to see all these needs.

"Trips to the dump simply started as a way to make sure the children had food. Then soon I began to understand that feeding them only made them feel better for a day. Finally, I began to think about their future, such things as jobs and skills, some way for them to take care of themselves. I realized then, that their behavior, education, and even the adults in their lives, all needed to be addressed. We also had to find a way to compete with the cartel. They were recruiting young men and girls at a very rapid rate. Then, there were all the spiritual issues such as illicit sex, drug use, and quick easy money through lives of crime, and so on. As we shared the Gospel, we could see lives changed, but we knew that the cycles of poverty, culture of corruption, immorality, and many other things, had to be addressed also. If Christians wouldn't do it, certainly no one else would. A holistic approach is the only way. It looks at mankind from birth all the way into eternity. The task is overwhelming, that is without God, but with God it all is possible.

"Take our prison work for instance," Jorge continued. "We kept running across children living in the barrio, on the streets, or wherever, because their parents were in jail. When we visited prisons to locate the parents, we quickly became acquainted with the appalling conditions there. It wasn't as if we didn't have some knowledge of it before, but when you see it with your eyes it becomes real. If you love, if you have the heart of God, you can't turn your head anymore. I think that is our biggest problem in the church. We think if we don't see it, then it doesn't exist. We both know that's not true.

"With the prison, we did a little homework and discovered this amazing work already going on. We called Prison Fellowship and they put a group together to train us to share the gospel in prison. It took a lot of pulling strings to make it happen. Finally, I had to risk calling my old ex-friend Pedro to get us in.

"On the day of that first meeting, as the men gathered in the yard to hear the gospel, we faced tremendous opposition. But Prison Fellowship's evangelist seemed oblivious to the fights, the profanity being shouted and even the fruit being thrown at him. He simply began to pray, and after about ten minutes a calm swept through the crowd. Over two hundred men were saved that day. Several of those men were beaten to death in the weeks that followed, but none denied their newfound belief in Jesus.

"A new wing had just been completed and we were able to talk the warden into setting it up for our new Christian brothers. I will not tell you that he had become sympathetic to our cause, but he had to do something because he was facing a full-blown riot due to the sudden amount of conflict. I hope you can see that Satan was pulling out all the stops to destroy what had been started. The work that was started on that day is now sweeping through the entire Mexican prison system. This is all an amazing display of the power of prayer."

We turned off the highway for our final leg of the trip back to the ranch. My head was spinning with all the information I was trying to process.

"Jorge, you know in Acts 2, when the church was born, it says 'they were all in one accord.' Then later it says those that had property sold it and no one had need. Later in Acts 4 it re-emphasizes that. In Acts 5, Ananias and Sapphira were struck dead when they misrepresented the sale of their property. I've struggled with all that for a long time. It seems that the early church was socialistic in practice. What do you think?" I asked.

"I think your right," Jorge answered, "but I think it can be dangerous to see these passages in a legalistic sense. Our community certainly operates in a socialistic pattern, but then again, we benefit from those in America who operate in a capitalistic fashion. Joe, Laura's dad, is a major contributor to our work. His building supply company makes that possible.

"I think one of the problems of capitalism is that in America it has caused a very selfish element within Christianity. This is totally against Biblical truth. On the other hand, men like Joe are able to take their blessing, and turn it into greater profit benefiting the entire Christian community," explained Jorge.

"Jorge, that brings up another issue. Maybe one of the biggest problems American churches have had to deal with, is that the dream of prosperity and wealth consumes church members to the point where careers and material goods become their definition of success."

"I think your dead on, Billy. I'm not sure how you could get Americans to buy into the sort of holistic approach we are doing here. One thing for sure Billy, what we are doing here resembles much more closely the culture that Jesus birthed the church into." Jorge said.

"I'm not sure how you can motivate Americans into the sort of generosity we see here," I said.

"That's something I think we need to pray about. God knows the answer for sure," Jorge said.

"Amen, Jorge."

"Billy we should get back around three. There's something else I want to show you, and since we are bringing up hard questions maybe you can help me with this one," Jorge said.

"What's that, Jorge?"

"I'd rather you see for yourself and then if you have some answers, tell me."

"Okay."

When we got back to the ranch, Jorge drove past the shop and along the edge of the lake to a building with a high fence around it surrounded by a hedge of flowers. "Billy, the people that stay here have mental disorders," he said. "They are either violent to themselves or others, or just too incapacitated to function. They need close supervision. We take care of them and do our best to treat them but I'm afraid many of them may never function normally. We've brought in a psychiatrist, but he is only able to alleviate some of their symptoms, and once they start using medications there are so many complications."

"Now, Jorge, that is a difficult issue," I said. "I can't say I have the answer, but mental health issues are rampant in the U.S. too. I've been asking the same question."

"We pray for their healing, but God doesn't always come through that way," Jorge said.

"I know," I said.

"I'm thinking it through this way," Jorge said. "Can Jesus heal them? Of course. He has before. Will He? I don't know. Certainly, much of evil's impact will be here as long as evil exists. We are making strides with Biblical counseling for Post-Traumatic Stress Disorder, but it is up to the person who has it to cooperate for it to work. As for chemical imbalances and neurological disorders, all we seem to be able to do is pray and keep them as comfortable and safe as possible. At least, as we take turns caring for them, it provides us with more opportunities to learn to serve Jesus."

"That makes a lot of sense," I said thoughtfully. "That's more than the mentally ill get elsewhere. Jorge, why don't you pull over. Let's pray about this now."

"Okay, watch out for the Cholla." Jorge pulled onto a bare spot next to the road and we bowed before a Holy God and prayed for the mentally ill in the compound and for those back in Tucson. There was a moment of silence after we were done.

"Billy, God's going to answer our prayer," Jorge said.

"I believe that too," I said. "I just don't know how yet."

"Isn't that how faith works Billy?"

"Yes, it is Jorge."

We went back toward the main hacienda and as we pulled into the driveway Laura and the boys ran up to greet me. Deep inside I knew that tomorrow I would begin my journey into the wilderness to meet with God.

"It's time, Jorge," I said.

"To meet with God, Billy?" he asked.

"Yeah."

"I have a special place for you to go to," Jorge said.

"Where's that?"

"I'll show you, I'll take you there."

"What makes it special?"

"It is where I met with God ten years ago," Jorge said.

"I'm ready, Jorge."

CHAPTER 20.

At dinner that evening, I shared my plans with Laura and we decided to spend our evening with just our family. Laura made hot chocolate and we sat with our boys in front of a roaring fire in the fireplace.

"Dad can I go with you?" asked Bobby. Bryan chimed in with the same question.

"Not this time, boys."

"Why not?" Bryan asked.

"This is not like our other camping trips," I replied. "It has to be just me alone since I am hoping to meet with God."

"But Dad, we love Jesus too! We would like to meet him too!" they exclaimed.

"I'm sure you would, and the time will come when I think you will. I think when a man goes to meet God, he needs to be alone. That's the way it has always been as men of the Bible met with God. Meeting with God is so sacred, so special, that a man needs to be able to give Him his undivided attention," I explained.

"I see Dad. We will pray for you, that He will be there and meet you," said Bobby.

"Perfect guys! That's exactly what I was hoping you would do!"

"Dad why is it so important to meet God?" asked Bryan.

"It's a little like meeting Michael Jordan only much, much bigger," I tried to explain.

"Who's Michael Jordan?" Bobby asked.

"Oh, I'm sorry, Lebron James," I said quickly.

"Oh, does Jesus play basketball?"

"I'm sure He could if He wanted to," I said. "The point is that He is so big, so awesome and so powerful that there really isn't any person to help you understand how great He is. After all He's God!"

"Dad I'm confused," said Bryan.

"How's that?"

"You say 'Jesus', then you say 'God' as if they are the same," Bryan said.

"They are," I replied.

"How can that be?" asked Bobby.

"We'll save that explanation for another day when your father understands how to explain it," I said, wishing I had a better answer.

"So, Billy, when are you leaving?" Laura asked, still smiling at my conversation with the boys.

"After lunch. I want to spend the morning here, and besides, I don't have my pack ready," I replied.

"Oh Billy, you're always the procrastinator! Nearly everything is in that back closet in our bedroom. I just have to stow it in your backpack and double check the list," Laura said.

"Laura, are you sure you're okay with all this? I asked.

"Not only am I okay, but I have been praying for this day. I am very excited for you and for whatever it is God wants to do through us. I just wish we could do this together," she said.

"I know. I will try to bring every detail back. I am sure there will be a lot for us to discuss when I get back," I assured her.

"Billy let's pray and call it a night. Are you good with that boys?" she asked.

"Yes Ma'am."

"Billy?" she asked.

"Yes Ma'am." I looked at Laura and then bowed my head. "Lord bless this family. Help us to know your will, to do your will, and to see your hands leading and empowering the work you have for us. Amen."

My eyes opened when my nose awoke them, with the

smell of pancakes and sausage drifting down the hall from the kitchen. We finished breakfast, and Jorge gathered most of the ranch members together to pray over me. We all joined hands in three circles around the dining room. Jorge prayed God's blessing and then everyone prayed out loud. Spanish, English, two hundred people praying at once, and I am sure God heard every word. I am sure that God was already working to answer all those prayers.

I said goodbye to Laura and the boys as they climbed in the bus to head toward the school. Jorge and I studied the maps on his computer, and after he explained where we were going, he printed out two copies for me to stuff in my backpack.

"Billy, I can drive to within five miles of your location but from there you will have to walk," he explained. "There are usually shepherds within five or ten miles. Take these three flares just in case you get in trouble. They should be able to see them to bring help. By the way, you won't need the tent, but I am sending this tarp with you. It will come in handy."

"How's that?" I asked.

"The place is a cave. The tarp will serve as a nice porch to build a campfire under. So, you've studied the books on edible plants and my recipes for wild game?"

"Sure have."

"Which rifle did you choose? Jorge asked.

"The 223-Remington," I replied.

"That's it?"

"I'm carrying the 20-gauge too," I said.

"Ammo?" he asked.

"Twenty rounds of each," I said, looking at my huge backpack and the guns, and wondering how I would carry them. "I'm good."

"Okay, let's load up and go," Jorge said. "You'll want to have camp set up before dark."

"Jorge, how did you find this place?" I asked when we got in the jeep.

"That's a long story but we have time. As we head up, I

will tell you."

We wound past the last of the buildings, headed north, and where we had turned left before we turned right. There the upper lake came into view. We crested the first peak and I could see a rugged road across a valley and up the next ridge. Beyond that, the mountains stair stepped higher and higher as each ridge was sky lighted above and beyond the next.

"The cave you will be staying in Billy is over seven thousand feet up. It will be cold at night but during the day it will be beautiful. That is unless you get a snowstorm. I've looked at your gear. You are well prepared. Back when I did this, ten years ago, I nearly froze to death. You are much better prepared than me. That kind of leads to my story.

"Truth is when I came, I didn't really care if I lived or died," Jorge began.

"Why is that?"

"Remember, I had just been caught by your father-in-law smuggling drugs. I had just become a Christian. Shortly after that, my wife and daughter had been killed. While I was still in Tucson, I had no reason to come back to Hermosillo. but God spoke to me. He said that I must leave or die in Tucson. If I had to die, I said I might as well do it at home. I called my friend, the Mayor of Hermosillo. He said that he could hide me on the ranch. I prayed, and God said 'yes' that he would meet me there. I was angry at God. I was afraid of Pedro who was hunting me in Hermosillo, but I was more afraid of God. There was nowhere to hide from Him. I went to the ranch for about a month and did nothing but pray and read my Bible.

"Then word came that Pedro knew where I was, and he was sending men after me. I packed up and headed to the mountains. I had my guns and a good bit of knowledge on how to survive in the wilderness.

"It is twenty-two miles to where we are going, I walked the whole way. There was no road then and I thought I could hide out here forever. Pedro could not find me here. And he didn't. But after I had been there a few weeks, my worst fear came true. I learned that I could hide from Pedro, but I could not hide from God. He found me there. He began to speak to me. He told me he had great plans for me, but I would have to learn to trust Him. Maybe I should have left my Bible at the ranch, but I didn't. Instead, I had been reading every day. God told me that for the loss of my daughter He would restore me with thousands of daughters. He told me not to fear Pedro. He was taking care of that. I came back, Billy. I trusted Him. The rest is history and it's not over yet." Jorge suddenly stopped.

"There it is Billy, up on the side of that mountain! There's the cave!" he exclaimed. "Here look at it through these binoculars." Jorge handed a pair to me and I searched the scenery. "You see it?" he asked.

"Yeah," I replied, "to the left!"

"You see the little spring?" Jorge asked.

"Yeah," I said, straining to make out a gully surrounded by greenery.

"It never runs dry. It is the sweetest water you will ever taste. I send my shepherds up here sometimes to bring home a few jugs for me," he said.

"It reminds me of Jesus," I commented. "Maybe that's His plan for me. Remember the woman at Jacob's well? He offered her springs of living water that would never run dry."

"This is it, Billy." Jorge started unloading my gear. "At least it is for me," he said.

"I know now why you brought me here, Jorge," I said. "This is where you met with God. This is where He spoke to you."

"That's right, Billy. And He ain't done yet! Let me pray for you Billy." Jorge looked up this time instead of down. "Lord, you met me here. I pray that you will meet with Billy here too. Amen.

"This is it Billy," he said again with finality. "You walk from here."

"Thank you, Jorge. Jesus couldn't have sent me a better friend," I said giving him a hug.

"That's the kind of God he is, Billy. He loves us."

CHAPTER 21.

Jorge pulled forward, turned the jeep around, and then came back to me and got out. "There's something else I need to tell you, Billy. No one has been here since me. I brought you here because it is so special to me. There is more to the story though. The crime I committed, that is the drugs brought into Tucson, and the grace Joe showed me, are all debts I need to repay. I prayed for God to send me someone I could give back to. Little did I know that it would be Joe's son-in-law. Can I pray for you Billy?"

"Sure," I replied. We knelt beside the Jeep and we prayed. Then I put on my pack, picked up my guns, strapped my survival kit around my waist, and started up the mountain as Jorge drove away.

Well, I am finally here Jesus, just you and me. I have some questions, but mainly I'm here just to listen and walk with you like Adam, Abraham and Moses. I know it's your timing not mine. I'm ready.

I could see from the trees that the stream must cross about a hundred yards ahead. When I got there, just as expected, the stream carved out a smooth pathway to the cave through a tall grove of mountain pines. There I turned and followed the gully slowly up the hill. The winding stream led me steadily toward my destination. The water fed an abundance of wildflowers. Six mule deer bucks jumped in front of me. They were still carrying their magnificent racks as it was late winter. After two hours, I reached the entrance to the cave.

Inside, a pair of raccoons scrambled to escape as I took possession of their home. After I cleared their nesting debris and poop, I was ready to call this home. I set my pack about eight feet inside the entrance and made my way back down the hill to the closest grove of pine. I had spotted a few dead trees that would serve as firewood for the next few days. With my hatchet and folding bow saw I set about cutting enough firewood for the evening. I figured the fire would discourage any unwanted visitors and warm me at night. I gathered kindling and some dried grass and started a fire with my lighter. I then went back down the hill to cut a couple of young pines as poles for my tarp. I anchored one side of the tarp with large rocks above the cave entry and stacked rocks around the base of the poles. I tied nylon string form the tops of the poles to large rocks on the ground and stretched them tight to support the other end.

My fire burned down to hot coals and I made a rack over it for cooking. I took some time to dam a pool at the spring, so filling my water bags would be easy. I then gathered more rocks and stacked them on the side away from the cave entrance. I stacked the rocks about two feet high so as to serve as a reflector wall to steer heat back into the cave. This setup worked very nice accept when the wind blew smoke back into the cave. The cave extended about fifteen feet into the mountainside and was six feet tall in the center. I learned to be careful after banging my scalp on a few hanging rocks. As night fell, I lit a couple of candles, read my Bible for an hour, and prayed myself to sleep. The blow-up mattress and the bedroll proved to be quite comfortable, so a tired man slept through the night and it was only the hint of daylight drifting in the cave entrance that woke me.

I poked a stick into the campfire, threw on a couple of pine logs, and it sprung to life. I poured a cup of water and began my prayer time. I had not planned on eating for the first few days. I had studied fasting and knew it could create a heightened sensitivity to spiritual things. My plan for the day included making a chair from green pine branches with willow branches for a seat and back rest. Thankfully, I had brought several rolls of nylon twine which would prove quite useful in the days to come. After finishing my chair, I again spent an hour in prayer. As I finished and tagged on an amen, my nose picked up a slight smell of gardenia. He was here, I knew it. I prayed for Him to come, but on this day He was silent. That was okay though, since I found great comfort in just knowing He was there. I wasn't alone. I thanked Him for His presence.

I emptied my pack and made my way down the mountain into the oaks. I needed better firewood and I knew the somewhat scrubby oak wood would be superior to the pine. I made three trips, and each time returned with a loaded backpack. This was to last a few days.

I had a few hours left, so I decided to do a little exploring. A few hundred yard below the cave, on a rocky outcrop just outside the pines, I found an old Indian campsite. There was nothing left of it but burn marks on the rocks and a hint of charred wood, but the site could have been a hundred years old. Then I found a couple of arrowheads. This did not surprise me, since chipping out new heads was a campfire pastime for the Yaqui's who had lived in these mountains for hundreds of years. The spring provided them with water and drew an abundance of wildlife. It was a perfect set up.

Back at camp I watched the sun set as I read my Bible. I lit candles and continued reading after dark while the stars appeared. The darkness before moonrise brought the stars out in all their abundance and glory. How could anyone see them like that and not believe there is a God? I suppose a lot of people never look up. I downed another cup of water, but hunger was starting to affect me. I prayed and once again the smell of gardenias drifted by. Yes, He was indeed here. A sense of the glory of God was beginning to make its presence known. My mind traveled to my family back at the ranch, then back to Tucson. With those thoughts, I fell to my face among the rocks and prayed more. Tears rolled down my face with thoughts of all the evil of the world in the city surrounding my church. At the same time the safety and protection of my family with Jorge on the ranch comforted me. It was time for some sleep.

I crawled into my sleeping bag but was suddenly rudely interrupted from my comfort as I felt a sharp pain near my left knee. I jumped out of the sleeping bag and shook it out, finally turning it inside out. Thus, I found the source of my pain. Four scorpions had found their way into the comfort of what was supposed to be my comfort. I pronounced a death sentence on the intruders and with candles, scoured the cave. Tonight, I would sleep on edge, but tomorrow I needed to figure out a better solution. "Lord protect me tonight, Amen."

CHAPTER 22.

I slept much better than I would have expected with the prospect of visits from more scorpion buddies. I started a morning routine of stoking the fire, putting on a pot of coffee and settling into my chair to pray and read my Bible. I was re-reading the early chapters of Acts to truly get a feel for those early days as the church was born. The coming of the Holy Spirit, the oneness they experienced, and the explosion in church growth were all elements I wanted to understand inside and out. I prayed for those days to come again. I believed I was seeing that at the ranch, but I longed to see it at home.

Right before I left the ranch, we talked about another school shooting in Florida, and I thought maybe the U.S. had awoken to the fact that this was the new norm. It was a totally unacceptable new norm but were we willing to address the problem? I longed to get back in action, but I knew that my heart needed more preparation. I didn't have answers, but I knew God did, and I did not plan on leaving the cave without those answers. The answers would ultimately have to be manifested in the church. They would not be found in a church that was fussing and fighting, but in a church that was truly aligned in unity as it embraced the power of God for change. This was my heart. This was my prayer. "Jesus, I need answers, Amen," I said out loud.

Next on the agenda was scorpion proofing my cave. I came up with a good idea. Scorpions like heat. I knew they would make their appearance as the sun warmed the air. I decided to expedite my idea. First, I took some coals from the fire and built a large fire inside the cave. I covered the entrance by dropping my tarp over it. Heat would bring them out and smoke would do them in. I needed to restock firewood and bring up a few gallons of water and doing so would allow time for my system to work. I did my chores and by the time I finished the fire had burned down. A few dead scorpions were inside the cave and more crawled out to look for a new home. The whole thing looked like success to me. I cleaned out the coals, brushed the ashes into the soil, and my cave became habitable again.

There was time left in the afternoon for a hike. I had spotted a herd of bighorns on the mountain to my east, so I grabbed my camera and a tripod which I had fashioned out of salt cedar branches and started my journey. I brought a zoom lens but wanted to get even closer pictures, so I edged down the back side of the mountain through pines. As the pines dwindled and scrub oak began, I found a perfect clearing for photography. I took a number of pictures and looked them over in my view finder. Satisfied, I moved on. I found another Indian site with flint strewn about. I thought it might be fun to make arrowheads, so I gathered enough flint to work on as a future task. On my way back over the mountain, I stopped in the pines to rest. It seemed the ill effects of not eating was starting to catch up with me. I prayed, and the scent of gardenias wrapped around me again. Maybe Jesus would soon show his face. My mind drifted and visions of Heaven flowed through my mind as I napped with a rock for my pillow. I felt a little like John in Revelation 4:1 when he was told to, "…come up here and I will show things to come."

I must have been really tired because when I awoke, the sun had already gone down. I made my way back to camp as the light faded, but to my surprise, when I topped the mountain, I could see my campfire blazing. As I got closer, I could see the outline of a man near the fire and a donkey tied to some nearby bushes. As I approached, a voice in perfect English said, "Howdy! Come on in here my friend. I've got supper cooking. My name is Josiah and yours is?"

"Oh, I'm Billy," I replied. "How did you find me? And I

don't mean to be rude, but why are you here?"

"I'm sorry," Josiah said. "I saw your camp. You know, seen the smoke and thought I'd come for a visit. I looked around for some food, saw you didn't have nothin' but this dried stuff, so I went and snared these two rabbits for supper. I figured you might be hungry."

"Well, my friend. You got that right but I'm fasting." I said.

"Now what's that? He asked.

"Not eating." I explained.

"Now why would you want to do a fool thing like that?"

"I came up here to meet with God."

"Billy, does God not eat? Maybe He'd show up if He could smell these juicy rabbits cooking. I got a Bible Billy, read the whole thang many times. I do recall stuff about fasting. Just never tried it myself. Frankly I don't know if it helps. I talk to Him every day anyway. He talks to me too. I never had to do anything special to talk to Him, nor to hear Him. Tell you a little secret Billy." The man leaned forward. "It was Him who suggested that I come up here to visit you. I knew you were here the first day you got here. I've been roaming these mountains for years, not too much goes on up here that I don't know about. You want to talk or eat?"

"I don't know. I'm not sure if it's right." I said.

"Billy, He's the one that told me to come up here and cook you some supper," said Josiah.

"You sure it was Him?"

"You see anybody else around here?" Josiah squinted out into the darkness. "I'm sure! Sit down let's eat!"

"Okay, Josiah," I relented.

"Can I pray first, Billy?" he asked.

"Sure."

"My father who is in Heaven, Holy is your name." he began. "Thy kingdom come thy will be done on Earth as it is in Heaven. Thank you, this day, for our daily bread. Forgive our sins as we forgive those who sin against us. For thine is the kingdom and power and glory forever, Amen."

I took a bite of rabbit that seemed roasted to perfection. "Josiah this is tasty!"

"Billy, I'm not that good a cook. You're just that hungry!" he remarked.

"You got a place to stay the night, Josiah?" I asked.

"Don't need one, Billy. I'm like a fox or a bird. I can sleep wherever I land. But if that's an invite, I don't get much company. I'd love to spend the night here."

"Then it's settled, Josiah. Welcome to my humble abode."

CHAPTER 23.

"Josiah, I'm thinking about bed, but I really want to get to know you," I said.

"Fair enough, Billy," Josiah replied. "Help me gather some fresh pine needles and I'll get my bedroll." It was dark, but we found the pines easily by a half moon and I began to strip the dry needles which were easy to pull off. "Oh no, not the dead ones," Josiah said. "Strip some from the lower branches. The green ones keep scorpions and other insects away."

"Now Josiah, why didn't I think of that?"

"Experience, Billy. I've been doing this a long time." We gathered up some armfuls and spread them out on the cave floor under our bedding. "There, that ought to be comfortable. You can douse the candles now," he said.

"So, Josiah, how long have you been up here?" I asked.

"A long time."

"Why here?"

"This is home for me Billy. I grew up here. I'm Yaqui.

"Are you a Christian?" I asked.

"I think you already know the answer to that question," he said.

"You said you've read the Bible many times. How many?" I asked, sounding a little nosy. But I really needed to know how much of an authority he was.

"I've lost count. I don't really know," he replied.

"Do you think you could answer some questions about the Bible?"

"I don't know until I hear the question. Give it a shot," he said.

"I know you say you talk to God every day. how well do you think you know Him?" I asked.

"Probably about as well as anyone." He put another log on the fire.

"Everyone always says that God is sovereign, meaning He's in charge, so why all the evil? Why doesn't He stop it? Can He?" I asked. I was getting a deep feeling that I could trust this man.

"Of course He can! But God did not create evil. He purposefully created beings that could make their own choices. Evil occurs when created beings, angels or men, choose to do life without Him," Josiah explained.

"Why is that? How can a created being choose right?"

"Creation is not eternal. It has a beginning," he said.

"I don't understand."

"The only way to make perfect choices would be to be all knowing. Neither angels nor men are all knowing," said he.

"But some know a lot," I said.

"Not really. They just think they do. Compared to God, angels and men know very little. Faith, asking God, is the only way to make perfect choices. Think of it this way pardner, the choices you make ripple through time impacting your children, your grandchildren, your great grandchildren and on and on. Doesn't the Bible teach that you are impacted by a choice Adam made?" Josiah asked.

"Yes, it does, and I believe it's true."

"How long has that ripple lasted?" he asked further.

"I don't know. A long time, right?"

"Doesn't the Bible teach that Adam would die when he ate the fruit?" Josiah asked.

"Yes."

"So, it's true for him and all his descendants since. That's why Jesus is called the second Adam, because although he was born into this fallen line, He was righteous. He gave His life to solve the problem of sin. It's really hard for us to think in these terms but in some sense, sin has value. It is through our consciousness of it, and its consequences, that we are pointed back to God and learn to trust Him. We have access to His wisdom, so we can talk to Him. We can know Him. He loves us, and we can love Him. It's the only way we can ever arrive at right choices," he said.

"Josiah, that's brilliant! How did you get so wise?"

"Billy, I am just an old man riding around on a donkey. I don't have a brilliant bone in my body. That's what I am trying to teach you. It's Him. I don't have to know much. I just have to know Him. Let's get some rest."

"Okay, I'll pray," I said, and bowed my head, still pondering the depth of all I had just heard. "Our Father, God who knows all, lives forever and has the power to speak the world into existence with mere words, holy is your name. Give us this day our daily bread, that is not just food but your word, your grace and mercy when we needed it most. Forgive us our sins. Thanking you for our Savior, Jesus, and His holy and righteous sacrifice in our rightful place of death. We forgive those who sin against us, because you showed us perfectly, how to forgive with the love you have for us. Deliver us from evil, as only you can protect us from our own ignorance, foolishness and the onslaught of powers of Satan and his evil servants attacking us. May your Kingdom come. Your will be done on Earth as it is in Heaven. Use us to do your will. Amen."

CHAPTER 24.

In the morning I woke up to the smell of breakfast drifting through the cave entrance. Mind you, this was not a traditional breakfast, but meat smoldering in the frying pan. Four tortillas lay to the side, ready to be warmed and receive the skillet's ingredients. Fresh desert cottontail with prickly pear fruit was seasoned with an assortment of peppers. Soon this was rolled tightly in the warmed tortillas. We thanked God for His provision and we ate. Over a cup of freshly poured coffee, I asked Josiah if he was ready to hear my dilemma.

"Josiah, how familiar are you with the work Jorge is doing?" I asked.

"Quite." Josiah said simply. "I visit him often."

"Then you understand his holistic approach to discipleship."

"I do," he nodded.

"In the U.S., specifically Tucson, I was pastoring a church of two thousand members before I came here. Though growth was good, I reached a point where it became obvious to me that serious Christianity seemed to be non-existent. I'm saying that folks were not all in. They were not sold out disciples of Jesus. As a matter of fact, even I had fallen into this trap of moderate Christianity. That's why I took time off to come here. I came to spend time alone, just seeking to be with God in a real and impactful way. Being here and looking at Jorge's work, has opened my eyes to a lot of real possibilities. The problem is, what he has accomplished has been done in a culture of poverty and hopelessness. So, the question is, can the same be done in a culture of prosperity like the U.S.?"

"That's a good question Billy. You're talking about doing it in the middle of prosperity. Might you be praying for the wrong thing? As I think my way through the Bible, I am seeing that those who seek God, are often those less fortunate. Is it possible that Christians in America might be living under an illusion? Josiah asked.

"What do you mean Josiah?" I asked.

"I mean that many may not be Christians at all but may be merely clinging to the traditions of their fathers and grandfathers, rather than discovering a personal encounter with God."

"So, are you saying that many of those people in my church may not even be true Christians?" I asked startled.

"Billy, it's possible."

"Hmm. That would explain their lack of commitment. If that's true, then how can I address that?" I wondered.

"You can't, Billy. You've never saved anyone, have you?"

"Not me," I replied. "Jesus does it with the Holy Spirit."

"Maybe that's the problem," Josiah said. "Imagine this. If pastors knew that only twenty-five percent of their members were saved, how do you think they would react?"

"Most of the pastors I know wouldn't say anything, especially at the pastor conferences."

"So, Billy, are you saying they wouldn't want to look bad among their peers?"

"Exactly," I said.

"Now wouldn't that be an ego problem before God, for those pastors?" he asked.

"I never thought of it that way, Josiah."

"Suppose you knew that hardship, personal crisis, cancer or losing children, would cause some of those people to see their lostness and find Jesus? Would you be willing to pray for that?" Josiah asked.

"Wow! I don't know!" I exclaimed, taken aback.

"Is it true that brokenness leads to salvation?" he asked.

"Yes."

"Then why wouldn't you be willing to pray that way?" Josiah asked.

"I suppose I wouldn't want to see them suffer," I said.

"What would be worse? some suffering here and now? Or a lot of suffering in an eternal Hell?" he pointed out.

"Then you think I should be praying for my people to suffer?" I asked. This conversation was getting more than a little uncomfortable.

"Not exactly, but for brokenness. I think you can leave the how part up to God."

I was relieved, but wondered further, "What about the saved? Should they suffer too?"

"Does the Bible tell us to die to self? What do you think that means, Billy?" Josiah asked.

"I think it means setting aside all our desires and replacing them with God's desires," I answered.

"Exactly. So, Billy, what do you think is the more powerful testimony, a Christian martyr? Or the "Christian" in prosperity?"

"The martyr of course," I replied.

"Is it possible that prosperity in the U.S. was Satan's plan at destroying the Church?" Josiah asked.

"I don't know, Josiah, but if it's true, it's certainly working well. Josiah, how do you know so much about prosperity in America?"

"I spent many years in Del Rio. You don't think I picked up this Texas drawl in Mexico now, do you? So back to my question Billy, are you willing to pray for your people to be broken?" he pressed.

"I guess I have to be," I responded with a reluctance I couldn't hide. "That is, if I really want to see my people saved and serving."

"Now Billy, it gets harder," he then added. "What about you? What about your own family?"

"Now that's really hard," I said.

"Do you believe Israel is God's chosen?" Josiah asked.

"Of course, Josiah, that's what the Bible says." I said, matter-of-factly.

"Do you not think that God knew that out of their brokenness they would come to Him? I think that is what He has done, and what He is doing. Now you will know how to pray for your family and church. It is when we truly see the heart of God that our prayers become real. His love runs deep for all of us. 'Oh Jerusalem, Oh Jerusalem, the city that kills the prophets and stones God's messengers. How often I wanted to gather your children as a hen protects her chicks...'"

"Josiah, you seem to understand a lot about God's calling. What about yourself? I mean wandering around in these mountains hardly seems like a calling!"

"It might seem that way to you Billy, but I am doing exactly what God wants me to do."

"How is that Josiah?"

"I wander. I wait. I spend time alone, just me and Him, and when He sends me to someone like yourself, I am ready. He prepares me for meetings just like this one. When you came, I knew you. Jesus and I had discussed the questions you would ask. The answers aren't mine, they are His," Josiah said.

"Oh," I said. "I don't understand. Waiting around for just for one person to show up, and then having these conversations with them, doesn't seem very impactful."

"You might be surprised, Billy."

"How's that?"

"You can't see what God has planned for you can you?" asked Josiah.

"No," I replied.

"What if this conversation carries you into ministry opportunities that lead thousands to Christ? Or what if maybe you just become God's man as a father, and through that, He directs one of your sons to be the greatest pastor, musician, or missionary in the world someday? Would you then say that this conversation was important?"

"Yes, I would," I replied, amazed at this thought line.

"We try to define value in our lives but only God knows. Why? Because He sees the future. If you evaluated Jesus' ministry based on twelve Apostles, starting with the one who was a failure, or looking at the one-hundred-and-twenty gathered in the upper room, would you consider Him highly successful? Can you imagine those first disciples' feelings as they watched him die on the cross? Then there is the resurrection! Do you see Billy? We don't get to define God's purpose. We don't get to understand His effectiveness. Our job is to trust Him, do as He says, and that's it." Josiah stopped talking, bent down and started to gather up his things.

"Well Billy," he said. "That's it. I'm finished. My work here is done. I have another appointment over near Durango."

"How do you know that, Josiah?"

"He told me Billy. In a week I will be there."

"How do these people know how to find you, Josiah?" I asked.

"Just like you did, Billy. God sends them to me, or me to them," he stated.

"I will miss you, Josiah," I said.

"Don't worry about that, Billy. We'll meet again when the work is done," Josiah smiled.

"You mean in Heaven, Josiah?"

"That's right, Billy, and you will know me, and I will know you. We'll catch up then. We'll have time to do it then," he said. "Adios, mi amigo!"

"Adios, Josiah!"

CHAPTER 25.

As I watched Josiah ride east over the mountain, I reached for my bag of flint to work on making arrowheads. I placed a large flat rock near the fire to serve as a table. I placed a piece of flint on the rock and chipped away at the edges with a fist sized round stone. A poor aim and a couple of blood blisters later, I trashed the malformed first piece and leaned back to reevaluate the process. I picked a new piece of flint and two new stones for shaping. One was a little larger than a golf ball, and the other was larger. I used the larger one as a hammer with and began to make progress. After seven or eight tries I made an arrowhead that looked halfway decent. Soon my flint was supply running low, so I decided it was time for a trip.

There was a good tamarisk thicket near my flint site, so I made a two-hour round trip to restock things. I managed to find a number of branches straight enough to make arrows with, and several larger ones for a bow. I soaked and steamed the shafts to straighten them. Looking down the shafts and spinning them proved to be a good way to assure their straightness. With my knife I shaped the bow, making sure the limbs were thin enough to flex well. Three twisted strands of nylon string proved to be right for a bowstring. After shaping the arrows, I placed them above the fire for hardening. I roasted the first six and made the ends pointed for small game arrows. Then I selected one with straight grain, split the end, slipped my prized arrowhead in the split, and tied it tight with string. I boiled agave to make glue and coated the string. On one of my trips I had located a Gould's turkey roost and found that there were plenty large feathers on the ground. I had found the site easily, since every morning I could hear the birds squawking before they left the roost. I collected a few nice feathers and split and shaped them, placing them for fletching on my arrows. There was nothing to do now but wait for the glue to dry.

A trip down the mountain revealed some snares Josiah had left, had done their job, as two cottontails and a jackrabbit had fallen victim. I dressed them and placed them on the spit to cook.

Now, there was a little free time, so I pulled up my chair to think and enjoy the comfort of the warmth. I thought about Josiah. He had probably made it over the next mountain by now. His next appointment divinely set by God himself, was waiting in Durango. Then my mind drifted to his appointment with me. Seven months earlier, God placed it in my heart to be here, and even then, he was preparing Josiah for the short but impactful meeting we just had. Amazing! Just amazing how God works! I prayed for my family, and once again I prayed for the meeting with God I had come here for. When the rabbits were cooked, I stripped the meat away and stowed them in zip lock bags for future use.

The glue on my arrows was dry. I tested my bow, and though not very powerful, my archery experience made me adequately proficient to try to go after some Gambrel's quail that were abundant. I snacked on some of the rabbit and made my way down the mountain to where I had seen the quail. I tried stalking them with little success, so I sat down to rethink my strategy. I knew that if I could get the quail to flush, they would not be so prone to run. As I sat there, I listened to the call of the birds as they regrouped from the wild misses of my arrows. I mocked their call and noticed that they responded. I continued calling and began to see them return toward my call. Soon I had several around me, so I backed into a bush and waited. As each one appeared, I drew my bow. Six arrows left three dead quail, and my mouth watered.

I thought about Israel and the manna. It really wasn't that different. I too, had been whining about God's provision. He is a good God, as just like he put up with the Israelites, He puts up with our whining, and sometimes blesses us in spite of our shallow minds. Oh well, quail tonight would be a nice change.

I dressed and prepared the quail and put them on the spit. Then I sliced some of the prickly pear fruit and put them in the skillet. I prayed, thanking God for his blessings, and enjoyed my dinner.

When the evening stars appeared, I thought how much I had changed in seven months. Tears rolled down my face, not tears of sadness but tears of joy, as a peace swept through the depths of my soul. I gazed at stars so numerous that they appeared to be clouds. You could see the bands of the Milky Way. I could barely imagine that my God, the one who made all this, was my friend. He was my Father. In all of His glory, He was speaking to me as if there was no one but Him and I. I supposed that in that moment that is exactly how it was. "Thank you, Lord," I prayed. "I will dream of you tonight. Amen."

CHAPTER 26.

"The word of the Lord came to Ezekiel the priest, the son of Buzi by the Kebar river in the land of the Babylonians. There the hand of the Lord was on him..."

The words of Ezekiel 1:3 where I opened up my Bible, caught my attention so I read the chapter through. It ended with Ezekiel 1:28.

"Like the appearance of a rainbow in the clouds on a rainy day, so was the radiance around him. This was the appearance of the glory of the Lord. When I saw it, I fell face down, and I heard the voice of one speaking."

I do not know what the glory of the Lord looks like. Ezekiel was trying to describe something so phenomenal, that adequate words did not exist. His response to his vision was the only appropriate response. I laid down to sleep but visions kept pouring through my mind. I didn't know if something like what Ezekiel had experienced would soon be in my future, but I was good with whatever God chose to do.

I remembered my grandpa. After my dad became an evangelist and spent so much time away, my grandpa and I went on fishing trips together and to the ice cream store. I remembered how he filled in for my Dad. I missed him. Grandpa had been gone for four years. How I wished I could see what he was already seeing. He was seeing Jesus and the glory and beauty of Heaven. We had been close, really close. I thought that missing him and wanting him back was selfish. The struggle and the pain were gone for him and one day they would be gone for me too. I would see him again. As I became sleepy, I smiled.

It's an amazing thing that right in the middle of this

messed up world, Christians can live with a huge sense of peace. My mind spun with visions of the righteousness of Jesus reigning in the hearts of those who were already in Heaven. What love! What grace! What unity! I had images of people smiling in the home they were made for. As the pictures in my mind drifted off, I thought, *Thank you, Lord. Amen.*

I awoke the next morning thinking how good some fresh eggs would be. I thought about the turkey roost, but I knew that since the gobblers were still silent, the hens wouldn't be nesting yet. I decided rabbit and cactus pears would have to be breakfast. But after breakfast I wanted to do something different. I needed some variety, I checked the traps and there were four more rabbits. This time I decided to do something different. I dressed them by cutting the meat into thin strips. I made a small fire pit and found a wide flat rock to cover it with. I placed coals in the bottom of the pit and loosely wrapped the strips of meat in foil. I cut some green mesquite and placed it over the coals. I then placed a smaller flat rock over the mesquite to set my wrapped meat on. I covered the whole thing with the large rock. Though crude, this made a good smoker and I looked forward to some rabbit jerky.

I had a couple of new veggies I wanted to try. I found an abundance of Yucca and used my hatchet to dig around them pulling them up by the roots. I trimmed the tops off and saved the roots to eat. I also found that the Cholla buds were tasty, so I gathered them to use like a salad. I collected mesquite beans to ground into flour. Christmas cactus produces a tiny red fruit. I gathered a knapsack full and headed back to camp. On the return trip I ran across a grove of Pinyon Pine and stocked up on pine nuts. I still had a good supply of seasoning, so it was time to create some recipes. There was quite a bit of prep work to be done, as some of the items had spines and some had hulls. After I prepared them, I gave them a taste test.

I checked my jerky regularly. When I ground the mesquite beans, I managed to produce over a pound of mesquite flour. There were a couple of hours left before my jerky would be fully dried, so I thought it would be a good time for a quail hunt. As my hunting technique was now refined, I returned with six birds. I stoked the fire, doubled up on my number of spits, and prepared the quail for dinner. Six birds were more than I needed but I saved whatever I didn't eat. They would keep longer cooked than raw. I removed the jerky and bagged it up. By then, the quail were done.

As I was removing the quail from the spit, and bagging them, I thought I heard cries from far away. They sounded like a cat or a bird, so I dismissed them until they became consistent. I went cautiously down the mountain towards the voice and it grew louder. To my surprise the voice was crying "help" in English. A man was lying in a dry gulch about a half mile from camp. I could see from his parched cracked lips that he needed water, so I reached into my pack and pulled out my water bag. I held it gently to his lips and he tried to gulp it but I made him sip it slowly. After a few minutes the color started returning to his face. He muttered some words I didn't understand. I said, "Don't speak till you feel better," and he nodded.

After a little while he pushed himself up to a sitting position. "Are you American?" he asked.

"Yes."

"Good, I'm safe for now. Did you see any men on horseback?"

"No," I replied.

"Good, maybe I've lost them!"

"Who?" I asked.

"The Guards from the prison," the man said.

"They're looking for you?"

"Well at least they were," he said. "I escaped from the prison at Hermosillo."

"You walked all this way?" I asked. "That's a long way!"

"No, I ran at least half the way."

"I think your safe now," I assured him. "Tell me when you feel well enough to walk."

"Give me a few minutes," he said. "It was the water I

needed. I haven't had a drink in two days." He leaned back and closed his eyes. After a few minutes, he spoke again. "Okay, I'm ready."

"What's your name?" I asked.

"Peter, Peter Graves."

"I'm Billy. I have food at camp," I offered.

"Okay, let's go," he said.

It was a slow walk but, in an hour, we made it back to camp. I handed him the jerky and warmed our dinner. He sat in my chair and I handed him the last of my tortillas, a prickly pear fruit and two quail. Then he began to tell me his story.

"Billy, I am a senior in college. Last spring for spring break, my friends and I went to Port Isabel. We made a few excursions to Matamoras. On the last trip, I decided to bring a little cocaine back with me. The border guards caught me, and I was put into prison there. After about six months they transferred me to Hermosillo, where I've been ever since. That is until two weeks ago when I escaped." He paused and looked for my reaction. "I've been two weeks on the lamb. That's what brought me here."

I was startled but I didn't show it. Instead, I set about making him feel welcome. "I'll gather some pine needles. I have an extra blanket. You can sleep with me in the cave tonight," I said.

"Thanks," he responded simply.

"You feeling better now, Peter?" I checked a few minutes later.

"Much. I have one question for you Billy."

"What's that?"

"What are you doing up here by yourself?" Peter asked.

"I came up here to meet with God."

"That's strange!" he said, a little sarcastically. "Does He live up here?"

"We'll talk about that later," I said. "You comfortable?"

"More comfortable than I've been in almost a year."

"Do you mind if I pray, Peter? I asked.

"I guess not," he shrugged.

"God, protect my new friend, Peter. Keep him safe and teach him that you are with him. Amen."

"Billy, you really think He's here?" Peter asked.

"He brought you to me, didn't He, Peter?"

"I suppose so."

"Don't worry, Peter," I said. "I prayed protection over you."

"Even if I don't believe in Him, Billy?" he asked.

"Peter, whether you believe in Him or not, doesn't make Him any less real," I said. "Goodnight Peter."

"Goodnight Billy, and thank you," he said.

"Your welcome."

CHAPTER 27.

I woke up early the next morning, but I let Peter sleep in. I thought I would play around with the breakfast menu. I made coffee, warmed some quail on the spit, and mixed my desert fruit until I found a combination that I liked. By the time I finished, I could hear Peter moving around so I invited him to my breakfast assortment. We ate. Peter said that it was different but good.

"So how did you sleep, Peter?" I asked him.

"Good, but I'm pretty sore." Peter replied.

"You up to taking a short hike?" I asked.

"Yeah."

"Come on, then. We'll check my traps."

"Okay, let's go," he said.

There were only three rabbits in the snares, so we relocated them about half a mile away.

"Peter, I am hoping that the relocation will keep us fed for a few days. It looks like a good spot," I said.

"How can you tell Billy?"

"You look for the droppings, trails, and the gnawed twigs and grasses.

"Oh, so the little brown pellets are rabbit poop?" he asked.

"Exactly."

"Well then it ought to work." Peter remarked.

When the snares were set up, I said, "Let's get back to camp and get these rabbits dressed and cooking."

"Okay, I need another cup of coffee anyway," he said.

We dressed the rabbits and put them on the spits. I poured

us a fresh cup and took a seat on the ground by the fire. "Peter, I think we need to make another chair. When I made this one, I didn't expect visitors."

"Is that easy to do, Billy?"

"Not bad. Grab my knapsack. My hatchet and bow saw are with it." We walked back down the hill, cut the right branches, and in an hour and a half we had another chair.

"Try it out, Peter," I suggested.

"Will it hold me up?" he asked.

"Faith Peter, faith."

"I thought Faith was a Christian thing, Billy."

"Not really Peter. All of us use faith every day. Sit in a chair. Turn the key on your car. Eat my cooking. It all takes faith. Everything we do requires some element of faith."

"Makes sense. So, this meeting God thing you mentioned last night. Seems like that would take a lot of faith! Seems like a fool's errand to me," Peter said boldly.

"I agree, at this point in your life it would be a fool's errand, but not for me," I replied.

"How's that?"

"I have been walking with God a long time."

"Literally?"

"If you mean 'physically', no, but you don't have to see something to know it exists," I said.

"Billy, that I get, air etcetera. If that is true though, we could believe in anything."

"Therein lies the rub," I replied. "We're not fools. We have to weigh the evidence."

"Billy, most of my college professors don't believe in God and they are some pretty smart men," said Peter.

"It all depends on motive," I said.

"What do you mean, Billy?"

"Let's say everything we can truly know can be verified. In order to verify you have to use faith," I said.

"Billy, explain."

"Until you sat in the chair we built, you couldn't be sure

it would hold you up until you used some faith. You had to sit down. All of life is like that. What about motive. What's your major Peter?"

"Biology."

"Perfect. Do you believe in the theory of evolution?"

"Of course, it is foundational to our whole biological system," Peter said.

"What's the fundamental precept?" I asked.

"Survival of the fittest. Take those rabbits we've been eating. They're survivors even when we and everything else want to eat them. They reproduce rapidly."

"I'll give you that, Peter, but somehow reproduction became their survival technique. Why didn't they evolve into huge animals with giant predator teeth? I think what we see is not survival of the fittest, but balance. Species adapt but they stay within their species. Reproduction does not cross the line of species. I probably shouldn't have gone there with my argument, but there is a reason. Science has had years to prove this theory right or wrong, but instead they continue to support it even though the evidence says otherwise. Why? The moment you chose biology as a major you were almost locked into evolution."

"Billy, I don't understand."

"It is what all of your professors were taught. It is what they teach," I continued. "Suppose they woke up one morning and discovered their entire career was based on a lie. You see I have the same challenge," I said.

"How's that?"

"Traditional theology has to be questioned. I can't believe it's true just because some old guy in a robe and a funny looking hat says it's so. Peter, I love a skeptic but if I am going to respect him, I am going to ask him to check out the evidence. But for a human being this is hard."

"Why is that Billy?"

"We have these prejudices and preconceived ideas. We rarely approach our search for truth without an underlying motive."

"What do you mean?" Peter asked. This was turning out to be rather complicated, but I needed to communicate truth to him.

"We're selfish, I said. "We want to prove our point. We want to win the argument. When we truly want to know God, we will find Him but if He's God then it won't be on our terms but His."

"We need to finish our rabbits so let's table this discussion for now. Can I pray for you, Peter?' I asked.

"I don't see what that would hurt."

"Good. God clear away the debris. Open Peter's eyes to know you. Amen."

CHAPTER 28.

"Peter would you like to see how I hunt the quail?" I asked.

"Sure."

"Let me get my bow and arrows. Let's take a different direction, I'm sure the quail down the hill are getting a little skittish," I suggested. We climbed over the top of the ridge and headed toward the next valley. About three hundred yards ahead, I could see a covey running down the hill. Peter and I grabbed some rocks and chunked into the middle of them. They flushed and scattered. "Follow me," I said. We set up in the area where they flushed, and I began calling. In about twenty minutes they began to dart from bush to bush. Thirty minutes later we had six in our bag. We went back to camp, dressed our quail, stoked the fire, and slipped them onto spits.

"Well Peter, it's time to get back to our discussion. Any questions so far?" I asked.

"Yeah. All the evidence for God and Jesus comes from the Bible, right?" Peter asked.

"Not all but most."

"So, what if the Bible isn't true?"

"I'll start this way. There are other books about other gods," I said.

"True," he nodded.

"Are those receptive to criticism?"

"No most are not," Peter admitted.

"The Bible welcomes criticism."

"Why is that important?"

"Because if it's true, it can hold up to criticism. You know what happens to those who question the Koran?"

"Yeah."

"That's my point," I said. "You know the Bible has been through many translations. For a long time, the earliest of manuscripts were not known. In the last few hundred years many of these manuscripts have been discovered. When held up against modern versions the integrity of what we now have is not just amazing, it is phenomenal! The Old Testament, for instance, according to the life and times of the writers, would date back anywhere from 400 BC to 1300 BC. Some scholars questioned that because there is so much prophecy in the Old Testament that predicted things far in the future. Critics were trying to date Old Testament writing at 400-600 AD. That is until the discovery of the Dead Sea Scrolls. These copies were as early as 150 BC. Geology has uncovered many of the sites described in the Old and New Testaments. Every time critics come up with a theory, God uncovers new evidence to blow it away. Peter, everything I'm telling you, you can check out for yourself. So why are intellectuals continuing to try and discredit the Bible? Why would biologists continue to hold to an antiquated concept in biology?" I asked.

"Ulterior motives?" Peter suggested.

"Exactly!"

"The quail should be done," I pointed out.

"Okay."

"Let me show you how to bone them. The easiest way is to cool them in a pan of water and then just pull the meat off with your fingers," I explained while doing just that.

"Like we do with the rabbits? Peter asked.

"Yeah, only easier." We separated all the quail meat from the bone and bagged it.

"Now let's get back to our discussion," I said.

"Fine with me, Billy. I'm learning a lot."

"Do you have any questions so far Peter?"

"No, keep going," he said.

"Well, I have one. Have you ever read the Bible or any part

of it?"

"No, but I know a few of the kid's stories from the two years I went to Sunday school with my friend down the street."

"Okay," I began. In Genesis 1:1, the very first verse, it says, 'In the Beginning God created...,' We'll stop right there because that already says a lot. First of all, the word for 'God' translated there is plural. It refers to the Father, Son and Holy Spirit."

"Why is that important?"

I explained, "Later it says they are eternal, as in past, present and future. Relationship, righteousness, justice, grace, mercy and love, are all words that are meaningless without two or more.

"The second word is 'created.' If God is not doing, he is not being. We are starting to see their character unfold. But God does create, and in creation another problem shows up, evil."

"Why is that? I don't understand!" he exclaimed.

"He chose to give Adam the ability to choose so he would not be a robot. Then He warned him not to eat of the Tree of Knowledge of Good and Evil, lest he die."

"Now I'm really confused,"

"I'll explain," I said. "The only way for man to avoid the snare of temptation was to trust what God said. But he and Eve did eat of that tree, didn't they? Yes, they did, and they brought the sin nature into all their offspring."

"And that's us Billy, right?" he asked.

"Yes. But God had warned them.

"Why were they so stupid?" Peter asked.

"Why did you try to smuggle cocaine across the border, Peter?"

"I see your point Billy," he responded.

"That's the thing, Peter," I said. "Choice carries with it the possibility of the rejection of God and running our lives the way that we want to. You see, created beings only know what they know. They don't know enough to make right choices.

"So, isn't that cruel on God's part, Billy? If they couldn't help it?"

"No, Peter, in order to create righteousness, He would have to create Himself. And yet, He is not created. He is eternal, self-existent. You see Peter, the only way for a man to be righteous is actually not by knowledge at all, but by faith in God. And not just in any god but in the only God!"

I could see I was confusing Peter with a lot of theology. I was glad he was kind of a captive audience. I decided to go back to our illustration. "Let's talk about sitting in the chair again. God is the chair that will never collapse or fail."

"Then why Jesus?" he asked.

"Because until Jesus came, man was trapped in his fallen state, that sin nature that Adam brought. Remember Adam's sin nature, and ours, brought with it the consequences of sin and the ultimate consequence was the death sentence."

"But Billy we're all going to die."

"Most men think of that as terminal. It's not. There's a second death, not of the body but of the soul. The second death is eternal separation from God."

"And Jesus?"

"Right. We needed a Savior. The death sentence was a given. We were trapped. That's why Jesus died in our place. Only God himself would be adequate to overcome the curse, and Jesus is a part of God. He died in our place! After all, we all trace our birth back to His creation."

"How do we know this is true?" Peter asked.

"It all hinges on the resurrection. Jesus rose from the dead, so we too could rise from death. Peter, do you believe in Jesus?"

"Billy, I'm still processing all this."

"You will understand when the time is right."

"I hope so."

"Oh, you will. Let's pray."

"Okay," he said.

"God take all of this knowledge you're giving Peter from his head to his heart. Amen." I said. "Now, Let's finish supper."

"Okay."

CHAPTER 29.

"Quail or rabbit?" I asked.

"Why don't we use some of both?" Peter suggested.

"Okay. Then stew it will be."

I started with Yucca leaves, since I knew they would need to cook a while. As they started to get tender, I added the prickly pear and Christmas cactus fruit. I mixed in some more water and some mesquite bean flour, seasoned it, and added my already cooked rabbit and quail. It wasn't exactly the tastiest meal I've ever had, but it was edible. The important thing was, I knew it was healthy and filled with nutrients.

"What do you think Peter?" I asked.

"Not bad, but then again I'm still trying to get my body back to normal."

"Peter, have you noticed how a lot of the best things for us are not the best tasting?"

"Yeah, this is definitely not a bowl of Bluebell Dutch Chocolate," he said.

"What's that?" I asked.

"A Texas delicacy, ice cream!"

"Oh. Anyway, as I started to say, what's good for us may not taste the best. I'm guessing this is the result of the fall. Earlier we were talking about the sin problem on the Earth."

"You mean Adam and Eve's fall?"

"Exactly." I said.

"Billy, you said 'Earth's' problem?"

"Right. When Adam sinned, all the Earth became fallen."

"Hmm," Peter looked at me curiously.

"The thorns, Peter. It's the thorns," I said.

Desert Dreams

"Do you mean on the Cholla?" he asked.

"Yeah, and everything else. It's all fallen, including us."

"So, we're stuck with that?" asked Peter.

"No, we're not, but we can't fix it. The answer is Jesus."

"How does that work?"

"Tell me about your stay at Hermosillo Prison.

"It was ugly," he said. "I was beaten by guards, other inmates and you name it. I am lucky to be alive. Sodomy was everywhere."

"You, Peter?"

"I am not saying," he looked down and replied.

"Did you know about the Christian section in the prison?" I asked.

"You've been there, Billy?"

"Yeah."

"I heard about it, but I never saw it. I even made application to get in there."

"And?" I asked.

"I'm a Gringo. You think they were going to cut me any slack?"

"I guess not," I said.

"No, my only hope was to get out. My dad even bribed the Guards, but they lied and asked for more money," Peter admitted.

"So how did you escape?"

"He bribed the inmates in the Cartel section. They got me to a gate and bribed the guard there. It was at night, but before I got out of sight the sweeping spotlight picked me up running. I heard horses coming. I managed to hide in a storm drain until they rode in another direction. Once I got to the mountains, there we're plenty of places to hide. The hounds would have caught me, if I hadn't spent a good bit of my journey covering my scent by wading in the river. Thank you, Billy, for saving my life! I was spent. I would have died in that gully if you hadn't found me!"

"I have more to say, Peter, but we'll talk about it later.

115

Let's clean up our dinner dishes first," I said.

"Okay."

When the work was done, I sat down to rest. "Works done, have a seat Peter," I said.

"Sure."

"Check out the stars!" I exclaimed.

"They are magnificent, Billy!"

"Yeah, I know. This is my favorite time each day. I look out there and remember just how small I am."

"No way around that Billy!"

"Right," I agreed. I saw another opportunity for an illustration. "When I see the stars, it tells me how big my God is. Science says this all started with a big bang. But you know, Peter, it all has order. The planets orbit. The earth is at just the right distance from the sun to sustain life. The galaxies and the whole universe are all in order. Big bang, garbage! There is order. Order does not come out of the chaos of an explosion. Order points at intelligent design. Obviously, intelligence far superior to any man. It's God!"

"But Billy, stars collide. They explode. They implode. There are supernovas and black holes," Peter said.

"Yes, and evil exists too," I said. Look throughout the history of mankind. Sin and evil show us that God is not finished yet. Creation is ongoing. When the day comes that evil is eliminated, creation will be completed. All will be perfected."

"You Believe that, Billy?"

"Yes, I do Peter. I've read God's word. He has not lied in six thousand years. I have no reason to think He will lie in the future."

"I suppose not."

"Let's go to bed Peter," I said.

"I'm ready," he agreed. "I've got some things to think about anyway."

"Good. Can I pray for you Peter?" I asked.

"Of course. It seems to be working," he replied.

"I'm glad you see that Peter."

"I do."

"God," I prayed, "Open the mind and heart of my friend Peter, that he may hear the words you have given me and take them into his heart. Holy Spirit do your work, and I know you will. Amen."

"Billy, thank you."

"Peter, you're welcome, Peter"

"Goodnight."

"Goodnight, Peter."

CHAPTER 30.

The next morning, Peter saw me reading my Bible as he woke up and asked, "Billy, do you read your Bible every day?"

"Every day Peter. Right after I pray and put a pot of coffee on. You want a cup Peter?"

"Sure."

"So why every day?"

"I always learn something new," I replied. "The Bible is no ordinary book. It's God's word."

"So, what are you reading this morning?"

"Glad you asked. Listen to this Peter. These are the words of John, the last living apostle. He was probably over ninety years old when he wrote this. All of the other apostles were dead. Most had died violent deaths with the chance to recant from their beliefs hanging over them. None did. Many were beheaded, crucified, or fed to lions in a Roman arena, but none would deny the reality that Jesus was Messiah. That's big Peter. Men don't die for a lie, but they will die for truth, especially when Jesus' resurrection carried with it the promise of their own resurrection. Anyway, listen as I read 1 John 1, verses 1 through 3. 'That which was from the beginning which we have heard, which we have seen with our eyes, which we have looked at and our hands have touched-this we proclaim concerning the word of life. The life appeared; we have seen it and testify to it, and we proclaim to you the eternal life, which was with the Father and has appeared to us. We proclaim to you what we have seen and heard, so that you also may have fellowship with us. And our fellowship is with the Father and with his Son.'"

"That's a lot Billy," Peter said.

"Not really. It's as simple as this. John is saying, I was there. I saw Jesus. I watched what he did, and I know He is Messiah."

"So, did John die a martyr's death too?"

"No, but the story is they tried to kill him by throwing him in a vat of boiling oil but couldn't kill him. I think that's why they put him on Patmos the prison island. It was there where he wrote this, his gospel, and the book of Revelation," I said.

"Now that's a story, Billy."

"But, it's true! God on a boring day is more exciting than anything man can conjure up." I paused to let that sink in.

"You hungry Peter?' I asked. "I've been warming our stew from last night."

"Let's eat, Billy."

"God bless the bounty of your wild provision, Amen," I prayed.

"Not bad for leftovers Billy."

"Thanks," I replied. "I added a little more seasoning, I think I've got this down now."

"You did good, Billy." Peter waited for a moment, then said. "So, I have a question. If all that you've been telling me is verifiable…"

"It is," I interrupted.

"Anyway, why do my professors, so many leaders, and the media, teach all this stuff to discredit the Bible?"

"Motives, Peter," I answered. "Just like I told you earlier, the truth is always critiqued because of men's motives."

"Clarify!"

"Take Atheists, for instance. If they don't believe there is a God, then why do they fight so hard against something they say doesn't even exist?"

"I don't know, Billy, but I see what you're saying," he nodded.

The truth is, Peter, it usually boils down to one simple

thing."

"What's that, Billy?"

"Moral law. God's law," I said.

"How's that?" he asked.

"If you have a lifestyle that violates God's law then the only way you can escape in the end, is to say that there is no God," I said.

"I have read the Ten Commandments," Peter said, "and actually they are quite sensible."

"They are."

"As a matter of fact, if men kept them, this world might be a pretty good place to live," Peter acknowledged.

"That's true Peter, but when men see a speed limit sign it makes them want to go faster," I explained. "It's only when they see the radar gun that they slow down. I discovered something amazing when I studied philosophy."

"What's that?"

"Well, it started with me trying to poke holes in the philosophy of Kant or Nietzsche, or Sartre. I could do that easily enough, but I struggled to understand how they came up with some of their stuff. Then I started checking their biographies and found that their immoral lifestyles perfectly explained their reasons behind discrediting God. It was the morals they didn't like. It's the same for all of us. We do fine with the God who loves us until we find out real love has boundaries."

I looked at Peter and smiled. "I'll let you in on a little secret, Peter. This is more fun to me, than the best party I ever went to."

"Teaching me about God?" he asked.

"Yes," I replied

"I don't see it, Billy?"

"That's because you have been so filled with the lies of the world that you can't see it."

"But Billy, it's a good life for you isn't it?"

"It sure is Peter, the best!" I exclaimed.

"Then how can I find it, Billy?" Peter asked.

"You will Peter, when you find Jesus!" I said.

"I already know who Jesus is, Billy," he said.

"Not really!"

"How's that?" Peter asked.

"Until you know him personally, I mean put your trust in Him like your best friend, then you don't really know him," I explained.

"My best friend lies sometimes," Peter said. "He's the one who got me caught at the border."

"Jesus will never lie to you. He takes the fall for you. Peter are you ready to put your trust in Jesus?"

"I am Billy," he said humbly.

"Then repeat this prayer. I am a sinner. I trust that your death on the cross paid for my sins, Jesus. I will put my trust in you. Amen." Peter repeated each phrase. Then he said.

"Billy, that seems too simple."

"It has always been simple. But at the same time, it's hard."

"How is it hard, Billy?" he asked.

"You've made a commitment to Jesus. He expects you to keep it, but he will help you every day because he lives in you. The Holy Spirit lives in you. You will want to do the Father's will now," I explained.

"Won't I fail sometimes?" Peter asked.

"Oh yeah, and you will ask forgiveness many times, but he does forgive. Do you feel different?"

"Much, but I can't explain it."

"You don't have to," I said.

By then the sun was pretty high in the sky and everything had warmed up since morning. "What's on the agenda today, Billy?" Peter asked.

"First, we need to check our snares."

"Let's go, then!" There was an eagerness in his voice I had not heard before.

"Okay," I said, and we gathered our things and went out into the scrub where we had set them up the day before. "Not bad. Five rabbits. Let's get them cleaned and cooked. We'll clean dishes while they cook."

"Are we de-boning them, Billy?"

"Yeah, that way we can eat them a variety of ways."

"Where's the bags?"

"They're on the little shelf above my bed," I pointed out.

"Are we quail hunting today?"

"Yeah, and we need to gather some more veggies too," I said.

"I heard a few gobbles this morning. Maybe we can find a hens nest!" Peter suggested.

"Maybe! You ready?"

"Let's roll!"

"I want to try that field of tall grass south of the turkey roost."

"For eggs?" Peter asked.

"Yeah, that's a great nesting site for hens."

We went down to where we could hear the turkeys roost at dusk and at dawn and hid out in the tall grass nearby. After about thirty minutes a hen suddenly flushed. When we inspected where she came from, she had already laid thirteen eggs. I pulled up some grass and created a layered nest in my backpack to put the eggs in without squashing them. The we made our way back to camp.

"Peter, I'm not taking any chances of breaking any," I said.

We made a hole in the cliff beside our cave and lined it with the grass. Then we placed the eggs in our primitive refrigerator.

"I can hardly wait to eat them!" I exclaimed. "But I will, at least until dinner. Now, let's go quail hunting."

It took us only an hour to fill our six-bird quota. We picked our usual prickly pear fruit, Cholla buds, and Christmas cactus fruit, and dug up some Yucca roots. But I kept checking my desert edibles book for something different. With fresh ideas in mind, we pulled seed pods from Chia sage, gathered some seed from the ground under several Ocotillo, and found about five pounds of remaining acorns in the scrub oak. As soon as we got back, we dressed and cooked our quail. We split and pulled the husks from the acorns and soaked them in water. The chia and Ocotillo seeds, we bagged. We set the acorns soaking on the fire, and after they boiled a while, dried them and ground them into flour. Now we had two types of flour with which to make tortillas. For dinner that night we had scrambled turkey eggs, prickly pear fruit, and quail. Altogether they provided a feast. Peter prayed this time. Then we ate and settled in for another stargazing conversation.

"Good supper, huh Peter?" I asked.

"Excellent!"

"You get enough?" I asked.

"I'm stuffed!" replied Peter. "Billy, I see your wedding ring. How's your wife feel about your stay up here?"

"She's for it. She knows my heart."

"Any children?"

"Two boys," I said. "Yeah, I miss them and especially my wife."

"When you plan on leaving?"

"After God comes," I replied matter-of-factly.

"What if he doesn't?" Peter asked.

"He will."

"How do you Know?"

"Remember, God doesn't lie," I said.

"Billy the stars look different to me tonight?" he said.

"Yeah, I know. You see them in their glory. You know the one who made them."

"Yeah, that's it," he said.

"What's next for you, Peter?" I asked.

"I don't know, you got any ideas?"

"A few," I said.

"What?" Peter asked.

"I need to pray about them before I suggest anything though," I said. "Are you ready for bed?"

"Sure," he replied. "I got a lot of thinking to do, and praying, Billy."

"Good night, Peter. I'm going to sit out here a few more minutes," I said.

"Okay, Goodnight Billy," Peter said with a fresh tenderness in his voice.

CHAPTER 31.

A red sun rose and reflected off of the surrounding hills. "You're up early, Peter," I said.

"Yes, good morning!" Peter said, stretching.

"So, did the smell of breakfast wake you up? Coffee is made!" I said.

"Pour yourself a cup and another for me."

"Thanks, Billy, I will," said Peter

"Breakfast will be done in a few minutes," I said. "I used some of the turkey eggs to make up tortillas. Give them a try!"

"Which ones did you make, mesquite flour or acorn flour?" he asked.

"I like them both, Peter, but the acorn is a little bitter so I used mesquite. We boil the acorns to remove the bitterness. I guess we need to boil them a little more," I said.

"Have you already done your Bible reading?" Peter asked.

"No, I thought I'd wait on you."

"Good," said Peter.

"You ready to eat Peter?"

"Yes."

"Let's pray and you can fix a plate. Lord thank you for saving my friend Peter. Bless this food. Bless this day. Amen."

"It's good Billy."

"Yeah, those turkey eggs are a blessing," I said.

"So, Billy, what's the plan?"

"After we eat, we'll have a Bible study and then talk. God's answered my prayer and we have to discuss the answer."

"Why's that?" Peter asked.

"Because the answer involves you."

"Oh."

We both took the tortillas and wolfed them down. "You done Peter?" I asked.

"Yeah."

"Okay, sit back down. I am going to read Acts 9. I don't have an extra Bible, so just listen. Peter, this is the story of Saul's conversion. Jesus changed his name to Paul. In another scripture Paul went into the wilderness to be personally tutored by Jesus."

"I thought Jesus was dead by then," Peter remarked.

"Oh Peter, he wasn't dead! He's still not dead! Paul had a calling on his life. It was so important that Jesus personally showed up and taught him."

"What's a calling, and what was Paul's calling?" Peter asked.

"A calling is God's plan for the rest of your life. Paul was to carry the gospel to the Gentile world."

"What's a 'Gentile,' Billy?"

"Everybody that's not a Jew."

"So, Billy, do I have a calling?"

"Yes Peter, we all do," I explained.

"I don't know what mine is."

"It's coming!" I said. "First, just like Paul, comes your time in the wilderness."

"Like now?"

"Exactly. Now don't be confused though," I said. The wilderness is the place where God trains us."

"Like Paul?"

"Yes. That's what my prayers were about, Peter."

"You have some answers, Billy?"

"Yes," I said. "But first I have some questions for you because God would not tell me the whole plan for your life. He will tell you. What he did tell me was the location of the beginning of it."

"Where's that?" Peter asked.

"You're not going to like this."

"Why?"

"It's Hermosillo Prison," I said.

"Woah! Wait a minute! I didn't sign up for that!"

"Are you committed, Peter?" I asked.

"I thought so, but now I'm not so sure!"

"You have to trust Him, Peter. There are things you don't know about, and things you don't understand."

"Such as?"

"Remember me asking you about the Christian section in the prison?"

"Yeah, I was trying to get in there."

"I've been there. It is one of the finest training grounds for discipleship I've seen," I said.

"Yeah, but I couldn't get in there. And besides, what would they do to me now that I ran away!" exclaimed Peter.

"Peter, I have connections."

"To the prison?"

"Yes. My friend Jorge. He knows the warden. He helped get that section started. Don't you have time left to serve? Don't you need Bible teaching?"

"Yes."

"What if you could do both at once?"

"Billy, I see what you mean, but they beat me there!"

"Sometimes you just have to trust God. Peter, pray this through. See if God gives you peace about it," I said.

"Okay. I'll try, but I don't know."

"I think you will once you've prayed about it."

"Alright, I'm going to go to the mountain top to pray, Billy."

"Good idea, I'll clean up. Then I'll check the snares," I said.

"Can I borrow your Bible?" Peter asked.

"Yes, for sure," I offered.

"Okay. See you after a while!" Peter took my Bible and a pack and disappeared into the brush. I didn't know if I would ever see him again.

I caught four rabbits and dressed them and put them on

the spit. Soon they were smelling good. I stripped and bagged them and waited. Finally, late in the morning, I saw Peter coming down the mountain.

"I have my answer, Billy. I can't believe I'm honestly saying this, but I'm ready to do it. What's next?"

"Take a flare off that shelf above my bunk and set it off," I instructed.

"You think someone will see them? It's daylight."

"I think so. I can see the shepherds across the valley. If everything goes right, Jorge could be here this afternoon. Set it off, let's do this."

"Okay."

"Let's grab our things and go down the mountain to quail hunt. Perhaps Jorge will be there by the time we are finished," I said. I took some water and some of our veggie collection with us and we followed the stream down to where the road ended. After we caught seven birds, we built a campfire, cut some branches and fashioned some spits. The quail were cooked and ready to eat when we saw dust coming up the road.

"Good afternoon Jorge," I said as soon as he pulled up. "Let me introduce you to my new brother in Christ, Peter."

"Glad to meet you Peter."

"Same Jorge," said Peter.

"You are a Gringo! What are you doing here?" Jorge asked.

"Yes, I am..."

"Peter, can I tell him your story?" I asked.

"Go ahead," Peter said, a little nervously.

"He's an escapee from Hermosillo Prison," I explained, "a college student from the U.S. doing time for cocaine possession. He has come to know Jesus and is willing to go back to serve the rest of his time."

"How long do you have left Peter?" Jorge asked, interested.

"Three years and two months or more, depending on what they do me for escaping," Peter replied seriously.

"I've prayed, and I believe God said he should serve his

time in the Christian section at Hermosillo," I inserted. "Do you think you can get him in without repercussions?"

"I'm sure I can," Jorge said confidently. Peter seemed slightly relieved but was still tense.

"How about joining us for some birds, Jorge?" I asked.

"Oh yes! Sure! And I brought some refried beans and some rice and enchiladas with me to add to them. I wasn't sure why you summoned me, or what you might need," Jorge said.

"Oh, that would be great!" I responded. "I sure could use a change of diet."

We all sat down around the fire and Jorge passed out the food.

"So, Peter you escaped the prison and made it all the way here?" Jorge asked.

"Yes, Jorge," Peter replied. "I can now see that it was God who brought me to this place. A divine appointment, as Billy would say."

"I agree with him Jorge," I said.

"So, you think you can get me in the Christian section of the prison without them beating me up?" Peter asked.

"Yeah, I don't think that's a problem," Jorge said.

"So, what's it like there?"

"Completely different than the rest of the prison, clean, safe and some very good men there. I really think it's a good idea Peter. Your greatest need is discipleship. There are men there who are highly educated, and depending on your level of commitment, in three years you could walk out with seminary level education. That's just one part though, with the spiritual maturity there you will have a great opportunity to build real and lasting strength for God's call on your life."

"And it's safe?" Peter asked again, this time referring to the inmates.

"Oh very. Prison fellowship oversees and supports all the work there. Pastors, seminary professors, amazing lay people all volunteer in the work there. So, where's your family from?"

"Austin, Texas," Peter replied.

"I've been there! Nice city. So, what's your dad do?" Jorge asked.

"My family's in the oil business, but right now Dad's serving on the railroad commission."

"So, did you go to U.T.?"

"No, I went to Rice," said Peter.

"That surprises me," Jorge responded.

"I wanted to get a little further from the house" said Peter.

"I see. How'd that work out for you?"

"Not so well. But then again, I might not have found Jesus had I not gotten in trouble," Peter said.

"Then you can make sure that Peter gets set up in the Christian section?" I asked, Jorge.

"I will," he replied.

"Then he's all yours," I said.

"Well! We'd better get on before dark," Jorge said, looking at me. To Peter he said, "You'll need to stay at the ranch for a few days while I make the arrangements for Hermosillo. The first thing you'll need is a shower and some better clothes!"

"That sounds great!" Peter said. "What about you, Billy?"

"I'm staying."

"You haven't met with God yet?" Jorge asked.

"I don't think so, no I haven't. Is my family okay?" I asked.

"Yes, just missing you. Don't worry they're taken care of. Even better, they are learning new things about God's work."

"Good, then it's adios for now," I said.

"Can I pray for you, Billy," Jorge asked.

"Yes, Jorge, and pray for Peter, too. He has a huge challenge ahead of him."

"Jesus, my Lord and Savior," Jorge began. "Visit my friend Billy soon. Show him your glory. Give Peter the courage he needs and keep us safe on our journey down. Show favor to Peter with the guards and the warden and have mercy on him as he begins his new adventure. Amen.

"See you in a few days, Billy!" Jorge said.

"Billy?" Peter asked.

"Yes," I replied.
"Thank you for everything."
"Your welcome, Peter. May God be with you!"

CHAPTER 32.

I watched as Jorge drove away. My thoughts drifted to the conversation going on in the Jeep. I trusted Jorge. Peter was in capable hands.

After making it back to camp I prayed for Peter, for my family, and about my future for a couple of hours. Then I decided it was time to hang my shower bag up and do a little personal clean up. It had been a nice warm afternoon. I thought that my guardian angel might be complaining and that if I didn't smell better, he would quit. Or, at least he was going to have to do his work from a distance.

After my shower, I cooked up my dinner, rolled up the veggies, quail and rabbit into tortillas and ate them. Then I cleaned up. Finally, I sat outside and watched the red sun set, thinking about when and how God would show up. I was growing a little impatient, but I knew my timing was not God's timing. When God was ready, He would show. Would He arrive dramatically, with flashes of lightning and thunder the way He came to Job? Or would He walk with me as peacefully as He walked with Adam? As the stars appeared, I sang quietly, "I Can Only Imagine."

The coyotes howled in the distance, serenading the rising of the moon. As darkness wrapped around me, the stars sang to the glory of God. They were a million billion miles out there, and they didn't even come close to finding God's boundaries. All of this and more was simply spoken into existence. All that vastness, and yet He personally loved me, talked to me, and died that I might live. At that moment it was beyond my comprehension that any man could see this and not believe. When I thought it through, though, I was reminded that I once was the same way. I, too, tended to forget or failed to see Him in all His glory. I crawled into my sleeping bag, and as I prayed, the scent of gardenias wrapped around me, stronger than ever before. He was there. Then as quickly as the fragrance came, it vanished into the night air. *God you are good, all the time. Amen.*

CHAPTER 33.

Sometime in the middle of the night the sound of a braying donkey startled me awake. The worst part was he had his head right in front of the cave entrance. He was obviously frightened and as I peered into the darkness at the edge of the shadows, I could see the outline of a cougar. I reached for my rifle and shotgun, chambered a round into my rifle, and pulled back the hammer on my double barrel twenty gauge. I hollered, but the cat lingered about forty yards out. I decided it was time to take action and peppered him with birdshot. With that he screamed and ran. I turned my attention to the still braying donkey, rubbing his neck until he calmed down. He looked familiar, and soon it dawned on me that this was Josiah's donkey. I stoked up the fire and said a prayer for Josiah. With the donkey calm, and the cat carrying a little lead and heading west, I decided it was safe to go back to bed.

As daylight came, I looked around and found that the donkey had made his way down into the grass filled clearing below camp. I grabbed some jerky, filled my water bag and set out to look for Josiah. As I started over the top of the mountain heading east, the donkey came running up behind me. He forged ahead as if to say, "follow me." I could tell he seemed to know where he was going, so I followed. After about an hour he led me to the edge of a canyon and stood there. I looked over the edge of the cliff and found the shape of a curled-up man below. I hollered, "Josiah, you alive?"

"I'm alive! I just can't walk!" came a plaintive cry. The donkey led as we made our way down a gully to the bottom.

"You okay, Josiah?" I asked.

"I'll be alright," he said. "I'm just beat up with a badly sprained ankle. I must have nodded off as we rode along this canyon! Best I can tell, I fell all the way down here. Balaam came after me, but I couldn't get on him. We stayed here a few days. I think I was about to starve or die of thirst. Finally, I told him to go find you. I didn't think he understood, but I guess he did. Once he left though, I began to worry. I knew I was a goner for sure if he didn't find you.

"How'd you find me here in the middle of nowhere?" Josiah asked.

"Your donkey led me straight to you," I said. "His name is Balaam?"

"Yeah, he doesn't talk but I guess he listens good!" he remarked.

"Let me help you get on him and we'll go back."

"I'm starving, Billy."

"Here, eat some of this jerky while we ride back to camp." I helped Josiah get up on the donkey.

"You okay?"

"Yeah, about as comfortable as a man can be with an aching ankle."

Josiah leaned against Balaam's neck weakly as we headed back toward the cave. Taking it slow, we made it back over the mountain in under two hours. "Camp getting close?" he asked.

"Yeah just over the hill."

"Billy, were you expecting me?" Josiah asked when he looked in the cave.

"No, why?"

"You made another chair."

"No, Josiah, I had a guest while you were gone," I explained.

"God?"

"No, his name was Peter. He was an American escapee from the Hermosillo Prison."

"He made it all the way up here?"

"Yeah, and left a believer in Jesus," I said.

"Billy, you've been busy my friend," Josiah said.

"Just doing what God called me to do, Josiah."

"You're the man, Billy."

"Thanks. Jesus gets the credit though," I said.

"That's true, Billy," he nodded. "Boy this chair's a good sight for these old weary bones."

I helped Josiah off of the donkey onto the chair. "Let me get a rag and we'll wrap that ankle in some cold water," I said.

"That spring water is nice and cold alright!" he remarked.

"Yeah, that will help get the swelling pointed in the right direction. Josiah, you being the mountain man you are, I'll bet you know a poultice we can put on that ankle."

"Just so happens I do. Pull some Lechuguilla leaves and get them in a boiling pan," Josiah said.

I stoked the fire and set some Lechuguilla leaves on to boil.

"Billy you know what Horsehound looks like?" Josiah asked, next.

"I already picked and bagged some. Made tea with it one day."

"Good, after the Lechuguilla boils, add some Horsehound to it and let it cool. When it does, put it on my ankle and tie it in the rag. It will take the swelling out. By tomorrow I should be able to get around with a crutch."

"What about supper, Billy?" Josiah asked when his ankle was wrapped.

"I've been playing around with some recipes," I replied.

"I heard you mention tortillas. You have any left?" he asked.

"There's just one," I said.

"Can I have it please? It'll tie me over until you get the cooking done."

"Sure thing, Josiah. By the way, it sure is good to have you back in camp!" I exclaimed, handing him the tortilla.

"Glad to be here. But guess you didn't plan on looking after an old cripple," he said.

"Actually, I'm glad. I feel like there's a whole lot we never got to talk about."

"That's true, Billy. I guess sometimes God has to slow us down to do what He knows is important," Josiah said.

"What about the man you went to meet in Durango?" I asked.

"If God brought me back here, then He's got someone else to handle that. Billy, His work always gets done. It's just a matter of putting the right people in the right place sometimes. Even when we fail to do what He asks, He'll appoint someone else for the task," Josiah continued. "Doing God's work is a privilege. Unfortunately, most people never get to enjoy it. So, what's for supper Billy?"

"Desert stew."

"Smells good!"

"I think you'll like it," I said. "Let's pray. You do the honors, Josiah."

"Lord, forgive me for jumping the gun, I guess I wasn't finished here. Bless Billy and bless the food you give us, Amen."

CHAPTER 34.

"Josiah if you're comfortable, I need to get some chores done," I said.

"Go ahead, I'm thinking about a nap," Josiah replied. "I saw that bow hanging in the back of the cave. You can shoot it?"

"Sure," I said. "See you in a little while."

"Those snares working?" he asked.

"Yeah, I need to check them now."

"Okay, see you in a bit!"

There were four rabbits in the snares. I dressed them and then I stuffed them in my pack. After that I went down the hill to quail hunt. I didn't do too bad. In two hours, I caught six quail and added them to the rabbits. I restocked my prickly pear apples, and I still had eight turkey eggs left. I used two spits to get them roasting and fetched some water. That wrapped up a productive morning.

"Josiah, how was the nap?" I asked when I returned and saw him sitting in the chair again.

"Good. I even mustered up the strength to take care of a little urgent business, if you know what I mean." "Yeah, not too close to camp, though?"

"A hundred yards, and down wind. You know the desert is a good provider for most things, except toilet paper," Josiah said.

"Yeah, cedar or pine is not too good."

"Better than cactus though!" he remarked.

"I'm not as tough as you Josiah. I've been using a rag and washing it."

"Downstream, I hope," said Josiah.

"I'm not that stupid."

"Just checking," he said. It was refreshing to see the return of his sense of humor.

"Let me see your ankle." I took off the rag gingerly. "Wow, the swelling is coming down!"

"Yeah Billy, like I said I can walk on it some."

"I still think relaxing is key."

"I plan on that."

"Sit down then!" I admonished.

"Okay."

"The quail are ready, and by the time they're deboned, the rabbits will be done. Here Josiah, make yourself useful. I'll get the bags." I handed him some bags and he worked quickly. Shortly we were finished. "Well, quail and rabbit done and bagged. I'll put the bags in the stream," I said. "That will keep them cool. Josiah, get your brain in gear. When I get back, we'll talk."

"So, Billy, tell me about, what's-his-name," Josiah said, as soon as I returned.

"Peter," I said.

"Yeah, Peter."

"Well," I began. "I got up one morning and could hear a man hollering. Tracked him down in the ravine. I gave him water and got him back to camp, fed him and nursed him back. Then I told him about Jesus."

"Now Billy, I know you. That's got to be the short version," Josiah said.

"I guess you do, Josiah. It turns out he was a college student, so I shared a lot with him. I started in Genesis with who God is, and how we can know He's the real deal. Then I told him about Jesus and how he died for our sins and rose again. With all that he had been through, the Holy Spirit was doing his work, and Peter believed. Jorge came and got him. In a day or so he should start finishing his time at Hermosillo. This time, though, he'll be in the Christian section."

"That's a good plan, Billy."

"I think it's God's plan," I said.

"I agree, Billy. That brings me to what I wanted to talk to you about."

"Okay."

"Did you feel more alive sharing the gospel with Peter, or when you were preaching in front of your church?" Josiah asked.

"I don't know," I replied. "One part of me says in front of my church, but another says that nothing is better than one-on-one, leading someone to Christ."

"So, what do you think the difference is, Billy?"

"Hmm. When I preach, the amens are coming. A thousand people are hearing God's word. That's a big deal. But then a divine meeting in the middle of nowhere, you can see God's providence all over that!" I said.

"Now, Billy, let's look at the difference. In the one situation, you receive all that approval from men, and in the other situation, no one knows about Peter, but me, Jorge and God."

"I'm sure a few others know by now, such as Laura."

"Okay, I'll give you that. But my point is an audience of Jesus watching, becomes all we need. How many people got saved in your church the last year you were there?"

"Ten."

"Then how did you grow your church so fast?" Josiah asked.

"Most newcomers were dissatisfied people from other churches," I said.

"Next question. Out of all those people moving their membership, how many do you think fully embraced a truly changed lifestyle?"

"Not many," I replied.

"Then why do you think they changed their membership?"

"I talked to most of them," I said. "They said they were looking for something more out of church than they were getting. Either that, or someone had hurt their feelings."

"Did anyone hurt their feelings after they came to your

church?" Josiah asked.

"Yeah, some have already left."

"Did any find what they were looking for after they came?" Josiah asked. "Let me ask that a different way. What kind of complaints were dominant?"

"There were two types, one about music tastes, and the other about not being plugged into leadership."

"Does that tell you anything, Billy? Like, why were they coming?" he asked.

Yeah. Come to think of it, there is one more reason. Many requested more stories and not so much Bible. That tells me they were there for entertainment or status," I admitted.

"Are those the right things, Billy?"

"No, they should be there to serve. At the very least they should want to be in training for whatever service God was calling them to."

"Exactly!"

"Josiah, that's why I became so discouraged. Me and my staff were having to do all the work."

"Now that you've identified the problem, Billy, how do we fix it? Josiah asked.

"I don't know, Josiah. Why don't we pray?"

"Good idea, Billy. It's all yours."

I prayed, "Jesus, this don't seem like a complicated problem, but I just don't have the answer. I need your help. I need your wisdom. It seems to me like every church in America is struggling with these same problems. Lord help me. Amen." I put another log on the fire and looked out at the scenery.

This next question hurt. "Billy, do you think you've ever been guilty of enjoying the status of being pastor too much?"

"I know I have," I admitted. "You know, on a Sunday morning after service when everyone shakes your hand and tells you what a great sermon it was, then what? When I got home, I would start thinking if that was such a great sermon, why couldn't I get my people to do it?"

"Billy, I'm not talking about them, though. I'm talking

about you. Let me put it a different way. Your assistant pastor, I hear he's a real fireball. How often does he preach?" Josiah asked.

"Now he's preaching all the time. But before, only a couple of times a year," I said.

"Why?"

"I'm the pastor."

"So, do you mean you've earned the right to preach, or you deserve it?"

"What do you mean, Josiah? And why did you say he's a fireball?" I asked.

Josiah ignored my question and went on. "What if you go back and your church doesn't want you back? How would you feel about that?"

"I'd be hurt."

"What if it was God's plan?"

"I'd still be hurt. Why, do you think it's God's plan?"

"Don't you see my point yet, Billy? There's no room in God's kingdom for big egos. Remember, He is God. Now Billy, let me pray. Lord help Billy to understand that in order to fully embrace your will, he will need a broken self so that he will be able to be willing to trust you, even if you call him to be janitor. Amen." Josiah adjusted the flames this time, and then said, "Remember, in the Bible it tells us that in the kingdom of God, the least shall be greatest, and the greatest shall be least."

After some silence, I asked, "One more question, Josiah, how did you know my assistant pastor was a dynamic preacher?"

"We'll talk about that later Billy," he said. "I'm hungry. Let's get supper ready."

"Okay, Josiah."

CHAPTER 35.

In the early evening we ate our main meal. "Supper was good Billy, Josiah said. "I can feel my strength coming back."

"How about the ankle?" I asked.

"Still tender. Before it gets dark maybe you could see if you can find a branch to make a crutch with," he said. I agreed and went out to find a couple of branches with forks in them. "Mesquite huh?" Josiah asked. "That will work. They are good and strong, as long as we get rid of all the thorns. Let me see your knife, Billy. I'll finish it up and give it a test." Josiah whittled and scraped and finally stood up with the two branches under his armpits. "They're good except the forks strike my armpit a little high. Where's that folding saw? It will be just right with two inches cut off."

"I'll get it," I said. I sawed the two crutches off where he showed me. "Josiah, how's that?"

"Perfect! Have a seat Billy. We have some more things to talk about.
You remember the question you asked?" Josiah said.

"Which one?"

"About me knowing that you're assistant Pastor was a dynamic preacher."

"Yeah, you acted like you have heard him speak!"

"I have."

"You've been to Tucson?" I asked surprised.

"Yeah, and a lot of other places," Josiah said.

"When were you in Tucson?"

"Last year. I sat in your church. I heard you preach! I don't think you noticed me."

"Now, Josiah, I always recognize visitors. It seems like I

would remember seeing you, especially if you were dressed like you are now."

"Billy, are you making fun of my attire?"

"Not exactly. I'm just saying that a man wearing a robe, I would have surely noticed!"

"I was incognito."

"What do you mean Josiah?"

"I mean you couldn't see me," Josiah said.

"Now you're really talking in circles!" I exclaimed.

"Not really."

"I mean really, Josiah, I think I would notice a man with a foot-long beard."

"Not if you couldn't see him," he said calmly.

"So, you were hiding?" I asked.

"Exactly, but in plain sight."

"Now you're really talking circles!"

"Not really."

"Josiah, would you please explain." I was becoming exasperated.

"Okay, I am an angel," Josiah said.

"You mean a bona-fide real come down from God angel?"

"Yes."

"Now Josiah, you don't look like any angel I've ever seen."

"How many angels you seen, Billy?"

"Well let me take that back, Josiah. I've seen pictures of angels," I said.

"Okay, but we come in all shapes and sizes," he said.

"But you look like a man, an old man, Josiah."

"Right you are, Billy. It comes with my role, my calling."

"Explain!" I demanded.

"Just like my call to you, Billy. I minister to God's chosen men. I come looking like a man so as not to intimidate men. My job is to show them God's will. I need to have real conversations in order to do that."

"Then why haven't I heard of more of you who do that?" I asked.

"There are not many of us."

"Why is that?"

"There aren't many men really wanting to do God's will. There's no need for a lot of us. Besides that, it's very dangerous. We're working in enemy territory," he said.

"What do you mean dangerous?"

"My injury is real, Billy. When I take on the form of a man, I face the same kinds of danger that you do."

"You can die, Josiah?" I asked.

"No, just like for you, Jesus paid the price, but I can lose my body," he said.

"So how long have you been around here, Josiah?"

"A couple of hundred years, Billy. It's a lot safer around here. God sends the men he needs for me to visit."

"And that's why I'm here, Josiah?"

"Exactly," he said.

"But it seems like I decided to do this."

"Doesn't work that way, Billy. Once you yielded yourself to God, he drew you to me. Now that you know who I really am Billy, we have a lot of ground to cover," Josiah said.

"We going somewhere, Josiah?" I asked.

"No," he said. "I've been laying the ground to prepare your mind for what's next Billy. God's plan for you."

"I need to ask you a question, Josiah."

"Yes?"

"Is this how it went down with Paul in the wilderness?"

"Yes, except in Paul's case, Jesus personally did the training."

My head was spinning with confusion and clarity all at once. I leaned back and look out at the stars once again.

"Billy, let's call it a night. I'm tired," said Josiah.

"So, you really do get tired, Josiah?" I asked.

"It's part of walking around in a man's body."

"I get that. I'm tired too, Josiah," I said.

"Let's pray, Billy," Josiah said.

"Me or you Josiah?"

"Both. You first."

"God, thank you for sending Josiah. Open my heart and mind to the words you have given him. May I always hear your voice and do your will. Amen."

Josiah prayed, "God, open the eyes of Billy to see you. Teach him the love you have for him, and the power you offer him as he learns to trust you. Amen."

"Goodnight, Josiah."

"Goodnight, Billy," Josiah said.

CHAPTER 36.

"Billy, you're up early," Josiah said.

"Yeah, I couldn't wait to get this day started. Besides, I didn't sleep well last night," I said.

"Why's that?"

"Thinking about sleeping next to an angel. And then the prospect of what you are going to be teaching me. Also, the prospect of seeing God. It's all pretty overwhelming," I said.

"So, the early breakfast is anticipation, huh? I'm good with that, Billy. I can see your going all out."

"Yeah, I broke out the flour and made some sabaquera tortillas with eggs and all the fixin's," I said. "In a couple of minutes, breakfast will be done. I'm ready to celebrate what I expect to be a momentous day in my life!" I passed out food. "Let's pray. Lord bless this day as I eagerly wait for what you have for me. May my mind and heart be ready for what I will see, learn and do with the rest of my life. Oh, and bless the food which you provide. Amen."

"Thank you, Billy," Josiah said. "Good breakfast!"

"Your welcome, Josiah, now let's get to the task at hand. Josiah, I spent most of the night thinking about you and the task God has given you. I've been thanking him for sending you, and I'm excited about what that means. So, what's next?" I asked.

"First, Billy, we have some problems to solve with the way you think."

"Okay."

"We're going to go back over three thousand years to the deliverance of Israel."

"To Moses?" I asked.

"Yes. Moses already knew God's plan to lead Israel."

"Okay."

"He takes matters into his own hands and kills an Egyptian. He goes on the run to Midian where he meets Jethro, becomes a shepherd, marries and spends forty years in the desert."

"Okay."

"Principle one, just because God has shown you a calling does not mean it's time to go. Taking matters into your own hands leads to disaster. All men think way too much of themselves. They are useless until they are broken enough to completely listen to the instructions of God. Remember Billy, you're still in the desert."

"I kind of get that, Josiah, I am looking for the burning bush." I said.

"Let's not call it a burning bush, because it may not take that form."

"Okay."

"So, Moses has his burning bush experience, but when God speaks, he forgets something important," Josiah said.

"What's that?"

"To take off his sandals," Josiah said.

"Why is that so important?"

"Until a man reverences a holy God, he will still try to do things his way. This is why worship is so important."

"So, I do need a burning bush experience?" I asked.

"No, you're missing the point, Billy. You must recognize the holiness, the sacred nature, the largeness of who God is. Then and only then will you be willing to hear him and do exactly as he says. Moses' leadership was dependent on complete obedience, and so yours will be too.

"Billy, in the past, how often do you think leadership in your church was modeled after tradition, your own thinking, the influence of your members, or the influence of the culture around you?" Josiah asked.

"Most of the time," I admitted.

"Do you realize each of those things are things of the

world?"

"I see."

"What about the authority of scripture, is that not God's word?"

"Yes," I replied.

"Then isn't it our task to allow God's word to rule our thinking?"

"Yes," I agreed. "Can I ask you a question Josiah?"

"Of Course," he said.

"You know God. You see him face to face."

"Yes, I do," Josiah said.

"And Jesus and the Holy Spirit too?" I asked. "Were you there when Satan and your brothers fell?"

"Yes," he replied.

"So, all that history, all of that wisdom, and yet you don't make some decisions on your own?"

"No."

"Why not?" I asked.

"Why would I? I have free access to God who knows all things. Why wouldn't I just ask him?" Josiah said.

"Hmm."

"I can get every choice made perfect by asking him," Josiah continued. "I would be a fool to rely on my own wisdom. Billy, you have to see, that's man's whole problem. They think they are far smarter than they are. That's not an intelligence problem. That's an ego problem. True intelligence is faith, trust in the one who knows all. Smart men are those who ask questions, the right questions. And if they are really smart, they will ask the One with the right answers, God. When Moses took off his sandals, he was finally ready to lead his people to the promised land, but not until then," Josiah said.

"Is it the same for me Josiah?"

"It is, for you and everyone else. And it will always be that way!"

"So do we need to take a hike, Josiah?" I asked.

"Billy, I still can't walk well, but why would we need to

take a hike?" he asked.

"The burning bush, Josiah."

"Billy, you need to get rid of that idea!"

"Why?" I asked.

"There will be no burning bush," Josiah said. "God shows his glory how and when he wants to. Whatever happens will be personal, unique to you. No one in the Bible except Moses saw a burning bush. For Paul, it was blindness, and then one on one with Jesus. For the other apostles, it was three years with Jesus. The list goes on"

"So, you don't know how God will meet me, Josiah?" I asked.

"I don't know, Billy. Remember this. Even though the apostles walked with Jesus for three years, until Pentecost they didn't understand what they learned. Then, in a light-bulb moment, the Holy Spirit made it all make sense. Even then though, faith became moment-by-moment, day-by-day obedience. We never see a time where God rolls out the entire blueprint for our lives. Billy, when I finish my assignment with you, I will go to Him, and He will give me my next assignment. We cannot, and you will not, move forward, until you learn to trust Him with what's next. I will tell you this, even now He is already working on what is next for you, your family, and your church. When you show up, you will find people ready to embrace whatever assignment he places before you."

"I guess I need to pray for humility then, don't I?" I asked.

"You do, Billy," he said.

"Will you pray first Josiah?"

"Gladly. Lord, break Billy. Humble him at your feet. May he see your glory. I know that when he does, it will put him on his face before you. Amen."

At Josiah's prayer, I fell to my face with the tears of a broken man. I prayed, "Lord may I die this day to all my selfish desires, and may I find my heart in you, to serve only you, with the message of the good news you give me. Amen."

As the morning sun passed behind a cloud, leaving the

cloud's edges glowing with a silver lining, I faced the heavens above and could see God's glory reaching all the way into my heart. The magnificence of the morning in the Sonoran Desert lifted its voice, and the birds sang to the glory of God.

CHAPTER 37.

The sun was moving high, so we slid our chairs into the shade under the tarp.

"Josiah, I need to gather some firewood," I said.

"Okay, would you do me a favor?" he asked.

"What's that?"

"In my saddle bags you'll find a leather case. Would you bring it to me?" Josiah asked.

"Sure." I fumbled through Josiah's bags. "This it?" I asked, holding up a small worn case of old leather.

"Yeah. Billy. Your welcome to take Balaam with you. You'll find straps on the saddle bags to lash the firewood with."

"Thanks, Josiah. That will make this an easy job."

"Are you gathering mesquite, Billy?" Josiah asked.

"Yeah, it makes the best firewood." I took Balaam's reigns and we headed out. "See you in a bit."

"I'll be taking a nap," Josiah said. "But wake me, when you get back."

I loaded the donkey with firewood in record time and returned to camp. "Boy that was a quick trip," I said. "Sorry to wake you."

"No problem. Remember, that's what I told you to do. Let me look at that stack of wood. See that piece right there?" he asked.

"The one in my hand?"

"Yes. Would you bring it to me?"

"Sure."

"This is perfect."

"For what?"

"You'll see," Josiah said. "Mark it here and here."

I put marks in the places he indicated.

"Okay, now could you saw out this piece?" he asked.

"Sure," I said.

"Yeah, that will do."

I watched as he unrolled his leather case, laying its instruments on the ground beside him. He held the mesquite piece in his left hand, and deftly began shaving off the outer layers. When he finished, nothing but a four-inch inner core was left.

"Billy, could you drag that backpack over here," he asked. "That will make a table to place my tools."

"What are you making, Josiah? I asked.

"Like I said, you will see!"

I watched with fascination as the orange center began to take the shape of a man. In about an hour he handed me a carved figure of a man. The features were very well defined, and had the man been standing in front of me, I could have easily recognized his face. It was balding on top with long hair on the sides, kind of stooped over, and looking to be about sixty years old."

"Josiah, is this anybody in particular?" I asked.

"Yes, Billy. It is the apostle Paul. I made this for you. I want you to carry it wherever you go."

"Now wait a minute, Josiah. We don't know what Paul looked like?"

"Correction Billy. You don't, but I do. Trust me this is what he looked like."

"I apologize, Josiah. I forget that you saw him."

"That's okay, Billy," he said. "When you get back to the ranch, carry it to the shop and drill a hole right through its ears. Then you can wear it around your neck."

"But, couldn't this be considered a graven image?" I asked, concerned.

"Only if your heart sees it that way, Billy. Paul was a man just like you, not a god. I just want you to able to see it, so it reminds you of how God can use a man with a willing heart."

Afternoon came quickly and Josiah asked me if I would

grab some tortillas and jerky. "It's time for an afternoon snack," he mentioned.

"Good idea," I said. "I'm on it."

"Do we have any fresh Prickly pear apples?" Josiah asked.

"Sure, plenty. I'll get a bag."

"Billy, have you eaten any cholla yet?"

"You mean the blooms?" I asked.

"No, the pods," he said.

"Josiah, my experience with the pods is not good," I said. "The barbs are harder to get rid of than a bad haircut."

"Not if you handle them right!" Josiah said. "Didn't I see you pulling them off your socks with a pair of needle nose pliers? Gather a few and put them in one of those plastic bags. Bring them here. I'll show you how to handle them."

"Is this enough Josiah?"

"For now, it is. Okay hand me the bag and pliers and watch. I pull them out of the bag with the pliers and with a thin skinny knife, I peel away that outer skin, like this. You see how the thorns come with it?"

"Yeah," I said, surprised.

"Grab it on the other end, pull off the last bit, and you have a tasty morsel!" He handed me one.

"Hmm, not bad Josiah! You would never think that such a devilish little pod could taste this good," I said.

"It's just the opposite, Billy. They taste so good that God had to give them extra protection or everything would eat them."

"Now Josiah, I am getting to see through your tactics," I said. "Is there an underlying spiritual message here?"

"How'd you ever guess, Billy?"

"Because, I know you, Josiah."

"Bet you never thought you would be good friends with an angel, did you, Billy?"

"You got me there, Josiah!"

"Okay, Josiah, spit it out," I said, wondering what the lesson could be this time.

"Billy, the work that God calls you into will be very difficult. You will be criticized, isolated, verbally attacked, persecuted and maybe even have to die for what you believe," he said.

"Josiah, I live in the good old USA where we have religious freedom. The church is not persecuted there."

"Billy you're wrong," he stated. "Jesus' true disciples are always persecuted. Right now, the protective grace which God gives, comes from the generations before you who sacrificed greatly on your behalf. That is soon to end. The judgement will come. Write this in your mind. The consequences of sin are God's most powerful tool to reach the lost. Judgement is needed. Judgement is necessary. Broken men hear the Gospel. Prosperity breeds indifference.

"Back to the cholla. Christians are called to be kind, generous and loving. When a man turns his cheek, when he gives and forgives, he is likely to be taken advantage of and abused. Billy, the only way for you to have peace and love in the middle of everything is that your protection will be God himself. Consequences are protection for the saints and conviction for the lost."

"That's not too clear, Josiah. Explain," I said.

"The ultimate consequence is death. For a Christian, there is no fear of death. Your accusers and your critics have no power over you," Josiah said.

"Hmm."

"What's the worst they can do to you? Kill you and send you to Heaven. Everything you do will be done before an audience of three, the Father, the Son and the Holy Spirit. They are the only ones that matter. All the good angels and all the saints before you cheer your efforts. All you do that is good, becomes eternal. Every prayer is written in stone. Evil will pass away. After supper we'll talk about the power you must receive."

This was all a little overwhelming. "You hungry Josiah?" I asked.

"Yeah," he said. "Bring me some more cholla. I'll peal them and you can take care of the rest. They're even better

Lonnie Barnard

cooked."

CHAPTER 38.

"Josiah, I forgot to check my snares today. Go ahead with prepping the cholla. I'll be back in thirty minutes," I said. As I approached the traps, I could see that I had caught five rabbits, but two of them were shredded. There was blood all over the ground. The telling tracks of a cougar pointed toward the culprit. I pitched the remains into the brush. As I removed the three remaining rabbits, I heard gunfire coming from camp. I rushed back to find a wounded dying man lying next to his chair. Josiah had been shot.

As I held him in my arms, he whispered, "It's warfare Billy, real warfare." As he breathed his last, he mouthed, "Jesus take me home." His body went limp. Then, suddenly, his clothing became vacant as he traveled home. His real home. I wept, but not with tears without hope. I knew one day I would see him again.

At the sound of horses, I looked up just in time to see banditos riding away over the next hill. I decided they must have been the ones that had killed Josiah. I reached inside the cave and grasped for a flare, but before the fireball had even hit the ground, I could see the dust of a Jeep in the valley below. I raced down the mountain. By the time I reached the road, there was Jorge sliding up to the roads end.

"Billy, get in! Bryan has been hurt!" he said.

"What happened?" I asked, noting the desperation on his face.

"Get in. I'll tell you on the way!" he said, keeping the jeep running. "He was riding a horse, and for some reason, one of my gentle horses spooked. It must have been a rattler. Anyway, when he fell, it was down a hundred feet into a canyon. They are taking him to Hermosillo now. We will meet them there."

When we arrived at the hospital, Laura was sitting in the lobby crying. I wrapped my arms around her, but she sobbed, "Bryan's gone, Billy! He broke his neck. He's dead! I reached for Bobby. Jorge slid in by us and we all cried.

After what seemed like a long time, Jorge knelt in front of us saying, "I want to pray for you. Lord we don't understand. A lot of times we don't. We trust you though. We know Bryan is in Heaven now. We live in a fallen world. None of us escape it's pain. We know that in this world even the good die, sometimes far too young. It won't always be like this because one day sin and its impact will be gone. We also know that this was your plan. Some days life down here is not pretty, but one day we will understand. Give this family, my family, comfort and peace in the midst of this life, this world of storms. Amen."

After a while, Jorge said, "Billy, I have made arrangements. My friend will make his body ready. You can have his service at the ranch if you like or we can take him back to Tucson."

"Laura what do you think?" I asked.

"Let's bury him here," she replied. "This has become home to me. Jorge, can we have a place on the side of the mountain to bury him?"

"Of course, and if you like, we will set aside places for all of you and any other family that might want that" Jorge said.

"Thank you, Jorge. We'd like that," I said. "There's something I need to tell you, Jorge. You too Laura. Let's go over to the family room. We can have some privacy there."

We settled into the chairs in the family room and I took a deep breath. "Laura, just before Jorge came to get me, a visitor died in my camp."

"Billy, I thought you were alone," Laura exclaimed.

"Do we need to go get the body and bury him too?" Jorge asked.

"No but I would like to get my gear and his donkey and bring them back to the ranch," I said.

"Okay, but what do you mean, we don't need to get his

body?" Jorge asked.

"There is no body," I said.

"Billy, are you losing it?" asked Laura.

"No Laura, I'm serious. There is no body."

"Then how do you know he died?" she asked.

"Laura, he died in my arms and then his body just vanished," I replied.

"Billy, I don't understand," Laura said.

"Laura, I think I'm beginning to see what Billy is saying," said Jorge.

"How's that Jorge?" Laura asked.

"Billy, was his name Josiah?" asked Jorge.

"Yes, Jorge! How did you know?" I asked.

"I knew him Billy," Jorge said.

"You did?"

"Guys, you're leaving me out," said Laura.

"Laura, Josiah is an angel. If he dies, there is no body, at least not what we think of as a body," said Jorge.

"Guys, it must be the stress. Maybe I'm the one who is delusional, but I swear I thought I heard you say Josiah was an angel."

"Right, we did," I said.

"So, Billy you did have your encounter with God. He sent an angel!" said Laura.

"I guess so. What do you think Jorge?" I asked.

"That is how it happened with me," Jorge replied.

"It's late," said Laura. "When will they will bring our sons body? Tomorrow?"

"Yes. Let's go home," I said. "I mean to the ranch. I'm still in shock."

"Billy, Laura, God's got this," said Jorge.

"I know, but it's still hard," Laura said.

"Trust me, I know," Jorge said.

As we left the hospital, the stars didn't seem so bright. The sights and sounds of sirens filled the night air of Hermosillo. The street orphans stood at the stop light intersections, begging for a handout. The drunks and addicts leaned against the walls and wandered in the alleys. The prostitutes advertised under the lights. "Lord take me home to the ranch where a little bit of Heaven shines in the beauty of the mountain air. Lord thank you for these reminders in the middle of a heavy heart," I prayed.

CHAPTER 39.

As we made the hour and a half trip back to the ranch, Laura wept lying in my lap. Bobby nuzzled against her side and then they wept in unison. My mind boiled with all that had happened. My thoughts shifted between anger and hope almost simultaneously. Jorge drove in silence. It was not time for talking but grieving. I wondered how parents with unsaved children dealt with this. Slowly the grief, the sadness, and the anger were replaced by visions of Bryan at the feet of Jesus. I could see my Lord holding Bryan in his arms, laughing and smiling. The anger began drifting away with the new images of my son protected and loved by a Father who would never fail, who would keep him until we all joined him.

Laura called her dad. The funeral was set for Thursday.

Maria had dinner waiting when we arrived. We prayed and ate in silence. After midnight, we made our way to our room. Maria made a pallet for Bobby next to our bed. It was no time for him to be alone without his brother. We sat on the couch in silence except for occasional sobs. Bobby sat in my lap and Laura stayed close by my side. Each of us prayed and then climbed into bed, but we all knew there would be little sleep. I looked over and Bobby had fallen asleep. The gentle snore of my wife, Bryan and Bobby's mother, finally gave me comfort to doze off on my own. The smell of breakfast woke me briefly, but I was soon back to sleep again. At ten I woke up and made my way to the kitchen, only to find Jorge weeping and nursing his cup of coffee.

"You okay, Jorge?" I asked.

"Probably no worse off than you. You lost your son Billy. I

lost my best friend," he replied.

"Josiah?" I asked.

"Yes. He's been here for the whole ten years, Billy. All of this, the ranch, the school, our work in the barrio, our work in the prison, are all visions he gave me. He taught me to walk with God. He will be greatly missed."

"I had no idea Jorge," I said. "I've been so busy feeling sorry for myself, that I hadn't even thought about your loss. I'm sorry, Jorge."

"No apology needed, Billy. We both have suffered great loss. At least we are here for each other."

"That's true, Jorge," I said.

"You remember Job's friends?" he asked.

"You mean so called friends."

"No, if you will remember, they wept with him for a week. They had it right at first. They were there for him. Their mistake was when they started trying to play God and explain why. Men don't have answers, Billy. The Lord gives and the Lord takes away, but only He knows why. God knows. He has the answers."

"I think it was time for me to quit relying on Josiah and look to the Heavens," I said.

"Maybe God took him home to watch after Bryan," suggested Jorge.

"Now that's a thought, Jorge," I said.

"Jorge, I hear some stirring in the bedroom," I said. "I better check on Laura and Bobby." I headed into the bedroom where Laura was just getting up. "You alright Laura?" I asked.

"You know Billy," Laura replied simply.

"Yeah I know."

"Hey Dad," said Bobby.

"Hey, Bobby," I replied.

"Billy, I was thinking," Laura said. "Jorge showed us a beautiful lake. I promised Bryan and Bobby we would go fishing when you got back. Do you think we could go, just the three of us?"

"That's a great idea Laura. Maybe we can chase away some of the sadness," I said. "Anyway, we need to be alone. Just us. Let's go ahead and eat breakfast. We'll have Maria pack us a lunch and Jorge can loan us some gear."

After breakfast, Jorge said, "I see that Maria has packed you a lunch. Where are you going?"

"We wanted to spend the day fishing at that beautiful lake you showed Laura and the kids," I replied.

"Good idea. Billy, you can follow me in my other Jeep," Jorge said. "I need to come back and use this one, but if you program the GPS, you'll be able to find your way back. It's only about twenty minutes north. Let's go. Bobby you want to ride with me?"

"Sure, Mister Jorge," Bobby said.

At the lake, Jorge said, "Billy we made it without anything bouncing off the Jeeps, so I'd call that a successful trip. This lake is well stocked with large mouth, I put my favorite lures in. You shouldn't have much trouble catching plenty."

I helped Laura and Bobby tie on lures, and by the time we had cast ten times, we already had three fish. I dug around in Jorge's tackle box and found a fillet knife. In the picnic basket was a sack of cornmeal and a couple of eggs. "Seems like Maria has done this before," I said.

While Bobby and Laura enjoyed catching fish, I built a campfire. We saved several nice ones and I cut some nice fillets. I broke an egg, coated them, and rolled them in cornmeal. Then I placed them on foil and arraigned them above the fire. Maria had made up rice and vegetables which I was not familiar with. All in all, it was a real good lunch.

We spent the rest of the afternoon catching and releasing what had to be nearly fifty Bass. As the sun began to set, we loaded our gear. Together we gave thanks to the Lord for helping us with the pain. I even heard laughter from my wife and son. Pain can only be replaced by joy, and for an afternoon there was joy.

I knew people would ask how I could go fishing the day

after my son died. But I would ask them, what do they know? What is right? What is proper? Men don't know but God knows. Bryan was in Heaven, He was smiling. It was right for us to embrace his joy because we would see him again soon.

CHAPTER 40.

That night I was half asleep. Or, was I asleep? I wasn't sure. I seemed like I entered in the presence of God. It was just as I remembered it from the Scriptures. God's throne, the Seraphim hovering above, with Jesus seated to His right. I knew it was all there, but I couldn't look. There was a great host of angels standing before God as He spoke. Josiah was standing there before him and God was saying, "It's good to see you my friend. I'm sorry I had to call you home, but your work has come before me. You have been doing an exemplary job with Jorge, and in the last days with Billy.

"The training assigned to you is completed. A great offensive is planned. Through the foundation you have established on the ranch and in Hermosillo, we plan a southern attack on the forces of evil to bring revival to the US. Jorge is key to our earthly attack, but Billy will lead. You have been chosen to lead our assault from the heavens. Satan and his henchman are aware of our plan and you must lead in the protection of all those we have trained for this assault. Even now Jorge is finishing the preparation we have with Billy. The previous host will need to provide protection at the ranch. Our offensive will be initiated there.

"Right now, Satan is gathering forces to launch an attack at the ranch. We need five hundred volunteers to go there immediately and drive out the demonic forces gathering there." Then God asked, "Any volunteers?" A large contingent of angels appeared before him. "Okay, angels you must go there now. As for you, Josiah, you will go there later but they should be able to handle the immediate needs. The balance of assignments will be at the Barrio and the prison in Hermosillo. Then we will need reinforcements at Billy's church, at the university in Tucson, and some for the oversight of Billy and Laura's families. Josiah, I want you to stay in close touch with me as we move forward in our efforts. Gabriel and Michael are on standby in case they are needed. Josiah you should now meet with the rest of your troops to update them on the work going on at the ranch, in Hermosillo and in Tucson. After that all of you should immediately report to your stations, Josiah?"

"Yes sir," Josiah replied. "You have your assignment?"

"Yes sir."

"Troops?" asked God's voice.

"Yes."

"Josiah, let's hear it."

"Okay, Angels"

A loud chorus rang out, "Holy, Holy, Holy is the Lord God almighty."

"Troops let's do our job! Remember, we're a team! Work together. Amen."

Josiah quickly moved to his group which was already over the ranch. They were already engaging the enemy. Profanity and insults were being hurled at them but as the hate was hurled it was met with stiff opposition as the angels quoted God's word. The demons quickly turned their attention toward earth. They conjured up a dry east wind filled with swarms of grasshoppers. The angels used the wind by meeting it with a west wind causing great thunderheads to rise, bringing rain with lightning and thunder. The grasshoppers were drowned as the rainwater swept down the gullies and ravines.

The verbal assaults came again but as God's word confronted Satan's forces, they turned and fled over the mountains. As God's word poured over them, light penetrated their darkness and a weak and whipped band disappeared. The angels turned their attention to the people on the ranch.

On the ranch, wind had scattered the livestock and there were fences down and roofs in need of repair. Angels ministered to the people giving them strength for the task they had to do, and order was restored to the ranch. Children were visibly shaken as adults around them held and gave them comfort. As the repairs were made, I saw that Laura and Maria gathered the women and held a prayer meeting. With the prayers the angels were quickly renewed in strength and ready for the next attack.

I did not know if all this was a vision or if I was dreaming. Then I saw Josiah gather his troops and explain to them not to expect the next attack to be so confrontational. The demons had not expected us to show up so fast. "I'm warning you," he said. "We must be very observant. I expect they will try to infiltrate the people and bring their chaos from the inside out. Watch for the attack to be subtle. I think they will use the cover of darkness to work their way in."

In the morning, I learned that winds had come during the night and livestock were scattered and roofs were damaged.

"So, Billy what do you think?" Jorge asked.

"Jorge, what do you mean?"

"That hot east wind, the grasshoppers, that's not normal this time of year," Jorge said. "Spiritual attack, Billy. God's going to do something big. Satan always shows up when God's about to do something big. I think we need to call a prayer meeting tonight."

"Sounds like a good idea, Jorge," I said.

"I'll get the word out, Billy. Six o'clock, right after dinner," he announced.

CHAPTER 41.

With dinner finished, and the tables cleared, everyone regrouped in the dining room. "Folks I know everyone is aware of the unusual events of the day," Jorge announced. "I would like to open this time for questions. If you raise your hand, we'll bring a microphone so everyone can hear. First question."

The mic was brought to a tall man standing in the back. "Can you explain what you think was going on and why?" he asked.

"I believe the dark forces of the world have discovered our work here, and planned on destroying much of our infrastructure," Jorge responded. "Angels intercepted their attempts and there was a battle in the air. For now, their efforts have been thwarted and we are safe. I do not think this is over though."

"But why?" asked a young mother in the front.

"The work here has progressed so well that there is now a significant force trained from which we can make a real Gospel push in Hermosillo, and who knows, maybe in the US someday," Jorge explained. "Up until this point, spiritual warfare has been mostly personal for us. Threats have been contained and dealt with, within our community. What many of you may not understand is that the angels have been protecting us from their stations above all along. A major offensive push was attempted by demonic forces last night. There will be more to come. Does that explain things?"

"Yes," several people replied.

"Are there any more questions?" Jorge asked.

"No? Okay, then let's gather in our prayer groups. We should pray for courage, protection, personal strength, and faith. Pray for the angels that protect us, pray that Jesus would give them great courage and strength. Keep in mind that the seriousness of the attacks tells us that God is doing something big, so we should take this very seriously."

Jorge sat with Laura and I. Maria and Bobby joined us. As the prayers poured up from those around us, we sat silently. I suppose each of us were still processing the grief lying in our laps. After a few minutes I could sense the presence of angels as they seemed to come down from their stations above the clouds and enter the room with us. A powerful peace flooded my soul. As I looked across the table, I could sense this great peace sweep around our table and then throughout the room. The room seemed as full of the Holy Spirit as it must have been there at Pentecost. There were no flames of fire, but we didn't need a visual. The oneness was there. Suddenly and spontaneously voices rang out, "Amazing Grace." I suppose most people sang in Spanish, but I heard the words in English as clearly as if this was our choir in Tucson. We made our way to our rooms silently. There was nothing left to say. God had spoken. He had spoken to everyone in that room.

Laura and I sat on the couch in our room. I pulled Bobby up into my lap. I as held him he cried again. Sure, we had explained that his brother was in Heaven, but his understanding of that had limitations. He had lost his brother, his friend. They had been inseparable. I needed to figure out a way to connect him with the other kids. He needed a fishing buddy. Daddy would do what he could, but that was not the same as a big brother. Laura and I prayed over our son and tucked him in to the pallet beside our bed.

"Laura would you like a cup of coffee?" I asked.

"I would," she replied. "Meet me in the kitchen. I'll put some on," I said. "There's a little table in there. We need to let Bobby sleep."

"Let me wash my face, and I'll be there in a minute," Laura replied. *I don't know why she wears makeup*, I thought, as she walked into the room. I always thought she was more beautiful without it. "Did you pour me a cup, Billy?" she asked when she got to the kitchen.

"Yeah, a little cream and sugar, just like you like it," I said.

"Billy, we haven't had time for you to tell me about your time in the mountains. I mean I know about Josiah dying and that he was an angel, but that's about it," Laura said.

"Josiah spent a lot of time with me Laura," I said. "I think he was my meeting with God. God sent him. He was my good friend. But mostly he taught me. He brought a very specific word from God. My future, our future is good. We will miss Bryan, but he's okay. Before we go back to Tucson, we need to make plans."

"Josiah didn't explain?"

"Not the details. He just helped me develop the framework. You and I will do the planning. That is, with a lot of help from Jorge. You okay, dear?" I asked.

"I'll be OK," she replied. "I trust God. He knows what he's doing."

"Your mom and dad will be here tomorrow," I reminded her.

"I know," she said. "They should be around lunch time."

"Let's pray. Your turn, Laura."

"Lord," she asked, "help my little boy, Bobby. Give him peace and understanding. God pour your Spirit over my husband and let our great loss bring us together to see, know, and do your will. Amen."

"Goodnight Laura."

"Goodnight Billy."

CHAPTER 42.

We ate breakfast and watched as the school children boarded the buses to the school, and workers made their way to their daily duties. Laura and I were to meet her parents in Hermosillo and have lunch there. We borrowed one of Jorge's Jeeps and drove to Hermosillo. We met in a park off the main highway. Joe and I went to the street vendor down the road and ordered hot dogs for all. Laura and her mother, Suzy, discussed all the things that had been happening. Tears poured down Suzy's face, but it was Laura's turn to be strong. We offered thanks to the Maker of the universe, and picked at our lunch, shaded from the warm afternoon sun by the trees in the park.

The plan was to drop Laura and Suzy at the Barrio, so Suzy could see the work there. Joe and I would go to the prison so Joe could see the work there.

When we got to the prison, I showed Joe the amazing work going on and we spent some time with Peter. I was amazed at how much scripture he had memorized in a week. I met his mentor Adan and was impressed with his skills. It was easy to see that Peter's time there would be an invaluable investment.

Meanwhile, the girls took a bus. This gave Joe and I time to talk. "So, Billy, are you and Laura coming home after the funeral?" Joe asked.

"We are staying here for a while," I replied. "God has laid a plan on my heart, but I need to learn more before we come back. To be honest with you, the ranch is such an awesome place that I would love to stay. Unfortunately, I think God does have plans for me back in Tucson."

"So, you're burying Bryan here?" he asked.

"Yes, and Jorge has set aside plots for all of us if we want them," I said.

"Billy, you don't seem to be struggling with this too much."

"That's true Joe. My faith has moved to a point where I know that this is part of God's plan," I replied.

"How's that?" he asked.

"Joe, I really don't know, but I trust Him. That's all. I mean, how bad can it be? Bryan's in Heaven. It would be selfish and cruel to bring him back. Laura's okay too. Bobby's got a way to go, but he will get there."

"About the prison, that was amazing! I've never seen a more dramatic illustration of the transforming power of the Gospel," Joe said.

"Yeah, it gives us a look at what we need in our churches in America doesn't it?"

"It sure does."

"Wait till you get your report from Suzy," I said. "They are stopping by the school on their way back to the ranch."

"Jorge has a school?" Joe asked.

"Yeah, he brings kids from the Barrio out there. He's training the next generation of great evangelists and true world changers," I said.

"And those are the poor orphan kids from the Barrio?"

"Exactly."

"That seems strange!"

"Not really," I replied. "Haven't you noticed the rag tag bunch Jesus chose his disciples from?"

"Hmm, I guess you're right. So, are you thinking that the next generation of earth-shaking Christians in the US may not be coming out of the fine middle class and wealthy neighborhoods?" asked Joe.

"Look at our country," I said. "It hasn't been working very well so far, has it?" I said.

"You're right," he said.

"If something isn't working, then we must do something different," I said.

"Yeah, you're right, Billy. So, is this what you've been figuring out?" Joe asked.

"Some of it, but there's much more. A lot of it I'm still working my way through. Wait till you see the ranch. You'll understand a lot more then," I said. We passed the school on our way to the ranch. "There's the school now!" I said. "Why don't I give you a brief tour. Looks like the girls are still here. There's the bus. When we finish, we'll give them a ride the rest of the way to the ranch. Might even take a detour, there's some things I'd like you to see."

Joe and I took a brief tour of the school and picked up the women and Bobby for the rest of the trip to the ranch. "That was pretty cool Billy," Joe said. "It's been a long time since I've been in a school with such well-mannered kids."

"That's just part of it. This evening I'll let you visit with some of the kids. You won't believe how bright they are!"

"Watch," I said. "After we cross this next ridge, look across the valley to the next ridge. There's usually a group of bighorns somewhere near the top."

"I see them Billy! Hand me those binoculars," Joe exclaimed. He focused in on the sheep. "Awesome! Suzy do you want the binoculars?"

"Of course, Joe," Suzy replied. "Wow, they're magnificent!"

"Before we go to the ranch house, I'll give you the fifty-cent tour of Jorge's operation here," I said. You see the crop fields, the orchards, and the lake below? The water resource, sewer processing, irrigation, and the electricity; everything is produced right here on the ranch. This whole place is self-sustaining. Even ninety per-cent of maintenance is done here on the ranch. They raise cattle, sheep, goats not to mention, chicken and turkeys. Even the kids work."

"With all this work, how are the kids so bright?" Joe

asked.

"There are no video games, no TV, and everything they are taught on computers is carefully screened. No junk," I replied.

"Then how do they have fun?"

"Just like you did when you were a boy, with soccer and all kinds of games. They also have hunting, fishing, and you name it, right outside their doors. Art classes, music lessons, shop classes, crafts, and trades, are all available to these kids. Just no Junk," I explained.

"You hear all that, Suzy?" asked Joe.

"I sure did. And the funny thing is, we all know that's how it ought to be done. Apparently, Americans don't think it's important enough to do things that way anymore," Suzy said.

"There's another important thing too, Suzy," I said.

"What's that, Billy?" she asked.

"Christianity here brings the adults into community. While some adults are here making sure these things happen on the compound, others are out there tending cattle, herding sheep, plowing gardens, or packing vegetables," I said. "None of this is possible without community, and community is not possible without Christians willing to live their lives together. Think about it. Here your neighbor is doing a better job with other people's children, than we do with our own. This is what God's plan looks like in action."

"Amen, Billy," Joe said.

CHAPTER 43.

Our arrival at the ranch was met with a mariachi band playing. The solemnness of the tragedy of our loss, mixed with the joyful sound of hope only God gives. Joe and Suzy met the warm embrace of their old friend Jorge. We moved to the dining room where Maria had prepared cookies and fruit juice for us. Jorge seated us at his table. Sounds of laughter rang out of the kitchen where the high schoolers were busy helping Maria with our evening meal.

Jorge produced an envelope which was addressed to Jorge, but was in regards to both Joe and I. "Billy, Joe, look at this letter that came in the mail today. It's from Durango," he said, "from the angel, Josiah."

"So, he did make it to Durango?" I asked.

"Maybe. But for sure his letter was there," Jorge said.

"Jorge, this is thick. Have you read it?" I asked.

"Not all of it."

"Whoa guys, you need to fill me in," Joe said.

"How's that Joe?" I asked.

"Who's Angel Josiah?" Joe asked.

"He's an angel," Jorge said. "He's been here instructing me for ten years."

"You seen him, Jorge?" asked Joe.

"Yeah, he wasn't an ordinary angel. He had a body. He visited Billy in the mountains. He died in Billy's arms," Jorge replied.

"Wait a minute. Angels don't die!" exclaimed Joe.

"He had a body. His body died, but he's still alive somewhere," Jorge said. "Joe there's a lot more but we'll have to get to that later. Right now, we need to deal with the letter. Actually, I need to meet with you and Billy.

"He told you that?" I asked.

"Yes, and I'm not finished reading, so if it's okay, can we meet in the morning? Say five thirty?" said Jorge.

"Okay," Joe and I replied.

"Meanwhile, it will be another thirty minutes before dinner is ready so why don't we take a quick trip down to the maintenance shop," I said.

We got back in the jeep and headed to the shop. There, Joe asked Jorge, "What's this man making?"

"Joe, Billy, this is my head machinist and mechanic, Louis. He is making a new shaft for a water pump. We always keep a spare. A few days ago, the bearings went out and cut into the old shaft. Keeping a shaft in stock allows us to make quick repairs. Our water system is essential. Something Josiah mentioned in the first part of the letter prompts me to illustrate it this way. The shaft must be precise. Failure to make it exactly right will result in the new bearings wearing out in a matter of hours. Josiah put it like this. 'If the devil is in the details, then God must be in the details.' Our lives, God's plan for each of us, will require us to be very careful to pay attention to every detail.

"Do you remember the story of Ananias and Saphira in Acts?" Jorge continued.

"Yes," Joe replied.

"Ever wonder why He was so quick to take them off the face of this Earth over their little lie about the sales of their property?"

"Yeah," we nodded.

"God is unveiling a new work in us. Details will be very important. This work will be important, and failure to pay careful attention to his instructions will be a big mistake. This is foundational. Laying the foundation right is essential. There's no room for error. If God treated the modern church like he did that foundational church, we might have a bunch of dead bodies in our pews."

"Josiah said this in the letter?" I asked Jorge.

"Yes, but he's been teaching me this for a while," Jorge replied. "I've been aware of the new work God is doing for a while. Look all around you. This is His work not mine. I'm now starting to see how he is bringing you in to take this work to other places."

"Jorge I am overwhelmed by your work here!" Joe said.

"Not mine, Joe, Jesus'," Jorge corrected.

"Okay, but the scope of all this and how smoothly it all came together is amazing," Joe said.

"Everything Joe, every detail. It's all by the instruction of the Holy Spirit," Jorge said. "He sent me Josiah as a visual, as a voice to make sure I got every detail right. That's what I'm trying to tell you. What's next will depend on you paying careful attention to the Holy Spirit's instruction."

"Jorge, it seems like things that I've had a lifetime to learn, you've learned in a few years. Why do you think that is?" Joe asked.

"It's all God, Joe. Do you remember that day you led me to Jesus?"

"Yes."

"You had fired your warehouse manager and called me into your office. You explained how you had uncovered our little drug smuggling plot," Jorge reminded him.

"Yeah."

"Why didn't you call the police?" Jorge asked.

"I don't know, Jorge. I was pretty mad," Joe said.

"I know, Joe!" Jorge remarked.

"Really?" Joe asked.

Yeah, it was God's plan," Jorge said. "He had something bigger on His agenda. Jesus didn't save me to sit. He had a plan for me."

"I can see that now, Jorge, but that's in hindsight," Joe said.

"Joe, I didn't know it then either, but now I look back and I see how it all turned out," said Jorge.

"That still doesn't answer my question," said Joe. "Your

spiritual growth, it's amazing."

"Not really Joe, it's all Him," Jorge said. "I'm just too dumb to know anything other than day to day obedience."

"I guess that's what spiritual maturity looks like to me." Joe said.

"Remember Joe, I knew nothing. I didn't know my Bible. I didn't know how to pray. I look back and realize that was an advantage. In America your churches are filled with traditions. Many of those traditions have nothing to do with scripture. Me? I just had my Bible, and so for me it was, just read it, believe it, and do it. When I went to the Barrio my heart broke for the children. My friends were drug dealers and hit men for the Cartel. I was dumb enough to believe they needed Jesus too. I shared the Gospel. Many believed. It was dangerous, but I wasn't worried about my life. Many of the men that wanted to kill me, were becoming my brothers.

"It's all about the details, Joe and Billy. But we don't know them. We don't have to. Jesus is our friend. if we walk with Him, He will tell us. Let's go have our dinner. We don't want to keep the others waiting."

CHAPTER 44.

I wish I could plug in a video of the scene that played out before us that evening after dinner. We had been asked to wear a coat and tie. We gathered in the entry to the dining hall, and High School boys escorted each of the ladies to assigned seats. Name placards were on each table, and as the ladies we're seated, the young gentlemen held their chairs and gently slid them forward to seat them. Young ladies in formal dress seated the men, and Jorge stood to offer thanks. Joe and Suzy were seated at the head of our table which was at the front of the room. On this night they would be our guests of honor. Jorge was showing the deep thanks he had for that afternoon in Tucson when Joe had led him to Jesus. To the right of Joe, was an empty chair with a placard, with the name of Jesus on it. The young men and ladies served each of us.

The words Josiah had given Jorge, suddenly struck me, "God is in the details". The reverence and courtesy with which these young men and women conducted themselves, was a sight to behold. In my mind, the difference contrasted with what I usually see in homes in America. A great hope swept through my mind as I witnessed the difference that could be made as we became eyewitnesses to the plan and impact of God. "Yes ma'am," "no ma'am," "yes sir," "no sir," "thank you," and "your welcome" are such simple things, but they were evidence of hearts that walked with Jesus. Jesus, in that empty chair, was showing us His glory. He didn't need to be there for it to be seen. The work he did two thousand years ago was on full display in the hearts of those who had truly become his disciples. Just think, only a few years before, these young people had been filthy, sickly kids, trapped in the poverty of the Barrio and all which that culture had for them. Not until all of us had finished eating and the tables were cleared, did they finally take their seats to eat in a corner of the dining room.

We made our way to the front porch. The mariachi band gathered under the patio in front of us. As their songs filled the night air, the people of God danced under the watchful eyes of stars God had hung in their place a long, long time ago; a little bit of Heaven. Jesus shows us glimpses, and it only gets better. I imagined Bryan dancing as he watched down on his earthly family and danced in unison with those who had gone before us.

"Joe, Suzy, how big is your God?" I asked.

"Billy, He's big, real big," Suzy said.

"Look through the telescope Jorge has set up," I said. "When you see what I've seen, He will get bigger."

"Billy that is amazing! Suzy and I want to capture that image in our mind," Joe said. "I think it's time to see the vastness of creation in our dreams."

"Goodnight Joe. Goodnight Suzy," I said. They turned and headed for their room.

I made room on the bench I was sitting on. "Laura, come over by me. Did you put Bobby to bed?" I asked.

"Yeah, we said our prayers," Laura replied.

"How long has it been since I told you how much I love you?"

"Yesterday."

"Well that's too long. Come up here and let me tell you all the ways you make me happy."

"Billy, you're silly," she giggled.

"Maybe, but I'm being serious now. I am a blessed man. I love you, Laura."

"I love you too, Billy." She paused. "So, when are we going home?"

"I don't know, but not yet," I said. "There's a lot more for me to learn here. I am hoping to have a clear plan when we leave. That reminds me, would you mind asking your dad about us staying with them for a while when we go back to Tucson?"

"I'll ask him tomorrow. But I'm sure it's okay. They have plenty of room."

"Joe and I are meeting with Jorge at five thirty, so I guess I need to get some sleep."

"Goodnight, Billy."

"Goodnight, Laura," I said. "Say your prayers."

"I will."

CHAPTER 45.

During the night, I had the most terrifying nightmare, but it had a wonderful ending. I dreamed that a demon brigade had gathered in the desert outside of Hermosillo. Three of them, named Thor, Valcon and Pultan, planned their strategy. They planned to create a diversion at the Barrio. Cartel recruiters would visit there looking for young men to carry their wares across the border. In my dream, when they showed up, they gathered a group around them and shared stories of wealth, cars and women. Five demons swarmed and laughed overhead. They hurled visions of a lavish lifestyle into the minds of the young men.

However, Josiah got word and sent word to teachers at the Barrio Bible study. Bible teachers confronted the Cartel recruiters, quoting scripture and reminding the young men of those who had died from among them. Meanwhile angels battled the demons overhead and the men made a hasty escape. At first the attack was working as the demon brigade made their way into the prison and filled men there with hatred for the Christians in the prison. After some cajoling and prodding they had the inmates stirred up enough that a plan was devised for forced entry into the Christian prison section.

In the yard where inmates exercised, a fight broke out. As the guards entered to break up the fight, the men rushed them, taking their keys. Forty men made their way toward the Christians they hated, but angels beat them there and delivered a warning. The Christian men knew the day would come for this to happen, and they had built a safe room under the floor of their dining room. By the time the forty arrived there was not one Christian left in the room. They were safely hidden away underground. Meanwhile in the air above the prison a full-fledged battle was going on. Josiah led his fellow angels with scripture, and the Word of God drove the hooligans away. Underground the Christians had bombarded the perpetrators, both in the prison, and in the air, with prayer.

A victory celebration took place in Heaven that evening as men and angels praised the power of God. Many such celebrations had taken place but none ever grew weary or took victory for granted. Every victory moved Heaven toward a time when the final victory would take place.

As I woke up my heart was beating fast. Joe and I went straight to the kitchen where Maria and Jorge were already up. They were praying together as coffee was brewing. It was still dark outside as Joe, Jorge, and I prayed together.

"So, Jorge, did you finish the letter?" I asked. "Has God laid a plan out for us in Tucson?"

"Probably not like you expect," Jorge replied.

"What do you mean?" I asked.

"There's a plan alright, but it's just how to start. Billy this has always been how God deals with me."

"How's that?" I asked.

"He never lets me get ahead. He gives me basic instructions to start and nothing else until I am obedient in them. I think that's how he teaches us faith. We don't move on until we do what he asks."

"So, what does it say?" I asked, impatiently. Jorge turned to Joe first.

"Joe, for you, he wants you to build a manufacturing plant. You are to develop jobs, provide incomes, and a base from which your workers can be influential Christians. Bible studies, prayer time, and families, are all to be part of the work. He also wants you to start a Bible group at your building supply company."

"What about me Jorge?" I asked.

"You will not go back to pastoring," Jorge said. "You will serve under David, your assistant, to bridge your church into the inner city. First you will learn to deal with addicts, the homeless, and people with mental health issues, all the while offering Jesus as the solution. The Gospel and saving souls will be your focus. After some experience you will train others to do the same."

"How long will this take, Jorge?" I asked. "That's up to you, Billy. Jesus will move you forward when you're ready. Oh, and Josiah's work with me is finished, he has been reassigned as your personal angel. Now I'll tell you what I think. Josiah is a very high up angel. Look at what God has given me. I expect you to be much further along than me in ten years. I don't know right now, but I expect that Joe's role, my role and yours, Billy, will all be connected, but I don't know exactly how. I'll leave the letter up on the table behind us. You're welcome to read it when you have time." Jorge said.

"I'd like a copy so I can frame it and keep it with me as a reminder," I said.

"Good idea, Billy. I'll make several copies. Gentlemen grab a jacket and meet me on the porch. We'll pray and watch the sun come up. Oh, and wake up Suzy and Laura. Breakfast will be ready in twenty minutes," said Jorge.

We prayed, watched a glorious sunrise. Then we went to the dining hall as the families gathered to begin their day. I knew that as we prayed, they were praying with their children. That's the way things were on the Rancho de Eden, high in the mountains of the Sierra Madre Occidental. "God hates a proud spirit but he gives grace to the humble."

CHAPTER 46.

I got a phone call from my Dad and heard that he and twenty-two people from Tucson, mostly from my church, including my assistant, David, were coming by bus to Hermosillo. I knew that somewhere Josiah must be praying for their safety. I couldn't help wishing my Mom was still alive to come too, but she had passed away when I was 14 and was in Heaven welcoming Bryan.

After breakfast, Joe and I took a bus, dropped off the ladies at school, and went on to pick up my dad and the rest at the bus terminal. Our timing was good, and soon, after a few tears we headed to the ranch. We would arrive just in time for lunch at noon. I sat with my dad as Joe drove us back. My dad, Paul, is a professor at Wayland Baptist in Tucson. He teaches church history and systematic theology. I went over the events of the past few weeks and he sat there speechless, now that's rare for my dad.

"Billy, when are you coming home?" was his first question.

"In light of all that has happened, I think I need to stay here a few more weeks," I replied. "I need to learn more of the details of Jorge's work here."

"Are you planning to bring something similar back to Tucson?" he asked.

"Similar, yes, but there will need to be some adjustments," I said.

"Why's that?"

"Jorge's work flows out of the poverty here. Figuring out how to implement that in Tucson might be tough," I explained.

"How are you processing that issue?" he asked.

"Prayer is where I'm at," I said. "After all that has happened, I plan to quit relying on my abilities. I don't know Dad, but I am sensing this is big, really big."

"Then I need to be praying too."

"Right," I said.

"What about Laura? How's she?" Dad asked.

"Sad, grieving, but I think she's beginning to see that somehow this is part of God's plan."

"Billy, the talk is that next year they are making me dean of Christian studies?" Dad said.

"Wow Dad! I'm proud of you," I said.

"Thanks Billy. I'm thinking that it could come in handy with your plan. What did you call it? Holistic Christianity?" he asked.

"Yes."

"Maybe God's got another revival in store for America," Dad said.

"Maybe. I sure hope so, Dad."

"Yes, Son."

"Watch for wildlife," I said. "The ranch turns off is just ahead. In about thirty minutes we'll be at the school. We'll pick up Laura and Suzy there."

We arrived at headquarters as lunch was being served. Jorge had a table ready for my family. Three extra tables had been set up for the rest of our crew. A delicious soup was served with Sonoran hot dogs. After lunch, David, my assistant, joined us as Laura led all the ladies on a tour of the family living quarters. I shared a little of the events with David, and Jorge read the letter from Josiah.

"Billy, he was a real angel?" David asked.

"No doubt," I replied.

"Hold on just a minute, would you mind telling that story to the rest of the guys from Grace?" he asked.

"Sure," I said.

David quickly gathered the group together, and I shared

Desert Dreams

my story. "That's amazing, Billy!" he exclaimed.

"I know. Here's what I want you to do," I instructed. "You guys gather up for an hour and pray. Maria will take you to a room where you can do that. After that I want you to see what is going on in the buildings down the road. We will pray too, but then we are going to try to put pieces together of what God is planning. We will carry this back to Tucson, and we will make a difference. Thanks Guys."

Four men sat at the table there in the mountains, each with pieces of a puzzle that certainly looked like the hand of God moving.

"Jorge, you take the lead," I said.

"Gentleman all that you have seen and all that we are now doing, is a plan God gave me," Jorge began. "I believe he brought you here to see, to learn, and to do this in other places. The keys are these. The love we have for each other, the humility before God to move only with his voice, and the willingness to passionately work hard at doing what he says."

Joe spoke up, "My part of this, is to take my business into an evangelism mode. I plan to train all my leaders to be witnesses. If they're not willing, they can find another job as it will be a private Christian company. Daily prayer and Bible studies will take place. Secondly, I want to develop a new business, and once plans are laid, build, train and hire with the same mission in mind. This will create funding for other ministries with the profits. Third, I am donating my old warehouse to use how you see fit."

"Joe, you mean the one going toward Nogales?" I asked.

"Yes, Billy," Joe said.

"Billy, you're up," said Jorge.

"Okay, this is what I know," I explained. "I am starting an inner-city ministry to help street people and address addiction issues. I intend to connect those to my church, and to what you are doing."

Dad said, "I think my job will be to train people to serve in your ministries."

David added, "My job is to help Billy draw our church into the plan. We will recruit help, help train, and create money for support."

"David," I said. "You don't know it yet, but you are the new pastor at Grace!"

"I'm not ready, Billy," David responded.

"How many people have joined the church since I left?" I asked.

"Three hundred," he replied.

"How many been saved?"

"Sixty-five."

"David, you're ready!" I said. "I've prayed this through. Just don't announce this till I get back. I want to handle this."

"No problem, Billy," David said.

"Gentlemen, let's pray," said Jorge.

"Okay Jorge. I guess its official now," I said.

"It needs a name," Jorge said.

"'The plan.' We'll call it 'The plan.' Why make it complicated," I decided.

As we were wrapping up the ladies returned. Laura looked at me and asked, "Are you guys finished?"

"Yes. I think Jorge wants to give us the tour," I replied.

"Perfect. I want to tell them your story, if it's okay, Billy?" Laura asked.

"Fine. I'd love for them to hear it," I replied. "Okay ladies. We're out of here!"

CHAPTER 47.

That evening, the largest group ever, gathered in the dining hall. Our guests from Tucson were there, and all except a skeleton crew from the ranch came from their duties, including those who worked in the mountains. The vaqueros mingled with the city slickers. There was laughter, as folks from my church kept translators busy learning about the people of Rancho de Eden. The binding of hearts through the love of Jesus showed off in this community of believers. As the meal wrapped up Jorge stood to speak.

He shared the vision God had given him ten years earlier, and that now this vision would cross the border. Then he pointed out that the community of God's Kingdom has no physical borders. Jorge pledged the commitment of those at the ranch to support God's work in new places.

The people of Mexico gathered around the people of Grace and my family, and they prayed. Their prayers were audible in Spanish, but the hearts of all understood, as they prayed for America, and for strength for my family to hold to God's plan in the midst of tragedy . I thought to myself, these are people who understand struggle and yet prosper right in the face of adversity. *This has to be the work of Jesus,* I thought. *Let his name be lifted high because this works, because of him.*

We sang a few songs in the yard under the stars, and bedtime rolled around. Our group was shown their sleeping quarters. Laura and I prayed with Bobby as the evening drew to a close. As I lay in my bed, the sense of community and the prayers for Laura and me, all poured through my mind. Tomorrow would be tough, but not as difficult as this day was, as Jesus would hold me and Laura in his arms.

Daylight dawned with Maria pouring Jorge and me our traditional early cup of coffee.

"So, you're really going to do this, Billy?" Jorge asked.

"You mean Bryan's funeral? Yeah. Laura and I together," I replied.

"I gave everyone the day off," Jorge said. "We will all be there, that is, except the few tending sheep and cattle in the pastures. Even they will stop at ten this morning and have a prayer time in honor of Bryan. Billy, they pray well. The vaqueros understand the cycle of life and death better than nearly anyone. It's everyday life for them."

"Hmm, I suppose they do," I responded.

"Oh yeah, they are our prayer team," Jorge said. "We make sure they know about our struggles on the ranch. They are out there close to God. Prayer is their calling; we couldn't do this without them. Think about it, when you get back to Tucson, I'll bet your seniors can do that for you."

"You're right Jorge," I answered. "They become the foundation to what we are doing."

"Prayer first, Billy."

"Right, Jorge. Let me wake Laura and Bobby. I see the rest are gathering for breakfast."

"Billy, after breakfast would you ask Joe to share his testimony? You know he's a hero to me," Jorge said.

"I'm sure he won't mind, Jorge," I replied.

"Good."

After breakfast Joe shared his testimony. Then we loaded into the buses and made our way to the Gym at the school. It took three trips but by ten everyone was there. The men in the wood shop had hand made a casket for Bryan. It was beautiful. His little body was beat up, so we chose to leave the lid closed. As the funeral began, Jorge introduced Laura, and acted as our translator. Laura shared many anecdotes of our life in Tucson, how Bobby and Bryan played in the desert, caught snakes even the sidewinders. Bobby cried as she shared our camping and fishing trip stories. She also shared the story of one night, she had prayed with Bryan before bedtime. He had asked, and she had shared Jesus. He had prayed that night and received Him. Then she turned to Bobby to remind him how two years later he too became a believer. "Bobby don't worry, your brother is waiting on you. One day our family reunion will take place in Heaven," she said.

When my time came, I shared battles of spiritual struggle. I showed how God gives us courage and strength, right when we need it most, as only He knows what lies ahead. My son was a gift from God. He loaned him to Laura and me for twelve years. Bryan was really God's child all along though, and when it was time to come home, He called him. I thanked God for sharing this with me. I then turned my attention to the school children there and reminded them that no one is promised tomorrow. A boy and a girl came forward as I invited them into a relationship with Jesus as Savior. They repented and put their trust in Jesus. It's hard to bury your son, but watching children get saved, keeps your priorities right.

We made our way to the burial site, where Jorge's crew had carved out a spot on the hillside, built an iron fence around it, and planted flowers. It looked like there was room for twenty more of our family. We said our prayers lowered Bryan's body into the earth, but knew he was already home. Laura, Bobby and I, each took a handful of dirt and pitched it in the grave. My mind jumped back to two thousand years ago when some women looked into a tomb and realized that Jesus was not there. Our hope is the resurrection of Jesus. Amen.

CHAPTER 48.

Dad and our other friends from Tucson took the bus back home after lunch. Joe and Suzy also headed back to Tucson in their own car. David stayed to check out the ranch some more. Laura, Bobby and I borrowed Jorge's jeep for an afternoon walk in the mountains. We drove all the way to the road's end, got out, and walked up the stream up the mountain to my cave.

As we walked, I recounted the events of those days in the cave. My meeting with Josiah and the place where Peter came to Christ became places they could now see with their eyes. I shared the details of Josiah dying in my arms and how he just vanished out of his clothes. There in front of the cave the evidence of the truth, his empty clothes, lay on the ground by my old campfire. Laura and I sat in the chairs I had made, as Bobby crawled into my lap. We prayed for each other and comforted our remaining son.

"This is a lot to take in in a few weeks, Billy," Laura said.

"Yes, Laura, it is," I replied. "But there is a sense of urgency. We can see it in the pace at which God is moving."

"Billy, when are we going back to Tucson?" she asked.

"We need to spend the next week or so learning everything we can about Jorge's work here," I replied. "I have spoken with Jorge about this and his guys are putting detailed notes together for us to take home. I think you, Laura, should spend more time at the school and on trips to Hermosillo, working with the Barrio mission. I am going to look at the details of the facility here. I will be meeting with Jorge and his staff to figure out how we can implement something similar when we get home. I'd like Bobby to attend classes at the school. The ESL classes would help him learn more Spanish."

That afternoon I set the snares, gathered some desert vegetables, and we had a mountain dinner before heading home. I showed Bobby and Laura how I had done things and took pictures to preserve the memory. We headed home, leaving enough time to make it back to the ranch before dark. I gave my bow and arrows to Bobby.

They were having a celebration when we arrived at the ranch house. It was Jorge's fifty-second birthday, and his huge extended family celebrated in grand fiesta style. It would be hard to leave this place. The joy and the spirit of God there, gave us visions of heaven. As the fiesta wound down, the people went home. Maria brought hot chocolate to Laura, Bobby and I and we joined Jorge on the front porch. The celebration had taken the edge off the grief of Bryan's funeral. There was a joy that can only be experienced by believers in Jesus Christ as they fight through the struggles of life.

"Billy, Laura and Bobby, are you all right?" Jorge asked.

"We're okay. It's a little tough on Bobby, but we have each other and Jesus," I said. "We're going to be fine. Besides that, we can't lose sight of the plan God has for us. We can't spend much time looking back."

"Yeah, I remember the struggle so well Billy," Jorge said.

"I guess you do, Jorge, and you were so young in Christ, and really had to walk through it alone," I responded.

"Not alone Billy, Jesus was with me. As a matter of fact, maybe that was the whole reason that I made it through. I didn't have anyone but Him to depend on. I think Jesus wanted it that way because all that he has blessed me with, has come because I depend on him."

"Hmm, I hadn't thought of it that way. Maybe that's why he took Bryan home, to teach us that we can rely on Him no matter what," I said thoughtfully.

"Could be Billy. I want to pray for you all," Jorge said.

"Sure, Jorge," I replied.

"Lord, thank you for the memory of my own trials," Jorge

prayed. "It gives me strength and a heart for my family in their loss. Lord, give them the comfort only you can give. Lord, give them courage to hold tight to the plans you have for them. Lord, give me the wisdom and ability to help them any way I can. Lord, thank you for saving my soul, and may every one of us tell the world what you can do."

"Good night, Bobby," Jorge said abruptly. "Goodnight, Laura. Goodnight, Billy."

"Goodnight, Jorge," we replied as he slipped into the house. Laura and I prayed with Bobby and found our way to our bed.

Thank you, Lord. Lord of the mountains in Mexico.

CHAPTER 49.

Morning began with Jorge and coffee. He had set up appointments for me and his staff. After breakfast we went down the road to the ranch offices. Jose, Armando, Juan, Adolfo, and Benito were waiting on our arrival. Benito handed us copies of Jorge's ministry plan. We went over each item considering ways to adapt them from Mexican culture into American culture. Juan and I played out some of the difficulties that would have to be worked out. Because of our plan to move fast, it was decided that food resources would be developed later as the plan unfolded.

The focus early on would be on income producing ventures. Manufacturing would be emphasized. We just need to figure out high margin, low impact, products. Three things were marked as primary, growing a community of believers who would work, train and evangelize as a team, emphasis on family and teaching faith to the children, and a school system within our community. It was planned that Jorge and Benito would travel to Tucson as soon as possible to scout out the warehouse Joe was donating. He would find out about adjacent property, water resources and other things we would need if this was to be our center. Juan would start searching for income producing opportunities. David Gorman, my new pastor, and I, had spoken about initial funding. Jorge volunteered some funding. My job would be for the next days to carefully study finances and operations at the ranch. Jorge and David would fill me in before they left for Tucson, and then the rest of the team would tutor me on their fields of expertise.

We prayed and I met with Jorge personally. He had an

overview of operations and ministries. Jose had a budget ready for each ministry.

We adjourned for a quick lunch. Armando and I visited, and he went over his plan for spiritual growth in the family setting. Families were clustered into groups which met once a week to pray for each other and address problems. Problems that couldn't be solved in this setting, were to be brought before a council. Once a week a Christian psychologist would come to address more difficult issues that the council couldn't solve. Prayer life, Bible study, work ethic and manners were to be the family emphasis. Adolfo then shared with me ideas for future development of farming and ranching. Mainly he outlined the types of property we should be looking for, if we were to undertake these ventures. We visited some families before dinner so I could watch families interact. We prayed with each family and they prayed for us.

Families gathered and we ate our evening meal together. Afterwards, communion was prepared and served. We remembered the reason for this community, and what it foreshadowed of the day when we would all take it with our Lord and Savior Jesus. We sang "Bless be the tie that binds." Laura and I had hearts that smiled as we listened to Bobby sing it all in Spanish.

We gathered on the porch later, and Laura shared details of the school. The amazing thing about the school was how well behaved the children were. "The hand of God is all over the school," Laura said. "The academics, yeah the standards like reading, writing and arithmetic are there, but there is also church history, and in the older grades, apologetics, philosophy, and intensive Bible studies. There are forty kids in the high school program and twenty are committed to be missionaries or pastors or evangelists."

When we got back to our room, Laura showed me the many curriculum materials they had copied for her. With a good copy machine, our school would be nearly ready to go. We said our nightly prayers and our day was done.

I lay in bed praying, and mostly listening, as Jesus unrolled more of the details of his plan for me in Tucson. Inner city ministry would be a big step for me. Sure, I had worked with addictions issues with members of families within my church, but most of the time, that had consisted of finding a rehab place or finding sober living houses. I knew the rate of relapse was high. I knew we needed to do a better job. To be honest, moving from prim and proper church members, to people who lived on the streets and didn't bathe regularly, was going to take some getting used to. I had worked in soup kitchens a few times, but it was easy to go home and forget about them. It would be hard when it became up close and personal. "Lord teach me how to love those that are so different from me," I prayed. "Help to teach the church how to love. Amen."

CHAPTER 50.

In the morning, Laura joined Jorge and me for prayer time. Jorge had another staff meeting set, with a working breakfast. Laura left to prepare for another day at the school, and Bobby and she joined the main group in the dining room. Jorge's staff joined Jorge and I in the kitchen. Juan and Benito's were to share some of their plans for construction, manufacturing and production.

Juan began by telling us that after receiving his computer training at MIT he had come to Hermosillo with his church on a mission trip. He said, "I was so struck by the living conditions at the Barrio that before I left, Jorge and I had met, and I already talked about working with him to create opportunities for the people here. Since graduating seniors at the school were already bilingual, I wanted to begin a program of software support training. We could rent space in town to set up a phone bank with an IT support service company. This would generate funding and soon should be able to add continuing education to the program. We would like to rent space to hold church services for people from the Barrio. We have started similar groups in Durango and plan to have another one in Guadalajara soon. To do this we have to be willing to move our brightest, most talented, and spiritual leaders into the new locations. A similar plan is being implemented in Nogales at our warehouse there, but I want Benito to share that story with you."

Then it was Benito's turn. "Good morning guys. From our distribution center in Nogales we are doing similar things with our warehouse workers and truck drivers. Besides our starter and alternator distribution we are adding other products produced in Mexico to our distribution line. We have started a church in Nogales, and another across the border. We have begun a program of work visas for those holding jobs in Tucson. The willingness of our people to work on construction sites and in other areas has established a connection to the Hispanic community in Tucson. Two Spanish speaking churches have been established there.

"The main thing I want to say is we have been very sensitive to opportunities that God has been presenting to us. When these doors open, we move, but none of this would be possible if we were not training people to fill those roles here at the ranch. Training and spiritual development are key. The last thing we need to happen is for our people to fall back into worldly ways in the middle of developing ministries. Leaders in these places are brought back regularly to train strengthen and encourage."

Finally, Jorge took over. "Thank you, Juan and Benito. I must add to what they have said in this way. There are now over fifteen hundred people involved in what we are doing. I cannot possibly keep track of them all. I pray for our leaders. I depend on each of them to take care of their role. I do not orchestrate all of this, the Holy Spirit does. When there are weaknesses, He tells me, and we pray for them. Most of the plan, the development, has come as we have merely observed areas that He is already working. Billy do not get too caught up in details of the plan but pray to see opportunities as they unfold. When opportunities come, they are open doors. Walk through them. Pray for the plan. Be quick to work where God is already at work. Trust those He gives you to lead and give them the freedom to do what God is telling them to do. Pray for the strength of their relationship to God for in those relationship the right decisions will come as He speaks to them. Trusting them is trusting Him. Billy, if it is alright with you, I plan on using Juan as our liaison between your work and our work. His dual citizen ship and skill in Spanish, should be very useful."

"Jorge that sounds like a great idea," I said.

"Good, then it's set," he announced.

"Thanks, Jorge," I said. "I need some help from you guys. I need video with some of your testimonies. I would also like video of each ministry in action. Detailed plans of the power systems and water purification would also be very useful."

"We can do that, Billy," said Juan. "I have all of the material already but will need to edit and translate it into English. I have software programs to do that, so I should have the videos ready by tomorrow morning. I think it would be useful for you to look at them in detail. I suggest you take pictures to go with the plans. My shop foreman will assist you in this today if that's alright."

"Perfect, Juan," I said. "Any other suggestions?"

"Yeah, I think our training manuals would be valuable to you too, so Jorge, can we provide that for Billy?" Juan asked.

"Sure, I will gather copies of that too," Jorge added. "Anything else?"

"Yeah," Juan replied. "I need to set up a secure internet link for Billy in Tucson. Billy, when you go home, you're going to be staying with Joe aren't you?" Jorge asked.

"Yes," I replied. "I'll contact Suzy and start setting up a direct link with her and Joe there. I'm going to give you two laptops to take home. I have them set up with WIFI connections through Joe's system. They will be video enabled so that we can easily stay in direct communication. Anything else?"

"No, that's it," Jorge said. "Then let's pray. God give all of us clarity of your plan. May we hear your voice daily and do your will, as we trust you completely, Amen."

CHAPTER 51.

We wrapped up our meeting, just as the school buses were bringing children back to the ranch. I sat on the porch and Laura and Bobby walked up to me.

"Laura, what's wrong?" I asked, seeing that her make-up on her face was a mess.

"Billy you're not going to believe my day. This place is wonderful. The hearts of these people are so right," she replied, joyfully.

"Sit right here and tell me about it," I urged. "Do you want some fruit juice?"

"Sure."

"Mom, Dad, Silvio and I are going fishing if that's okay," Bobby said.

"Go ahead Bobby, as long as your homework is done," I said.

"Did it at school," he replied.

"Okay, Bobby. Go catch a big one!" I said. "So, what about your day, Laura? Your eyeliner is all over the place. Have you been crying?"

"Yeah, Billy, but they were tears of joy," Laura answered.

"Tell me about it," I said.

"When I got to school this morning there was a note in Josie's room to meet in the gym. When I got to the gym, the whole school was there. They started clapping, and I was invited to sit in a chair on the stage. Armando took the mike and prayed. He then presented me with a jar of coins. It seems the children had been saving their pesos for us. They have collected four thousand pesos for us. That's over three hundred and twenty dollars!" Laura exclaimed. "It's for our work when we leave. Billy, I know it's not much but it's a lot because they don't have much. It turns out they have been doing extra chores to earn that money.

"It gets even better though. Every family has been gathering after dinner to pray for us. These poor people here in Mexico are praying for children in America who have so much. I asked why. Several of the high school kids spoke. They said that they had so much on the ranch that they wanted to share, but it wasn't the money that meant so much. That was just their way of saying that they will pray.

One of the boys said, "We hear that children in U.S. schools are bullied, classrooms are crazy, kids aren't learning, and drugs are everywhere. Those kids have problems we don't have here. We have peace. We are happy. They don't have these things. We are praying that you and Mr. Billy can help the U.S. kids get what we have."

"Billy, you know they're right," Laura said.

"That's why we home school, Laura," I said.

"I know Billy, but that doesn't help the rest."

"Laura, I'm proud of you. You are seeing God's heart. You're seeing what He's put in my heart," I said.

"But Billy, the problem is so big," she said.

"I know Laura, but our God is bigger, much bigger," I replied.

"How was your day, Billy?" Laura asked.

"Learning, Laura. A plan is coming together. Jorge is committed and all his men are committed. Laura, I think help is on the way. God's handprints are all over this," I said.

In the evening we walked toward the dining room. "You ready for dinner, Laura and Billy?" someone asked us. As families walked by us, each one greeting us by name.

"You see Billy, they know us. It's personal for them," Laura said. "I'm embarrassed that I don't know their names."

"That's okay Laura," I said. "They don't expect that. Let's eat."

"Okay. Where's Bobby?" Laura asked suddenly.

"Oh, he's sitting with Silvio and his family," I replied.

"Good. I'm glad he's found a friend," she said.

We sat at Jorge's table where Jorge, Benito, and Juan were gathered in prayer. Being as quiet as we could, and listening, we soon learned that they were praying for us. We could hear from the tables around us, that they too were praying for us. As the prayers wrapped up, the kitchen staff began serving dinner. Laura leaned over and whispered, "Billy, I have never felt so loved in all my life as I do now. I love this place."

"I know, Laura. It would be nice just to stay here and enjoy this, but God has a plan," I replied. "The good thing though is, we have a place to come to when times get hard and our spirits need renewal."

"I know, Billy. Until Heaven becomes reality, this will always feel like home."

"That's a good way to put it, Laura," I said.

We met on the porch for our customary watching of the sunset. Jorge opened his Bible and read Psalm 19. We worshiped silently in the quietness of our hearts as the words of God spoke to us. Wispy clouds shrouded the tops of the mountains across the valley. The sunset bathed them in glorious colors as another day on Earth ended. The twinkle in the stars emerged first in dimness, but as darkness surrounded them, they became millions of tiny lights.

I thought, *He knows each star by name, just as He knows each one of us by name. He loves us. Oh, how he loves us! That means me and Laura, and Bobby, and every one of us. Jesus didn't die just for everyone, but for each one of us.* Now that was beyond the scope of my comprehension.

Bobby spent the night with Silvio and his family, and Laura and I had our first night alone in a while. We prayed together and let the romance and love we had for each other take its natural course. God is able to comfort, not just when it's hard, but especially when it's hard.

"Goodnight, Laura."

Lonnie Barnard

"Goodnight, Billy."

CHAPTER 52.

It was four o clock when God woke me up. I slipped into the hallway and as I passed Juan's room, I could see the light on, so I gently knocked on the door. "Come in," Juan said. "Good morning, Billy. What gets you up so early?"

"I think God woke me," I said. "I was headed to the kitchen to make coffee when I saw your light on. Juan, have you been up all night?"

"Yeah, had a lot on my mind," Juan said. "I needed to finish this for you. My assistant finished your video material yesterday, and I gathered all the blueprints and made copies. I kept thinking about your problem of adapting the plan here to American culture. I have been praying, and when God answered, I wanted to write it down. I've been checking real estate listings in downtown Tucson and have located a vacant old building that I think we can rent cheap. About the warehouse Joe donated, it's about fifteen miles south of town in the desert. When I prayed, God said these are parts of the plan. I want to go there as soon as possible and look at both buildings. I texted Joe and as soon as he gets up, I expect a call from him."

"Juan do you sleep?" I asked.

"Not too much. When I get something on my mind, I'm a little OCD. I'm hoping Joe can meet me today. I can get a driver and sleep then."

"I'll make coffee and be back in a few minutes," I said.

"Bring me a cup, please!" Juan asked.

"Okay." I went to the kitchen and came back with two cups of hot coffee. "Here you go Juan. Do you want it black?"

"Yeah. Oh, Joe called already. I'll be leaving in thirty

minutes."

"Did you get a driver this early? I asked.

"Yeah, I got a driver," he said. "I made an outline with a tentative plan. Look it over, and when I get back this evening I'll know more."

"What do you think the problems are?" I asked.

"First, the condition of the building downtown is in question," he said.

"How much money will it cost to make it usable?" I asked.

"It hasn't been occupied in five years." Juan explained. "Second, a water source for the warehouse will be needed. I mean, it has city water, but that's too expensive for the plan I have there. Jorge is usually up by now let's pray with him before I leave."

"We filled Jorge in, and then we carried it before God. We prayed for safety and answers in Juan's journey. Joe was going to meet him at the warehouse. He was going to look over the building in town before first and take pictures of it.

"Laura and Armando joined Jorge and me for breakfast. When breakfast was done, Laura checked on Bobby and they left for school. Armando gave me a two-dollar tour of the farming operation. He showed me the composting operation, and how they used the waste plant in their process. Waste from the barns and even sawdust from the wood shop was used. The most important part was the lab where testing was done before the fertilizer was used. They also kept medical records on everyone to show their added health that was ensured by eating organic foods. In ten years on the ranch they had built quite a case for their methods.

Armando then took me to the lab and showed me some of the organic medicines they had developed. This was a pet project for Armando, and he shared how many of the cures and treatments had been gathered from the Yaqui Indians. He gave me detailed paperwork on their methods and formulas. He showed me how these methods were also used on the livestock.

We had lunch with the vaqueros and shepherds in the

mountains. After lunch we joined them in their prayer session. It was amazing to see these men pray, and even though I didn't understand their words, I could sense the power that came from the prayers of these men.

We arrived back at the ranch as dinner was being served. Laura and Bobby joined Jorge and I, and midway through our meal Juan showed up. We finished and met with Juan after dinner.

"Well, what's the verdict Juan?" I asked.

"When Joe met me at the warehouse, he informed me that he had bought the building downtown. Turns out the city had condemned it, and he was able to get it for a song. He said it's structurally sound but will need to have all the mechanical items upgraded, like the sprinkler system, the AC and the electrical system. The warehouse is a huge old warehouse with a large concrete parking lot. The building is okay, but it will need a lot of work. I was right that water could be our biggest problem. Also, lot of the wiring has been stripped by thieves, and the only plumbing left is what the thieves couldn't get to. I have a good idea of what it will need, but if we can't get water it will be unusable."

Jorge said, "Then that's what we will pray for. Men join me in prayer. God of all creation, we know it's the middle of the desert, but your plan needs a water source. We don't know how or in what way but we know you have the power, and so we look to you for answers. Amen. Men keep this on your prayer list. Let's call it a night."

Laura and I prayed with Bobby, put him to bed, and prayed together. "Billy," Laura said.

"Yes, Laura."

"I guess if God can give us water in the desert, then He can do just about anything," she said.

"Laura, He can do it," I said. "That might not be how He answers, but for sure He can. I think this is a wait-for-a-miracle time in our life." A few minutes later I said, "Goodnight, Laura."

"Goodnight, Billy."

CHAPTER 53.

Early mornings were getting to be a habit. At four thirty, coffee was on. This morning Laura joined me. "So, Billy we're going back to Tucson soon," she said. "I love this country and especially the mountains. Could we take a trip back to the cave before we leave?"

"I was thinking about that Laura. Do you think Silvio's family would take care of Bobby for a few days?" I asked her.

"I'm sure they would, but we can ask them at breakfast. Why? What are you thinking?"

"I was thinking you might like to camp with me in the mountains for a few days," I suggested.

"Billy, that would be wonderful!" Laura exclaimed. "Are you still thinking God might show up?"

"Not really. I was just thinking about us spending time together. We need to go home with a lot of spiritual strength, and I thought it might be good for both of us," I said.

"I'm up for it, Billy," Laura said.

Just then Jorge walked in. "Good morning Jorge! Laura and I were just talking about spending a few days in the mountains before we go home," I said.

"Sure, Billy. That can be arranged. Are you going back to the cave?" Jorge asked.

"Yes, I want Laura to enjoy a little of my experience," I replied.

"What about Bobby?" he asked.

"We're going to ask Silvio's parents if Bobby can stay with them," I said.

"Good family. I'm sure they won't mind. They're up. I'll

ask them now." Jorge darted into the dining room and returned shortly. "They said they would love to," he said. "So, it's all set. When do you want to leave?"

"After breakfast okay?"

"Sure. I'll drive you up myself," Jorge volunteered.

After breakfast we loaded our gear and headed up the mountain.

We arrived at the road's end, slipped on our backpacks, and made our way along the stream toward the cave. I set snares on the way up and found camp pretty much as we had left it, though I had to run some racoons out of the cave. I tightened the ropes on our awning, sent Laura for more firewood, and lit our campfire. She returned with enough to make it through the night. I laid a layer of pine boughs to get rid of any scorpions. With our bedrolls laid out it was official. We were home.

We hiked down the mountain to gather vegetables and fruit for our dinner. Then when we reached the traps, we found meat. I gave Laura a lesson in dressing rabbits, and we headed back to camp. After I taught Laura how to do it, she prepped the cactus. I pulled the skillet out to make dinner. I had remembered to bring some onions and peppers. We made a Sonoran goulash over the campfire. "Tomorrow, Laura, I will teach you how to make tortillas," I said. We prayed and enjoyed our mountain meal.

Before the sun set, you could see a line of clouds moving in from the west. "Billy, do you think it might rain?" Laura asked.

"It does look like it, Laura," I agreed. By the time we had cleaned up, raindrops were bouncing off our porch tarp. A chill entered so we slid our chairs close together. In the distance I could see lightening striking the mountains across the valley. The rain picked up and the wind blew harder. We were glad to be inside the cave as the chill and lightening increased. We prayed together and used up batteries in our flashlights to read our Bibles.

Laura was filled with questions about the mission that

God was calling us into. We talked about what I knew, but many of her questions went unanswered. "Billy, doesn't it scare you to go into something with so much uncertainty?" Laura asked.

"Of course, Laura, but I think that's part of the deal."

"What do you mean, Billy?"

"Faith, Laura. God doesn't explain it all to us. Trusting Him is part of the deal. Our job is to trust Him. We don't have to see around the blind curve to move forward because He's there before us, clearing the way."

As I finished this statement it began to hail. It was marble size but there was a lot of it and it was turning the ground white. We slid into our sleeping bags as the tarp flapped loudly. We lay there talking for a while because the noise made it hard to sleep.

Sometime toward midnight we heard a voice!

"Hello!" A young man came bursting into the cave. It nearly scared us to death, and we were glad our flashlights still worked.

"What are you doing out on a night like this, and how did you find us?" I asked.

"My name is Daniel. I was sent here. You are under attack. I'm here to protect you," he said. Then it hit me, the smell of gardenias.

"You're, you're an angel?" I stammered.

"You guessed it," he replied. "What you can't see is there is a war going on above us, above the clouds."

"Josiah must have sent you!" I said.

"You could say that, but I'd rather you say God sent me. Josiah works for Him."

"Okay, I get it," I said, trying to adjust to the whole thing. I gave Daniel a change of dry clothes and hung his wet ones on some roots hanging down over the cave to dry. I didn't think it would do much good because it was raining sideways and threatening to extinguish our campfire. Daniel prayed for us and we settled in to try and get some sleep.

"Daniel, do angels sleep?" I asked.

"Only when we come in human form. We have to deal

with all the problems of being human when we take human form," he said.

"Just wondering," I said sleepily.

"That's okay, Billy. I'll be sleeping with one eye open tonight though. If any demons escape from the battle above, they will try to slip in and harm you and Laura."

"Daniel, is that possible?"

"Harm, yes, but only to the extent God allows," he replied.

"Daniel, why would He allow demons to harm us?" Laura asked.

"It would only be to toughen you up. Laura, you and Billy have a battle ahead of you. Your spiritual preparation is in the works. Anyway, I'm an accomplished warrior. You should be fine. Get some sleep."

As the storm grew even fiercer, Daniel dragged one of the chairs in front of the cave and we could hear him softly saying, "In the name of Jesus flee demons flee." Eventually, Laura and I fell asleep.

We woke up to the sounds of birds singing beautiful morning serenades. Daniel was gone. My clothes were folded and lying in the chair. It had been a long night, but the sun was up and a mist hung over the mountains as the warmth lifted the moisture of the night storms. Under my folded clothes was a bag of wafer like chips. A note said, "Enjoy your breakfast." I made coffee and Laura and I sat there eating the wafers.

"What is it Billy?" Laura asked.

"That's what it is," I replied.

"Billy, I mean what do you think these are?" she persisted.

"What is it," I replied.

"Billy, I don't need the double talk. I asked a question."

"And I answered, Laura. Don't you remember my sermon on manna?"

"I guess not," she said.

"Manna means 'what is it.'" I explained.

"Okay, so you think it's manna?" she asked.

"What else would angels eat?" I said.

"Billy, this was surely not what I was expecting. What a night! But I'm not the least disappointed," Laura laughed.

"Me neither, Laura." I laughed too. Thus, we both started our day joyfully.

CHAPTER 54.

In the morning, we set about our daily routine. I took my knife and hatchet and peeled wood shavings off of wet wood to restart our campfire. Downed trees blocked the rabbit trail, so we cleared the debris and set new snares. We found a turkey nest with fresh eggs. We stole one and gathered mesquite beans. We gathered more desert bounty, and Laura got her lesson in tortilla making.

We spent some time praying for Tucson, our church, and what God was doing there to prepare hearts for his plan. We prayed about the water situation at the warehouse, and finally when Bryan's name came up, we wept and continued the process of healing. We needed to keep moving forward.

"Billy, I love you so much," Laura said through tears.

"I love you too, Laura," I replied drying my face.

"Billy you know this is it," she said.

"What do you mean, Laura?" I asked.

"The way we love each other," she replied. "We can do this for each other, but the love our brothers and sisters have for each other is key to this whole plan. I wish I knew how to make that happen, Billy."

"Me too," I said.

"Maybe what we have learned about each other is the key," Laura said.

"What do you mean, Laura?" I asked.

"I mean, the time we spend together looking into each other's eyes, commitment to stay, to working through the problems, putting up with each other on the bad days, and enjoying being together. The church, our church fails because it fails to live in community, to live together, to work together, to worship together, and to pray together," Laura explained.

"That's it, Laura. Oneness is life together," I said. We were both quiet for a moment. "Laura, those tortillas should be ready!" I said suddenly.

"Yeah, they're done," she said.

"Get a plastic zip lock out of my pack and put them in there," I instructed.

"Yes sir."

"Let's go check the snares," I said.

We walked down through the scrub and the downed trees to our traps. "Oh, Billy, we got four!" Laura exclaimed.

"Reset them and we'll come back after dinner," I said.

"Okay, like this?" she asked.

"Yes."

We stopped along the stream, dressed our rabbits, and made our way back to camp. "Laura, I'm putting the rabbits on a spit. Keep an eye on them and I'll get some cholla for you to prep," I said.

"Billy, I hate messing with those things," she said.

"Yeah, but you like how they taste!"

"Sure do," she said.

"Just be careful skinning them," I said. "As nasty as those thorns are, you'll learn fast. I think I'll get a couple more turkey eggs and we can scramble them with the roasted rabbit and cholla."

"That sounds good, Billy."

By the time I got back, Laura had lunch finished. She had roasted rabbit, cholla and onions, all rolled in fresh tortillas. We prayed together and ate. I brought two more loads of firewood in, and we took an afternoon siesta under the warm mountain sun. I checked the snares and brought three rabbits and two turkey eggs in for dinner. We watched the mountain sun set after dinner and held hands as the stars made their first appearance. As the darkness wrapped around us, the coyotes sang, and the stars glistened in all the glory God gave them. Off in the distance, a cougar screamed as she looked for her evening meal. She was answered across the valley by something I'm sure she knew. Desert bighorns probably shuddered at the voice of their mortal enemy.

I turned to Laura as she strained her ears, listening to the sounds of God's creation. "A penny for your thoughts, Laura," I said.

"Billy, I was thinking about it all, the sights, the sounds, and even the taste of dinner still lingering in my mouth. God gives it all to us. How could anyone not understand what God has given us? How can men possibly even consider that there is no God?" she said.

"Laura, not many see what we've seen. Not many hear what we hear."

"But Billy, it's there," she said emphatically.

"I guess when men choose to go the way they want to go they have to ignore truth," I said.

"That's right, Billy. They have to ignore the truth," Laura said. I put another log on the fire. "Billy, is Jorge picking us up tomorrow?"

"Yeah."

"I wish we could stay longer," Laura said.

"Me too, but we have work to do," I said.

"I know."

"Don't worry, Laura. We'll be back," I assured her.

Then, later, "You ready for bed Laura?" I asked.

"Yeah."

"Let's pray. Lord thank you for visions of Heaven. Shadows of the real thing are seen in the glory of your creation and it just gets better, so thank you again. Amen." We crawled into our sleeping bags and I leaned over and kissed Laura goodnight.

"Billy, do you think he's out there?" Laura asked.

"Who, Laura?"

"Daniel!"

"I can guarantee you he's out there, Laura," I said. "He's

keeping watch over those whom God loves. That's us."
 "Amen," she said.

CHAPTER 55.

When morning dawned, we cooked breakfast and prayed together. Laura and I took down the tarp, extinguished the campfire, moved the chairs inside the cave, and made our way down the mountain. As we worked our way around the debris from the storms, we were reminded of the spiritual warfare we were likely to encounter. When we arrived at the road, Jorge was waiting for us. He had his tripod set up fifty feet behind the Jeep and was taking pictures of a band of mule deer and some bighorns across the valley.

"Good morning, Laura, Billy. How was the excursion?" Jorge asked.

"Interesting, Jorge. We'll tell you about it on the way back," Laura said.

"How's the picture taking?" I asked.

"Oh, I'm taking these for you. I'm going to blow them up and frame them for you to take home," Jorge said. "I have pictures of the cave too. You've seen the ones I have on my office wall. They inspire me to stay true to God's plan. I look at them when I'm down. They take me back to my time with Josiah. They'll serve you well too."

"Thanks, Jorge. I would love for you to throw in a picture of you too," I said.

"Why's that?" he asked.

"You are an inspiration, too," I replied.

"Thank you, Billy. Tell me about what was interesting, Laura!" said Jorge.

"We had a visit from one of Josiah's warriors," Laura said.

"Really?" Jorge asked.

"Yeah, his name was Daniel," Laura explained. "He protected us from the storms."

"What storms?"

"You didn't have storms at the ranch night before last?" I asked.

"Not that I know of. Why? Did you?" Jorge asked.

"We had horrible storms! Daniel said we were under a spiritual attack."

"Wow, that's amazing!" exclaimed Jorge. "He sat at the mouth of the cave quoting scripture," continued Laura.

"That is so cool Laura!" said Jorge.

"You better believe it Jorge," I added. "The demons take this personally, don't they?"

"Oh yeah. I've been there many times. Trust me this is just starting. The good news is, we win," Jorge said.

"Laura, Billy would you like to have lunch with the vaqueros?" asked Jorge.

"That would be great," we both said.

"Good. I needed to meet with them, and they always love a little company."

When we arrived, the group was gathered around a campfire, putting finishing touches on a substantial meal. Jorge pulled out a blanket and we sat on the ground eating lunch. Of course, we had prayer first. After lunch Jorge shared some pictures of the buildings in Tucson. Then thirty-two vaqueros surrounded us and began a special prayer time. Laura interpreted for me, so I understood that they were praying for our future work in Tucson. Once again, the smell of gardenias drifted in, but my sense of the presence of God was there before the aroma. It was strange to think that once the work began, we would have a prayer group totally committed to supporting us.

As we headed back toward the ranch, a peace swept over me and I knew it was time to go home. "Laura, are you ready to go home?" I asked.

"Not really Billy, but I know it's time," she replied.

"Billy, can I spend the day with you tomorrow before you

go?" Jorge asked.

"Sure, Jorge. Why?" I asked.

"There are some things I want to talk to you and Laura about before you go."

"It's a deal," I said. "We will leave after breakfast the next day."

"Good, then we're all set," Jorge said. Suddenly he slid to a stop. "Look at that ram standing up on the rock!" he exclaimed. "It's almost as if he is saluting you. I think when we obey God nature does salute us."

"How's that?" I asked.

"In Romans it says that all of nature waits for the day of redemption," Jorge explained. "The mountain lion kills to survive, but there was day when he ate the plants and fruits. Sin ended that day and nature waits for the return of paradise."

We arrived at dinner time after Jorge gave us another tour on the way back. As we ate dinner, I didn't have much to say. I was enjoying listening to the people of the ranch loving each other. Considering how many times I had sat with my church members, trying to sort through differences, the oneness of this group was striking.

I would miss the glorious sunsets and the billions of stars, but memory would let me take them with me. That night Bobby joined Laura and I, and I pointed out the galaxies and planets to him. We used Jorge's telescope to draw them closer. Bobby looked at me and said, "I'm alright dad. Bryan's at home with Jesus!"

"It doesn't get any better than that," I responded. "I'm glad he's there. I just wish I could be there too. Ready for bed?"

"Yes sir," Bobby said.

"Come on Laura, let's put this boy to bed," I said. We all prayed together.

"Goodnight, Bobby"

"Goodnight, Dad."

"Goodnight, Laura."

"Goodnight, Billy."

CHAPTER 56.

It was the last day at the ranch. Jorge and I had our traditional early morning coffee. Maria was a gracious a hostess with her happy smiling face.

"After breakfast, we'll meet in my office, if that's okay with you?" Jorge asked me.

"Sure, Jorge," I said, and headed that way.

"I would like to pray for you," he said, when we reached his office. "Lord of Heaven and Creator of all things, fill Billy with your Spirit. Fill him with passion and courage to lead in your plan. Protect his family and may they come alongside him in one mind and Spirit, your mind and spirit. When attacks come, let them serve to encourage him. Satan does not oppose those who are no threat, but You are there in our times of need. Help him to pay careful attention to the details of your plan and hear your voice. Help him to keep himself pure and holy, so that no snare destroys the work you choose to do through him. Help him to be oblivious to the naysayers and critics. May the work you have appointed for him bring many souls to you, and may their passion be your passion. Lord help me to be his friend, his supporter, and always be there for him when he needs me. Watch over all that are involved in your plan, and may we work together in perfect harmony. May the love we have for each other clearly state to the world that Satan cannot steal our joy because he didn't give it to us, and he can't take it away. Amen. Time for breakfast Billy.

I thanked Jorge and said, "I'm going to check on Laura and Bobby." Laura and Bobby met us in the kitchen.

"Good morning Laura, how's my little Bobby?" Jorge

asked.

"Feeling fine, Mr. Jorge, but I'm getting big. How are you today?" Bobby asked.

"I'm filled with hope and the joy that Jesus gives me, Bobby!" Jorge replied.

"Me too, Mr. Jorge," Bobby said.

"Maria are those for me?" I asked, pointing to what she was making.

"No, they're for Bobby," Maria said. "I made your favorite, Senor Bobby, blueberry pancakes."

"Bobby, I think Maria thinks your special," Jorge said.

"Senor Jorge, Bobby is special!" she said.

"Maria, I guess you're right. Laura, would you say grace for us?" Jorge asked.

"Sure. Lord thank you for our family here in this wonderful place. Bless them all and bless the food you give us, Amen."

We ate silently, thinking about the day ahead. Then Jorge asked Bobby, "How were the pancakes?"

"Awesome Mr. Jorge," replied Bobby.

"Laura, do you have plans for today?" asked Jorge.

"Yes sir," Laura said. "This is Bobby and my last day at school. There will be a lot of goodbyes and thankyous today."

"Billy, you ready to get our meeting started?" Jorge asked me.

"Yes sir." We got up and went back to Jorge's office.

"Come on in, Billy. Have a seat. First things first. Billy, take this envelope," Jorge said.

"Yes sir," I said wondering what it was.

"Go ahead and open it."

"Two hundred and fifty thousand dollars!" I exclaimed. "I can't believe this. Jorge you shouldn't have!"

"Oh, I should have. It's part of God's plan. Just consider that it's from the poor folks of Mexico," Jorge said. "Use it wisely."

"I promise I will, Jorge," I said.

"Second thing," Jorge went on. "Your leaving will not be

any easier for you than for me. I will tell you that."

"Jorge, I don't expect it to be easy!"

"I'll be in touch with you every week, Billy. We will pray for each other," he said. Jorge then excused himself with some things to attend to but said I could use his office.

Just then Juan appeared. Juan had experience at the ranch and in the U.S. and was to be key in our transition.

"Billy, I have researched water issues at the warehouse," he said. "It turns out there is groundwater at about a thousand feet. The problem is we have to apply to the state of Arizona for rights and amounts. I have the application, but we may have to set up a nonprofit group first."

"Juan, we have to do that anyway," I said, "So go ahead and download the application and we will fill it out."

"I've started taking bids for the downtown building rehab," Juan said. But we need to have a plan. What do you think?"

"I'm thinking the top two floors could be living quarters with the bottom for meetings, such as a church. The second floor could be made into classrooms," I said.

"That's what I was thinking," Juan agreed. "Downtown power and utilities will come from public utilities, but I am working on an off-grid system for the warehouse."

"I'm thinking we need living quarters there too, to minimize expense and maximize Christian community," I said.

"Billy, that's a start, but we're waiting on a lot of people to get back to us before we can do further planning," Juan said. Let's get those forms so we can fill them out and mail them," I said.

"They're already printing them, Billy," he said. "Walk with me to my office and we'll fill them out now."

"We need to pick a board. You, Laura, Joe and myself, for a start," I said. "I would like Jorge but he's not a US citizen."

"That'll work. Billy," Juan said.

After filling out the forms I said, "I hate paperwork, Juan."

"Me too but you gotta do it!"

"I know, I've filled out the application and put it in the mail."

"Come on down to Benito's office," Juan said. "Joe sent warehouse prints and he's been working on power grid stuff."

We reached Benito's office and saw that his desk was covered with plans. "Morning gentlemen," Benito said. "Here's what I've got. With a combination of solar and wind generators we can start out with about two hundred and fifty thousand watts. We'll do everything in 220 volts and the larger loads with 440. That will save money on wiring."

"Guys that's Greek to me," I said.

"Billy, the higher the voltage the smaller the wire size," Benito said. "We'll keep a lot of stuff DC, but a lot of the smaller motor loads will need to be AC. Anyway, Billy, you don't have to understand all this. This is our department."

"Good, because if I needed to understand it, that might delay us twenty years!" I exclaimed.

"The first business I want to get going is Hydroponic vegetable growth," suggested Benito. "LED lighting has made that very profitable since it will significantly reduce lighting costs. Speaking of food, you guys ready for lunch?"

"Let's go, Jorge is meeting us," I said.

CHAPTER 57.

As we sat down to eat our lunch, the kitchen behind us was in a flurry of activity. "What's going on Jorge?" I asked.

"They're planning a party," he replied. "A farewell party." The ovens were cranking out Tres Leche Cakes and other ingredients for a fiesta. We prayed and finished our lunch. My compadres returned to complete their daily tasks. With things on my agenda completed, I went to my room and brought my Bible back to the dining room. I opened it to Joshua and read the story of Israel battling against Jericho and crossing the Jordan. I watched as my new family worked so effortlessly side by side. After reading and praying among the bustle for a while, I made my way into the yard. There next to the porch, I picked a spot. I began gathering large rocks and stacking them in a pyramid shape. This would be my memorial, my Jordan to crossing to my promised land back in Tucson. Tomorrow we would leave but the promise God had given me would be fulfilled as I embraced the detail of doing it exactly as He instructed. The promised land was possible, the giants were real, but God is Lord of the giants too. Little men can do big things if they hold on to a big God.

Men and women made their way to the dining room. They set up tables and placed the chairs. Tablecloths were spread out and vases of flowers were placed on each table. Decorations appeared throughout the room, and the stage was set for celebration. Everyone pitched in to accomplish a mammoth task in short order. Cabritos roasted over open fires on spits behind the kitchen. This was a feast!

Laughter once again filled the room as harmony filled

hearts. When the school buses arrived the children soon realized a celebration was on the agenda, and they quickly began decorating the yard and hanging lights from the trees. Like a finely tuned orchestra working in perfect harmony, the plan came together. The mariachi band set up on the porch and music began to flow as the balance of God's people made their way to the fiesta.

They shoved Laura, Bobby and I to the center of the yard and dancers circled around us. Jorge took the microphone and blessed the food as everyone made their way to a buffet style serving. We three were seated at the top of the room as honored guests. There were Tres Leche cakes for everyone, and the celebration moved back into the yard where the band played once again. The evening ended as Jorge took the mike and led a prayer time. In ten concentric circles the people, our people gathered and prayed for our safety and blessing. We thanked them and shared that we would be back. I spoke and reminded them of the task God had set before us and our need for their continued prayer and support. I thanked them all for the money Jorge had handed me and told them that every one of them had become a part of our lives and the work Jesus had given us.

Laura found Bobby asleep in a chair on the porch, so we made our way to our room. We all prayed together, and angels above prayed with us. I noticed the smell of gardenias and fell fast asleep.

CHAPTER 58.

Before breakfast, Laura and I had our gear loaded into Jorge's Jeep. We woke up Bobby and went into the dining room. After a good breakfast, a few tears, and a lot of prayers, we were on our way to Hermosillo. We stopped at Jorge's house and there switched to our Suburban. On the way out we stopped at the barrio and said goodbye to the people there. They prayed for us and we headed north. As we passed through Nogales, the Sierra Madre faded into the distance. The street children of Nogales were busy on the corners begging for handouts. The border crossing went by fast and we were suddenly back in the US. The skyline of Tucson made its first appearance and soon we were at Joe's house. He and Suzy were waiting for us. They offered us lunch and showed us to our rooms. We unloaded our things. Joe told us there was a welcome home party for us at the church that evening.

"We have time, Billy, if you would like to run downtown and look at the building," Joe said.

"Let's go," I replied. "The girls can get our stuff put away while we're gone."

When we pulled up in front of the building, I could see that Joe already had workers there. "What's going on Joe?" I asked.

"They're setting up temporary lighting and plugs for the work," Joe said. "We already have power and they are bringing circuits online as they are ready. I expect to have power to all the floors before the end of the week."

"How'd you get the city inspectors to okay that?" I asked.

"I've got a little pull in building inspection," Joe replied.

"I had to call in a few favors." As we got out of his truck, I could see a sign over the door. It said, "Future Homeless Shelter Under Construction." A lot of homeless people were already hanging out in the area, and we brought folding chairs to the sidewalk to visit with them. I asked a lot of questions and got to know two guys named Sydney and Patrick. Both of them were veterans with disabilities. Their injuries from Iraq had left them addicted to painkillers and finally Heroin.

"Joe, we have lighting on the first floor, don't we?" I asked.

"Yes."

"Okay guys, can you get the word out that at twelve o'clock tomorrow we will meet here? Bring as many other homeless people as you can. Lunch will be provided."

"We'll do it!" they both exclaimed.

"How many people do you think you can get?" I asked.

"Oh, we can get a couple of hundred since your feeding us," they answered."

"I'll call David and see if we can get chairs and tables from the church," I said. "We'll run to the wholesale store and buy lunch meat. We can ask some ladies to make sandwiches in the morning at the church. I think we can work out the rest of the details at our homecoming party this evening."

"Boy, Billy, you're not letting any grass grow under your feet, are you?" Joe remarked.

"Joe, there's no time. Those guys told me somebody dies almost every night from a Heroin overdose. That needs to stop now."

"Let's look at the rest of the building," Joe said, overwhelmed.

"Joe, the set up on this building looks perfect for foam insulation," I said.

"Yeah, I know," Joe said. "I have a truck mounted sprayer and have ordered the foam. Next week we should be able to start if we get the rough-in on electrical conduits and CPVC for water set up."

"What about air conditioning and heat?" I asked.

"Were running pipes for that too. I have a lot of questions though," Joe said.

"Juan, Benito and Julio are going to be here at ten tomorrow. They can help," I said. "Good a friend of mine, who is a mechanical engineer, is supposed to meet me at nine in the morning."

"Are you talking about Jeff Piniot? He's a church member," Joe said.

"Yes."

"Good, he'll have some answers," Joe said. "Billy, we'd better get home and clean up. We're meeting at the church at six thirty."

"Okay. The ladies are cooking dinner there. We don't want to make them wait," I said.

"Jeff will be there. We can probably get started with questions there," Joe said. "I've got a set of preliminary plans I'm bringing. Let's go home."

"Okay, Joe. Do we have time to run by the warehouse?" I asked.

"Yeah, it's only about eight miles past the house. We do have two hours before we have to be at church."

We stopped by the warehouse. It was a massive metal building, and to my delight, I learned it was sitting on forty-five acres with an acre of concrete parking lot.

"Here it is, Billy," Joe said. " There is a lot of work to be done to make it usable, but the Lord told me to donate it, so I did. I have no idea how you intend to use it but here it is."

"When Juan saw it his mind already went to work," I said. "He's already making plans."

"Like what?"

"There is a group of high school seniors he's been training in software support. As soon as we get some air conditioning and rooms set up, we'll set up a phone bank for software support. We're supposed to meet with them this week and sign a contract," I said. "Then he wants to set up hydroponic farming systems for food and we're working on an organic health supply company to utilize some of the herbal medicine formulas learned from the Yaquis."

"Good. My friends down at city hall have been working with the state to establish our water rights limits," Joe said. "I've got the solar panels and wind generators coming next month. Hopefully the state will answer by then. At least we have city water to begin the work. As soon as the electricians get temporary power downtown they are coming here to start."

"What about money?" I asked.

"We're fine," Joe said. "Most of the labor is being donated and material costs have been well within my means so far. I've got about seven hundred thousand in the bank. I'll need to get the non-profit set up to avoid paying taxes. You've got the two hundred and fifty-thousand-dollar check Jorge gave you. Hold on to it until the non-profit is official. We'll set a new bank account up as soon as that happens. Come on Billy. Let's go home and get ready for church."

"Yeah we're running out of time."

CHAPTER 59.

When we arrived at my old church, it was evident that David had been doing an amazing job. The crowd was much larger than I expected. David prayed and we began preparing our plates in a buffet style line. After the meal David asked if I would share some of my experiences and the plans God had laid on my heart. There was so much that had happened. I told them about the work of Jorge, Bryan's accident and funeral, meeting the angel Josiah, and the young Peter now saved and finishing his Prison sentence. "There's much more, but I'd really like to share about God's plan," I said. "God has called me to do inner city ministry. I am hoping that all of you will be my best supporters. I am resigning as your pastor but will continue to be a member of the church. The vision God has given me requires a lot of workers and I would love for many of you to serve with me.

"We have already acquired a building downtown and a warehouse south of town. These are part of the plan. By Sunday, I hope to have a rough outline with some of our goals. My hope is that our church can model for other churches a solid Biblical plan for taking Jesus back to the U.S. We will be partnering with Jorge's work in Mexico. Most of you know him since he has been in this church many times. As a matter of fact, he is a member here since he was baptized here. Anyway, he has established a phenomenal work there that gives us a pattern for the work we will be doing here. That's all I have for now, but there will be more as the plan becomes clearer."

Our head trustee stood to speak. "I am James Clark. Most of you know me as Jimmy. We have some business to take care of. First, Pastor Billy, I want you to know we started a fund to raise money for whatever work God was putting on your heart. Right now, we have raised five hundred and thirty thousand dollars. I move that we go right into a business meeting at this time, since most members are here. I am going to make a blanket motion, and then give everyone fifteen minutes to pray and ask any questions they may have. I move that we appropriate the money for Billy's ministry, that we officially elect David as our new Pastor, and appoint Billy as our Urban missionary."

A second sounded out from the audience. There were a few whispers in the general silence. "Any questions?" Jimmy asked. "None? Okay, I know that Billy and Jesus have already discussed this. What we have done anticipates the moving of God's Spirit on Billy, and at this time each of us should pray to be in unity to support the moving of God among us. I will again give you fifteen minutes to pray, and then if everyone is ready, we will vote."

Prayers filled the fellowship hall in our church and the familiar smell of gardenia's filled the room. After fifteen minutes the vote carried unanimously. Our music people took their place and we spent the balance of our evening praising the Lord of all creation.

Pastor David and I met for fifteen minutes afterward, and he explained how the Spirit had been moving. "David that explains the ease of the vote," I said. "I'll be honest with you. I was shocked at how well that went!"

"Billy, while you were in Mexico God has been preparing our hearts for the plan you would bring back," David said. "I have really been teaching them about the need for change and how the power in the early church was to be our model. I believe we are about to see God do some miracles in Tucson."

"Me too, David. By the way, you're invited to our first inner city meeting tomorrow," I said.

"I know. The ladies are already planning to meet here to make sandwiches in the morning," David responded. "The trailers are loaded with tables and chairs. I'll be there. Are you preaching?"

"No, this will be a question and answer session," I said. "We need to get to know and understand the needs of the homeless if we are to make a difference."

"One thing we'll agree on already, is that they need Jesus!" David said.

"Amen. Goodnight David. See you in the morning!"

Laura and I drove home and joined Joe, Suzy and Bobby on the back patio. The stars were out in all their glory.

"Billy?" Joe asked.

"Yeah Joe," I said.

"That was amazing."

"How's that?" I asked.

"How smoothly all of the plan went," he said. "I was afraid it would take weeks to get the church on board with the plan."

"Joe that was totally a God thing," I said. "I knew when I smelled the gardenias, that something amazing was about to happen."

"Billy, is that what that smell was?" Joe asked.

"Yeah, it's been happening a lot lately. Isn't that right Laura?" I said.

"Sure has, Billy," said Laura. "Dad, that's God's way of letting us know he is there."

"Well baby girl, He certainly was there!" Joe exclaimed.

"Big things Dad, big things are happening!" Laura said.

"Should I sell my house too?" asked Joe.

"Not unless God tells you to. Besides, we're glad we have this place to come to," I said.

"Old men need to get to bed," Joe said. "Goodnight everyone."

"I'm right behind you, Joe," Suzy added.

"Okay Suzy."

"Let's go to bed too, Laura," I said.

"Okay Billy," Laura said. "Bobby's already asleep. Can you carry him to his bed?" I picked up Bobby and carried him to his room.

"Goodnight, Billy."

"Goodnight, Laura. I am praying for you," I said.
"I'm praying for you too, Billy," Laura said.

CHAPTER 60.

Joe had coffee on when he woke me. We poured two to-go cups and went downtown. Although we stopped to buy breakfast taquitos, we still managed to beat the morning traffic.

The electricians and plumbers were already starting their workday. We now had functional lighting on all floors. Joe and I walked the building one floor at a time. A mass of conduits was in place, and the 4-inch pipes for AC and heating had been stubbed on each floor. I carried a note pad as Joe barked instructions. Joe called the man in charge of electrical over to inform him to focus on the conduits that ran along the exterior walls.

"I am scheduling foam for Friday and Saturday, so we need to be ready by then," Joe said. "Billy, we need to decide on finishing materials so I can get them ordered."

"Joe, I trust you to make right decisions so do whatever you think best," I said.

"I'm thinking keep it cheap and durable," he said.

"Exactly, Joe."

"Stained concrete floors, all metal framing and sheet rock walls would be good," Joe said. "Of course, sheet rock is not so durable, but it's easy to repair, and requires less fireproofing."

"Okay," I said. "I've got some AC and heat ideas I want to throw out, but we'll wait for Juan to get here. He helped with the ranch. He can help us a lot. He's done a lot of this type of thing before. Juan and Benito should be here in thirty minutes."

"Good, that gives me time to meet with Jimmy and Bud our electrician and plumber," I said. "Joe I'm going to find a corner to work on my notes for our meeting with the homeless. Plus, I need a little prayer time."

Desert Dreams

"Okay."

I prayed and went over my notes. They were pretty much all questions except for some basic instructions. Joe had set up a small temporary office, so I made copies of the questions. Soon I heard the voices of Juan and Benito. I met them just as Joe was walking up. Juan said, "Why don't we take a quick tour so I can get my mind wrapped around a visual for our discussion."

We quickly walked each floor and made our way back to the small office. There was barely room enough for us four to be seated around a table with the prints rolled out. "Joe, I see you have installed four heating/cooling pipes from floor to floor. That means you plan a water-cooled system," Juan said.

"Yes, and boiler heat," Joe replied.

"Joe, that brings up something important," Juan said. "I've done the math, and you can do solar panels to heat water for the winter. If they're not enough, you can always add covered parking with solar panels on top of the roofs. There's technology of variable speed compressors I'd like to implement for the chillers. That in combination with evaporative cooling should keep HVAC costs at less than thirty percent of Tucson norms."

"Juan, I'll leave that up to you," Joe said. "I just need some assurance of reliability."

"Good. I have a Japanese firm working out the details," Juan said.

"What about you Benito? Any questions? Ideas?" Joe asked.

"Just some questions," Benito said. "Is the flooring going to be stained concrete?"

"Yes."

"What about the walls?" Benito asked.

"We'll be using metal framing, sheet rock, texture and paint," Joe said.

"Sprinkler system," Benito asked.

"Yeah, the city requires it even though most of the building is fireproof," said Joe.

"Juan?" asked Benito.

"Yes Benito?"

"Is there a way to combine sprinklers with AC?" Benito asked.

"Not a good idea, Benito, since we'll probably go with a dry system," Juan said. "Water makes a real mess."

"Okay, gentlemen, we're done," Joe announced.

"Hey Joe," said Juan. "Can we use your office at your building supply?"

"Sure, and feel free to use my staff to help you," Joe replied.

"Besides that, I want to see your foam rig," Juan said.

"It's in the parking lot," answered Joe.

By this time a large crowd had gathered on the first floor and the people of Grace were serving lunch. Pastor David offered thanks and we joined them. After lunch, I spoke before the group.

"God has laid it on my heart to help you folks out. Here are some of my thoughts," I said. "I do not have the right to impose my lifestyle or what I consider normal on you. It is your right to live in a way that makes you happy, that is unless it infringes on someone else's rights.

"I have spent some time among you and know there are a variety of reasons that folks become homeless. Take a look at the question sheet you received when you came in. There are questions like: 'Are you happy with this lifestyle?', 'How did you become homeless?' and, 'If you would like to escape homelessness, what do you think it would take?' I want you to answer honestly. Do not put your name on the sheet. We will be taking your pictures as you leave, to put with your name and where you usually sleep. You do not have to participate in that, but I would love for you to do it for me. Please answer as many of the questions as you can. We will be using your answers to develop our program.

"Starting this Sunday, we will be holding church services here with lunch provided. Everyone is welcome and bring a friend. Thank you all for joining us. If there is anything you would like help with now, write it down with your picture. Our people will be in touch with you about it."

I was proud of Grace Church. Fifty of our folks made the meeting and helped with the food and tables. I prayed for them and dismissed them. Several of the homeless people asked for help and Pastor David and I stayed busy talking with them for the rest of the afternoon.

David and I met afterward to go over the questionnaires. Very quickly patterns began to emerge. Many were addicts who used drugs and/or alcohol. Some were just poor, jobless. Some had felony convictions or no skills. PTSD and other psychological disorders were common.

"So, what jumps out at you David?" I asked.

"We will have to get involved in drug and alcohol treatment, job training, and in some cases just teaching people to work. We will also have to find ways to deal with mental health, physical health, and children's education."

"Yeah, those are my thoughts, and if we're going to make a real difference we have to address as many of those areas as we can."

"This is strange," David said. "Look at these answers. Most of these people are okay with living on the streets. It's not that they're really happy or it's good. It's just that many are used to that lifestyle."

"David, the Gospel will change their lives," I said. "They need that so much! Let's pray."

CHAPTER 61.

Juan and Benito stayed with us at Joe's. Joe and Suzy invited Pastor David and his wife, Tina, over for dinner. Suzy sorted through the answers from the homeless questionnaire, while Laura cooked dinner for everyone. Juan and Benito got there about five thirty. Dinner was set for six thirty. Juan and Benito had made phone calls on the way and gotten materials lined up quickly. They already had firm dates for shipment arrivals. They went over all of this with Joe and me.

A chiller package was to arrive in thirty days. Solar panels for electricity and hot water were found locally. Each of the top two floors would have living quarters for twenty families. The first floor would be wide open except for the entry and the restrooms. The second floor would have multiple classrooms, restrooms and a kitchen. Each floor was 12,000 square feet. The first floor would seat around six hundred people. We were setting it up so it could be used as a gym, an auditorium or a dining room.

Pastor David and Tina arrived, and dinner was served. After dinner the ladies had a prayer meeting and the men went over some ministry plans. I looked at some of the graphs that Suzy had prepared from the questionnaire and opened our meeting with prayer. Since David had also interviewed some of the homeless, I asked him to tell us about his interviews and what feedback he could give.

"The interviews pretty much followed the data I saw on the graphs," he said. "If we are to do this right, we are going to have to be willing to do rehab, train workers, teach parenting, teach spiritual growth, provide jobs, and have a school for the children. We will have to find doctors and Psychiatrists. We will have to provide food, clothing, housing and more."

"My thoughts exactly," I agreed. "What about you Joe?"

"The buildings, construction, and even some jobs I can do," Joe said. "The rest is Greek to me."

"I understand there is only so much you can do," I replied. "That's why a significant work force is needed."

"Billy, that's why I made sign-up sheets in the church," David said. "As you know, we are one of the snowbird capitols of the world. We have all these retired people with so many different skills. Over 200 people have signed up to help us."

"What about you Benito or Juan?" I asked.

"Well, we have been through this at the ranch, so we know that the hardest part is training people, getting them to stay committed, and then helping them to make it personal," said Juan.

"What do you mean by making it personal?" I asked.

"Many things can be done in a classroom or group setting but the homeless problem will only have great success if folks are willing to look people in the eyes with compassion. Personal mentoring is key," Benito said.

"That's a lot of people, Benito," I responded.

"Yes Billy, it is, but moving too fast will produce a bunch of half-committed disciples. Do it right from the beginning and a year later growth can happen exponentially. It's the New Testament pattern," Benito said.

"Then that settles it," I said. "Pastor David, you and I have a lot of work to do. We will take the volunteer list and make a plan. I'm sure the halfhearted will quickly weed themselves out, because we need an eight-hours-a-day, five-days-a-week training plan started as soon as possible. Let's meet in the morning at the church and look at the list."

"Will do, Billy. Seven o'clock?" David asked.

"That works." I turned to my father-in-law. "Joe, did your secretary get the paperwork filed for our non-profit?"

"Yeah, she mailed it today," Joe said.

"Any other comments or questions? No? Then let's pray.

Get the ladies. Let's do this together," I said. The ladies came in from another room. "Laura, would you pray for us?" I asked.

"Yes dear," Laura said. "Lord Jesus, King of all the Earth, bless your plan, give these men your wisdom to make right decisions, give them the courage to do what they need to do, and give them faith to know it's your will, Amen."

"Goodnight all," I said. "Juan and Benito, Suzy will show you your rooms. Thank you, gentlemen."

"Laura did you pray with Bobby before you put him to bed?" I asked a few minutes later.

"Now, Billy, you know the answer to that," Laura replied.

"Yeah, I guess I do."

"So, Billy, how was the meeting?" she asked.

"It was very good Laura, but there's one area that I want you to really pray about," I said.

"What's that Billy?" Laura asked.

"That every one of us will truly have hearts of love as we deal with the street people."

"So, do you think that's a problem, Billy?" Laura asked.

"Yeah, I know it is," I said.

"How's that?"

"I met with several of them today. They hadn't had a bath in a while. They smelled really bad. That may not seem like much, but it was really distracting," I admitted.

"I've got a good idea, Billy," Laura said.

"What's that?"

"You know that corner between our building and the one next door?" she asked. "Don't we own that property?"

"Yeah."

"Why don't we put a free laundry and showers there for the street people?"

"Laura, that's a great idea!" I exclaimed. "Thanks."

"Goodnight, Billy."

"Goodnight, Laura. Say your prayers."

"Yeah, Billy."

CHAPTER 62.

At six o'clock I was up. I made a to-go cup of coffee and headed toward the church. I picked up four breakfast taquitos and met Pastor David there at six forty-five. He unlocked the doors, turned off the alarm and we went to his office. On the way, I opened the door to my old office and ran my hand across my desk. My palm was covered in dust. Everything seemed different now. I stopped by the restroom to wash my hands and met David. He offered grace and we ate our pastor's breakfast.

"David I've been going over the first parts of our plan comparing them to those early days when Jesus called his disciples. His words were simple, but the disciples seemed to understand, 'follow me'. They gave up everything, leaving their homes and families. Their days began to take on an entirely different flavor," I said. "When Jesus taught, he did it on the move. What he taught was immediately wrapped in living breathing examples. He reached people heart to heart. He healed. He forgave sin. He said go and sin no more. He is God. The things he offers are supernatural. I see two missing elements in our plan. Supernatural empowerment and making it personal."

"Billy, I'm following your thinking," David said.

"Thanks David. You know, these are things that are missing in our church," I said.

"I see that, Billy, but how do we get them back?" he asked.

"Our people have lost the personal touch. They see ministry as mowing the yard or painting the building. Even teaching a Sunday school class can lose the personal touch. If teachers don't see the needs of families and pray for them, we're not utilizing the power offered to us," I said.

"But Billy, we're not Jesus," David observed.

"No, but did he not offer the power for us to do his work? Is he not in us? Is he not sitting at the right hand of the Father making intercession for us?" I asked.

"Billy, I think I can see where you're taking this, won't our people need more training to do this?" Pastor David asked.

"Training helps," I said. "But the empowerment of the Holy Spirit fills the need while we are learning."

"Explain Billy," he said.

"Remember how Jesus sent the disciples out two by two? Then he sent out 72 very early in their ministry. Remember Luke 7 and Luke 10? Remember how they were amazed at the miracles they were able to do? Do you remember what Jesus said when they expressed their amazement at the miracles?" I asked.

"Yeah," he said, 'do not be amazed for I was there when Satan fell like lightening,'" Pastor David said.

"Exactly," I said. "He's saying, 'Realize this. I am God. I am the Son. Don't you understand what I am offering you?' David, we don't get that. He said that when you come before kings or leaders do not worry about what you should say. In our divine appointments, God will also give us the words to say."

"I remember that, Billy. So, how does this impact our plan?" David asked.

"It's faith, boldness, courage, and willingness to do the work, David, that brings power. Our love for those in need will bring the mindset of Jesus right into our work," I said.

"Here's my thoughts David," I continued. "While the building is being finished, we need to assess our volunteers today so that tomorrow we can bring those who were saved yesterday to the church to help and train them, so they will be ready to serve when the building is finished."

"I'll get the list of church volunteers so we can organize this," David said, finally catching my vision.

"Okay, David. I have the list of those who were saved. Let's plan on bringing them here to the church tomorrow," I said.

Desert Dreams

"What time?" he asked.

"Let's make a day of it. We'll try to have everyone here at 8:30 am. We'll need to spend this afternoon locating street people and have the vans downtown at 8:00 in the morning," I said.

"I'll get the staff calling church volunteers for when they get here at 8:00," David said. "I'll also bring kitchen folks in for breakfast and lunch. Let' see that list."

"Look at this, David. I'm counting 82 street people who made a commitment to follow Jesus yesterday. 61 of them admit they are dealing with addiction issues," I said.

"Billy, I know a man who runs a faith-based treatment center. Let me give him a call!" David exclaimed. David made a quick call and announced immediately, "Okay. Hey, Billy, he can meet with us in thirty minutes!"

"Good. Hopefully he can help us with what we need to do," I said.

Half an hour later we were shaking hands with Kevin Powers. "Billy this is Kevin Powers," David said. "He runs a treatment center near Joe's warehouse."

I explained our situation right away. "Kevin, we have 61 people who want to begin treatment immediately."

"Unfortunately, I have no room," Kevin said.

"How many do you have now?" I asked.

"94 altogether. 52 men and 42 women," he replied.

"Are they separated?" I asked.

"Yes. We have slabs poured to double our capacity," he said.

"Billy, what about all those FEMA trailers Joe has stored at the warehouse parking lot?" David asked suddenly.

"I'll call Joe," I said.

"Good."

I picked up my phone, "Joe, you think you can get us permission to use some of those FEMA trailers for temporary housing?"

He said, "I'll see."

I turned to Kevin. "So, Kevin, are they going to need supervision?" I asked.

"About half of my people are four months into treatment. In an isolated place, they could work to supervise. Plus, that would free up half my staff to move them there," Kevin said.

"Is there water sewer and electricity?" I asked Joe on the phone.

"It's there," he replied. "The trailers will have to be hooked up."

"Okay," I turned to David and Kevin. "He's writing an emergency order for us to use the trailers, but we will have to fund." I turned back to the phone. "Thanks, Joe. I'll call back in a few minutes."

"Billy, about 50 volunteers are here! They are praying in one of the classrooms," David said.

"Good, David. Let's meet with them," I said.

The three of us went to the classroom and I spoke to the group. "Thank you for being here on such short notice. Here's the situation. 82 street people were saved downtown yesterday. 61 are dealing with addiction issues. This is Kevin. He runs a treatment center and is willing to help us start rehab. We have permission to use the FEMA housing stored at Joe's warehouse. We need volunteers to hook up electricity and plumbing there. We need volunteers to transport the new converts that are addicts in our vans. We need volunteers to buy groceries, and to provide security at the warehouse. We are setting aside a couple of classrooms for the other converts. There are fifteen children who are not attending school, so we need volunteers to teach and care for those kids. Signup sheets are on the table in front of me. We really need your help. Take a moment to pray and ask how God wants to use you. Thank you."

My phone rang and I answered it. "Excuse me, everyone. Hello Joe. Okay, so you are sending materials and a crew of six to the warehouse to begin hooking up trailers?" I repeated. "Good we will send some help from the church. Thanks Joe."

I turned to David. "David, I'm going to need you to coordinate things at the church. I'm going to spend my afternoon getting a list of people willing to leave the streets. Keep me updated. Let's pray. Lord we don't have to question whether this is your will. We need your power. We need your strength. We need your people to get involved. Holy Spirit, fill us all, Amen."

By 10:00 am, more volunteers were showing up at the church. David was organizing and assigning tasks. Jorge was coming from the ranch and would be with us by dinner, so I called him to ask for volunteers from there. He said he would bring men with work visas to help. I called Laura, and she and Suzy brought Bobby and met me downtown. I had assembled a team of three to help us locate the street people who had been saved. I took a few minutes to walk through the church building, watching people busy with their tasks. I marveled at the activity and paused to thank God for his faithfulness. *Amazing! Just amazing! Thank you, Lord, Amen.*

CHAPTER 63.

I drove by the house and picked up my mission team. We arrived at the first homeless site. Laura and Suzy were soon talking to the ladies while Bobby and I spoke to the men. Using the pictures we had taken, and the names we were given, we started locating people on our list. We bought gift certificates to give out, from a nearby McDonalds, and in about two hours we had made contact with many of the people. We were assured that the others would be notified to be at the downtown building by 8:00 in the morning. New people we met were invited to a midday meal and repeat of the previous day's church service. We spent the last two hours just getting to know people with a new list of questions I had prepared. It asked; "How did you become homeless?" "What would it take to get you off the streets?" "What kinds of legal problems do you have?" and "Have you trusted Jesus as savior?" Three people were saved that afternoon, and we added those to the group to be brought to church in the morning.

In the evening we returned to Joe's with Tex-Mex take out. Jorge had arrived with seven men. Joe was talking to Jorge when we arrived, and Jorge was filling the men in on work detail for the next day.

Ten FEMA trailers were already hooked up and ready. There were plans to have twenty more ready for tomorrow. With the extra help we hoped to make it thirty. We prayed and ate our meal.

Spray Foam would start tomorrow downtown. They would start at six and the plan was to have the first floor finished by ten so we could set up for services.

Two of the men Jorge had brought had set up the power system at the ranch. With solar cells locally available, they planned to do installation tomorrow afternoon. We filled Jorge and the others in on the salvations and how Grace Church had stepped up. Jorge did the necessary translating, filling in the others. We used the balance of our evening to pray for all of the events of tomorrow. Some prayed out loud some silently, some in English and some in Spanish. The smell of gardenias swept through the house as God put his stamp of approval on the work, He had given us.

Joe had picked up inflatable mattresses and sleeping bags for our guests. Furniture in the great room was pushed to one side to make room for our brothers from Mexico.

I had appointments set to meet with Pastor David and two Christian counselors at 7:30 in the morning. Joe delegated his daily responsibilities at the building supply to his warehouse manager so he could take construction over-site. Jorge planned to help set up housing at the warehouse. A rehab indoctrination was arranged at the church. The plan was to house the new converts at the warehouse. Classrooms would also be ready to start there tomorrow. Two Church attorneys would start sorting out legal issues for the homeless in the afternoon.

Laura put Bobby to bed, and we made our way to our bedroom. We prayed together, said our good nights, and called it a day. My mind was so filled with details that I lay in bed for two hours just talking to Jesus. I saw visions of hundreds being saved, people living good Christian lives and a Church revival sweeping across our city. The last thing I remember as I nodded off, was Jesus assuring me that all was well, that He was in control and I was simply to do what He said. I heard Him say, "Billy I've got this, don't worry, I love you my son."

CHAPTER 64.

We had breakfast at six so our whole group got up early. It was a traditional breakfast with bacon, eggs, and biscuits, with picante sauce on the table. We prayed together and ate our eggs with the excitement of conversation. Everyone seemed to anticipate that Jesus was doing something special here. An eagerness to start our day showed on our faces.

Everyone headed in different directions, but every one of us was working toward common goals, God given goals. I went to meet Pastor David. Upon my arrival, I also met the counselors, Travis and Tamara. David had sorted out some of the more difficult cases from our street guests, and after prayer began sharing details of various psychological issues.

"I have one question guys," he said. "Some of these cases are so bizarre that I go back to New Testament times and demon possession."

"Billy," said Travis, "if these folks were truly saved yesterday, the possibility of demon possession no longer exists in them."

"Okay Travis, but I want to hear your explanation," I said.

"Salvation brings the Holy Spirit," Travis said. "The Holy Spirit is fully God. I don't believe demons can live in the same body as God," Travis said.

"Travis, I like that," I said. "I wanted to hear that from you. I wanted to know if you're the right man. I think you are."

"Thank you, Pastor Billy," Travis said.

"So, what if that person still shows symptoms of demonic behavior?" I asked.

"Billy, that's possible," Travis said. "Have you ever dealt

with someone coming off drugs or alcohol?"

"A little," I replied. "Okay, well until the drugs are no longer present, that person will exhibit behavior that makes no sense. Craziness and temporary insanity are common," Travis said. "Once their system is clean their thinking begins to return. There is also the impact of how the brain processes the loss of the drug and it continues to affect them sometimes for a while. Sometimes the impact even leaves permanent damage."

"What do we do then? We need a miracle?" I asked.

"We pray. I don't believe there is anything that God cannot do, but He sometimes leaves damage to help us, like He does with a Down's Syndrome child. He uses the impact on those around him for good," Travis said.

"I can see that. Thanks, Travis," I said. "I can also see a parallel in how we see the Holy Spirit. All believers have Him, but few know how to use the power He gives them."

"Exactly."

"I have a question for you and Tamara," I said.

"What's that?" Travis asked.

"Would you be willing to help us full time?" I asked.

"We have prayed about that Billy. We believe that's what God wants us to do, but we don't know how we can support ourselves doing charity work," Travis said.

"We need you, and so I think we can find a way to make that happen," I said. Tamara's your wife, Travis?"

"Yes."

"Do you have children?"

"Yes, two girls," Travis said.

"What age?"

"Four and six," he said.

"What if we get them in school here at the church and make sure they're cared for while you work?" I suggested.

"That would be awesome!" they replied.

"What kind of house do you live in?" I asked.

"A nice 3,000 square foot home near the mountains," Travis said.

"Would you be willing to move and downsize," I asked.

"Absolutely!" he said.

I turned to David and asked. "Pastor David, would you pray that God open these doors?"

"I sure will!" replied David. "Lord, it's your work. It's your plan. Help us make this happen exactly like you have planned, Amen."

"Thanks for your time Travis and Tamara. Let me have your numbers and we will be in touch," David said.

"Thanks Pastor David. Thanks Pastor Billy."

"You're welcome," I said.

Pastor David, the new Christians should be arriving by now. Let's gather them in the dining hall and have a meeting with them after they finish breakfast," I said.

"Billy, do you have some things in mind to go over with them?" Pastor David asked.

"I do," I replied.

We moved from table to table getting to know them better, and when they finished eating, we had them clear and clean the tables.

"Ladies and gentlemen, welcome to Grace Church," I announced. "Each day for the next two weeks, Pastor David will be teaching you some of the basics of Christianity. He will teach you how to pray, how to study your Bible, and some basic house rules. First, I want to say this facility will be available to you to begin your journey walking with Jesus. Please take care of the property here. Always leave things as good or better than you found them. Second, always treat each other and the people here who are serving you with respect. 'Yes, Sirs' and 'Yes, Ma'ams' are in order. I expect you to use these words liberally. If you fail in these, it will be addressed.

"We will be offering counseling in every area. Alcohol, drugs, psychological help, job skills and anything else that will help you be productive Christians. A long-term treatment center is being set up for those with addiction issues as we speak. Those needing treatment will be moved this afternoon to begin treatment. Housing and food will be provided. Those entering that program will be given assignments. You will be expected to fully participate. Repeated failure to work will land you back in the streets. We can't help you unless you are willing to take this seriously.

"I have two attorneys coming this afternoon who will be available to help you with any legal problems. Once you are far enough along in treatment, you will be expected to help us with the next ones coming to treatment. Don't worry about your ability to do that. You will be trained how to do so. Any Questions?"

"What about those of us with children?" one woman asked.

"As you already know, a nursery has been provided. School age children will be assimilated into our already operational church school," I explained. "Those going into treatment will leave your kids here while in treatment. They will be well cared for and twice a week you will get to see them as you will be attending church here. After services we will give you some one on one time with your kids. Any other questions? Okay, then let's make our way to the basic Christianity class where Pastor David will begin teaching. Thank you everyone, for being here. You will find that our folks will love you and take good care of you.

"You have thirty minutes before class starts. Down the hall, you will find restrooms with showers. Please use them. In the rooms just beyond the restrooms are a lot of donated clothes sorted by size. Find clean clothes and take what you want. If you want to save the clothes you are wearing, you'll find permanent markers there to write your names on the inside of them. By the time you finish class, our ladies will have washed and folded them for you. Have a great day and I will see you tomorrow morning!"

CHAPTER 65.

The next morning, I went downtown. When I got there, Jorge was with Joe looking over the work. Foam was going in on the second floor. Windows were open. They would be finished by eleven thirty. I walked with some of the workers and we talked. "Billy, we want to be here when the street people get here at noon," they said. "Serving lunch with you, will give us a chance to put faces with what we're doing."

By eleven, some people were already gathering outside. We sat with them and used the workers as translators to interview several of the Hispanic men. Most were illegals, which brought a whole new problem to us. I decided that using Jorge as a translator would be a good idea when we shared the gospel after lunch.

By noon, every chair was taken, and we used every available extra chair we had. There must have been over 50 people who had to stand. Almost 400 people had crammed into the first-floor space. Another 60 folks came to know Jesus as savior that afternoon. Grace folks took pictures, filled out questionnaires, and told them to meet us at eight the next morning at the vans.

I texted Pastor David and he responded that he had just finished speaking, and was turning the training over to Jeff, his education director. He was on his way downtown. We he arrived, we gathered in the small office downstairs and prayed together, giving God thanks for those who had been saved. I wanted to talk to Pastor David about a few things, and I invited Joe and Jorge to stay. Joe said he needed to get to the warehouse, but Jorge stayed.

"David, there are things going on here that I don't know about and I need you to explain," I said.

"What's that Billy?" David asked.

"How is it that so many volunteers from Grace are stepping up?" I asked.

"Okay. Right after you sold your house and left, I explained why you had gone to the ranch in Mexico, in a Sunday morning service," David said. "What followed next, was the most amazing thing I have ever seen. I don't know all the details, but the next Sunday, offerings tripled. I'm guessing our folks are following your lead."

"So, David, are you saying that it was all about setting an example?" I asked.

"I think so, Billy," David said. "Julie and I have downsized ourselves. What you did impacted us too. When you get to church tomorrow morning, I want to show you the bank statement. We have all kinds of surplus money. Even with all the projects we are working on, there is not a money problem. Billy, we had twenty retired tradesmen show up this afternoon to begin skills training. They plan to teach until 8:00 this evening."

I looked across the table at Jorge. Tears were streaming down his face.

"What do you think Jorge?" I asked.

"It's just like Josiah showed me two years ago, Billy," Jorge said. "I saw God's vision, and this is just the beginning."

"Listen," said Pastor David. "That's not all. There is a group of women who started holding two-hour prayer meetings every day since the day you and Laura left. I know as preachers we often blame their people for the church's failure, but I am seeing that it was us, the leaders, who were failing them. We had lost our vision. We no longer expected miracles.

"Billy, every time in scripture, when God moved in a mighty way, it happened through the men he called to lead."

"David, you're right," I said.

"Amen," said Jorge.

"Gentlemen," I said.

Lonnie Barnard

"Yes, Billy."

"We must travel to the warehouse."

Shortly thereafter, we met Kevin at the warehouse. When we got there, he had set up chairs in a corner of the warehouse and started a modified twelve step class. Everyone had a notebook and was taking notes. He handed us four extra folders, so we could review and keep his material. Kevin introduced us to the men and women gathered for the class. As soon as we were introduced, hands shot up for questions.

"Mr. Billy, we need some Bible teachers," one man said.

"Okay, guys. Let's pray for that," I responded. Everyone prayed out loud, and as they prayed, two friends who were retired pastors came to mind. I stepped outside, dialed their numbers and both said they would be there with their wives in an hour. While I was outside, I noticed three members of our church security team keeping an eye on things. I walked out to thank them and learned they had already set up twenty-four-hour security at the site. I also noticed that some carpenters had built the frame for a 2,000 square foot building on the back side of the warehouse. I walked over to thank them, and found Joe pouring over a set of hand drawn plans. He was conducting an orchestra of nail guns and skill saws.

"Hey Joe. Thanks! And be sure all these guys get thanked!" I yelled over the din.

"Billy, did you notice the wiring already in the warehouse? The foam guy will be here the day after tomorrow to start this building," Joe said. "Back up. I want to show you something. I backed up far enough to see that Juan's guys were moving along, installing solar panels on the roof. I walked back into the warehouse, just in time to see that Kevin was wrapping up his meeting. Everyone was moving toward tables to do their homework. When I heard a diesel truck pull up, I went back outside. It turned out to be a motor home with "Arizona Baptist Disaster Relief Team" painted on the sides. They had brought along a full kitchen feeding team. I turned to Pastor David, but from the smile on his face didn't have to ask who called them.

Two of the men and women that stepped out, were familiar faces from Grace Church. I bowed my head and thanked God. I was in utter amazement and total awe. Three days, all of this in just three days. *Amazing Jesus! just Amazing!*

Pastor Phillip and his wife Maurine arrived. A few minutes later, Nathan and Louise showed. I introduced them and they gathered together our group for Bible class.

"Ladies and gentlemen, 'In the beginning God created...' That's where we'll start," said Phillip, as the others passed out written materials already in folders to 60 men and women. The weather was beautiful so I set up a folding chair where I could see the most people at one time. On the roof, behind the warehouse, and in the parking lot, a hundred men and women had come together as one, all doing God's will. I called Laura. "What are you doing, Babe?" I asked.

"Sitting here with two women who have lost their children to foster care due to their homelessness," she replied. "We're meeting with some lawyers in a minute to start the process for them to get their kids back."

"That's awesome," I said. "What's next?"

"I'm going home," she said.

"How about stopping by Julio's and picking up some chicken? I'll meet you at Joe's and we'll take Bobby to watch the sun set in the desert. Billy," I suggested.

"That's a fabulous idea! I'll meet you there."

By the time Laura and Bobby arrived, I had folding chairs and a table loaded onto the Suburban. We headed out into the desert. We drove out to Saguaro national forest and eased up a road on the side of the mountain. I knew just the right spot, facing west to watch the sun set. We blessed the food and ate our meal as the sun set to our west. A wisp of cirrus clouds brought out orange and violet colors as the sun fell below them. The silver lining symbolized the work God was doing. In silence we worshiped, each in our own minds, as the Creator of the universe showed off a little. *Thank you, Lord and Creator of all things.* We drove back in awe of our God who loves us, as the stars ap-

Lonnie Barnard

peared in their billions.
    "Goodnight, Bobby."
    "Goodnight, Laura."
    "Goodnight, Daddy."
    "Goodnight, Billy."

CHAPTER 66.

With much of our operation functioning, we had time to enjoy breakfast as a family. Jorge and the group from Mexico joined us, as they didn't have to be anywhere until 8:00 am. The pleasure of breakfast with brothers and sister in Christ, reminded me of the place in Heaven that Jesus was preparing for us. We prayed together English and Spanish, piercing the gates of Heaven, as God, who understands all, embraced the words of those He had chosen to do his work. Smiles and laughter have no language barrier and we joined hearts in ways that only God himself fully understands. We loaded into our vehicles, with each team headed toward the tasks that God had set before us. Laura, Bobby, Suzy and I headed toward Grace Church. The others went downtown and to the warehouse.

I arrived at 7:45 am, just in time to see the first group of new Christians arriving for their day. Pastor David greeted them and pointed them to where breakfast was being served. I thought of the group at the warehouse standing in front of a mobile kitchen, receiving their breakfast. The third and fourth floors of our building downtown would be foamed today. Interior framing had already begun on the first and second floors.

I found the group of women prayer warriors at the church and joined them. I gave them a brief update and then prayed with them. After David's indoctrination talk, I met with him, and learned that 30 more would be moved to the warehouse for rehab. I prayed about our rehab facility. If the numbers being saved held up, we would be out of room for them shortly. I called Joe and he told me he had been praying about that, too. He had located a hospital that had been closed down when the new government healthcare insurance had been mandated.

"Billy, I talked to the owners and I think we can get this building cheap," he said. "It's in a bad neighborhood, and they have no intention of reopening."

"Why don't you set up a meeting with them, Joe?" I asked.

"I was hoping you would say that, Billy. The building is pretty much move in ready. It's only been vacant six months. The owner kept a security force there to prevent vandalism," Joe said.

Suddenly I noticed Pastor David standing in the room looking at me. "We need to be downtown in twenty minutes," he reminded me.

When David and I arrived, lunch was being served. We grabbed a quick bite. David was about to preach that afternoon and my mind was in prayer for his message. 32 were saved. We interviewed them and only eleven would need to go through treatment.

A large group of teenagers who lived together in their own tent city were among the saved. Most had been kicked out of their homes and had dropped out of school. David and I discussed their situation and decided they needed to stay in our program and attend the church school to finish their high school education. David called the church for a van and rode with them back to the church. Joe called, and said we had a 2:30 appointment at the hospital. When we arrived there, I noticed that the hospital had kept the utilities on and the building was intact, hospital beds and all. The building had one hundred and twenty beds, and a full kitchen. Joe negotiated a twelve-month lease with an option to buy at the end of the twelve months.

A temporary security fence was installed around the building. We could start moving people in as soon as tomorrow. Joe called his plumber, electrician, and air conditioning man to check out the building. I called Benito and Juan from the warehouse to do an inspection.

Joe and I went to the warehouse to meet with Kevin, our treatment supervisor. Travis and Tamara, our counselors met us there as well. We discussed how things were going, and Kevin went over some rules we needed to implement. Drugs have a tendency to sneak into rehabs. Anyone caught bringing them in would be kicked out. They would have the opportunity to re-apply in a month if they stayed clean and could pass a drug test.

"So, you did get the hospital?" Kevin asked.

"Yes," I replied.

"Good. We can set up a detox unit there. The next time we find out that someone knows about drugs filtering in, and doesn't report it, they will be given dish washing duty at their first offense and kicked out at their second offence. They will then have the same reentry procedures as the one who sneaked them in.

"I need two things, Billy," Kevin said.

"What are they?" I asked.

"I need a safe to keep prescribed medication in, and a doctor to evaluate those needing them."

"Billy?" Joe interrupted.

"Yes Joe?"

"Why don't I call Dr. Dudley. I'll bet he'll volunteer to evaluate them."

"Yeah, Joe, isn't he a Doctor and Psychiatrist?" I asked.

"Sure is! A good Christian man too," Joe said.

"How long will you need him, Kevin?" I asked.

"A couple of days at first, but after that, an afternoon a week will do," Kevin replied.

"I'll call him now," Joe said, punching the number into his phone.

"I left word with his secretary. He'll call back soon."

"Anything else?" I asked.

"No. Oh, they got thirty more trailers hooked up," Joe said.

"When do we start bringing folks to the hospital?" I asked Kevin.

"I think I've got that figured out," Kevin replied.

"How's that?" I asked.

"I have a friend working at another rehab that is not faith based. He wants to work for us," Kevin explained.

"What will he cost?" I asked.

"Food, housing, a car and a hundred bucks a week," said Kevin.

"That's all?"

"Billy, he's committed. He's been waiting for an opportunity like this!"

"Kevin, give him a call he can start tomorrow," I said. "He can help get things set up at the hospital. Oh, and I read through the manual. It's great! We're making more copies for future use. That's a wrap guys! Let's pray."

"Billy?" Joe interrupted.

"Yeah, Joe," I said.

"Dr. Dudley called. He will start tomorrow after lunch," Joe said.

"Good! Where's Jorge?" I asked.

"He's visiting with the staff."

"Can you get him?"

"Sure." Joe left and returned with Jorge right away.

"Afternoon Jorge! We were just fixing to pray. We want you to do the honors," I said.

"Okay," Jorge replied. "On your knees please!" We all knelt. "Lord fill these men with wisdom, your wisdom. Give them faith to know and do what You want, as You give them each a vision to see your plan, Amen."

"Gentlemen, you ready to call it a day?" I asked. "The girls should have super about ready."

"Let's go, Billy," Joe said.

"I'll be along in twenty minutes," Jorge said. "I have two groups left to pray with."

"Okay, Jorge. See you at the house," I said.

We finished dinner and I led a Bible study out of Acts. Jorge translated. We prayed together, and tired men and women found the comfort of beds.

"Goodnight, Laura."

"Goodnight, Dad."
"Goodnight, Bobby."
"Goodnight, Billy."

CHAPTER 67.

At breakfast Friday morning, Joe, Jorge, Laura, Suzy and I talked about the things God was doing.

"Billy what's going to happen if 200 are saved today? Where will we put them?" they asked.

"I've made phone calls to Texas Baptist Men," Joes said. "They are sending a feeding team with a large tent, tables, and chairs. I've ordered another hundred blow-up mattresses. Local help centers are scrounging all the blankets they can," Joe said. "We need to get the restrooms and laundry set up downtown. Texas Baptist Men are bringing their mobile laundry center and Arizona Baptist Men will be teaming with them. They will have six mobile stations and 35 men and women here this evening. We are preparing for as many as 500 at lunchtime services downtown. We need to be in prayer for those souls this morning."

"Yes Joe," I agreed.

"Materials are being delivered for framing and sheet rock downtown and at the warehouse this morning," Joe continued. "Materials for the restroom laundry room are already there. They start framing this morning. The plumbing is roughed out."

"Jorge what are you doing today?" I asked.

"I am going to the warehouse this morning. I need to learn more about Kevin's treatment program. I'll meet you downtown before noon to translate," Jorge answered.

"Good, Jorge. Ladies, what are you doing?" I asked.

"Oh, were going back to the church to help in the school," Laura answered.

"Suzy would you pray a blessing on our day?" I asked.

"Sure, Billy. Lord bless the work of your hands. I pray safety over all the workers, and especially convict the hearts of those we will share the good news of Jesus today, Amen," Suzy prayed.

Joe and I headed downtown. We looked at the progress on the laundry room construction. Then we turned our attention to laying out the location for the 300 by 200 foot tent, due to arrive that morning.

Wall materials were already at the warehouse, and workers were busy placing them on the three upper floors. The freight elevators had been repaired the day before, and quick work was being made of material distribution. The same would happen on the first floor as soon as noonday services were over. Fifty volunteers from various local churches showed up with tools, and Joe abandoned me to lay out walls with a marker on the floors. I grabbed one of the workers and finished marking off the parking lot for the tent set up. One of the framers helped me read the tent plans and began setting lags in the concrete. A number of the homeless showed up early wanting to help, so we had extras setting up tables and chairs.

Today our church band was coming, so a crew was busy setting up sound equipment. They had a portable stage on a 16-foot trailer which they backed in through the roll up doors on the east side of the building. I thought about how four years earlier, we had built this trailer for street revivals, and how God knew then that one day it would be used here. We had all worked hard all morning, and I was thinking how I wished those showers were already in place. One thing was for certain. We could now better identify with the street people. With the lags in place we joined the others for lunch, and I stood and introduced our band. They rocked downtown and by the time I stood to preach a couple of hundred downtown secretaries and businessmen had joined the 400-street people. I stood and gazed across the crowd. Before I could catch myself, I was audibly weeping. The sight of men in suits and ties and women in office attire, dispersed throughout the mass of dirty, disheveled, and smelly street people, overwhelmed my heart. I pulled my work rag from my overalls to wipe my tears and stood before them all to share the gospel.

I was not dressed appropriately for the audience but that didn't matter. The message was universal. Over 90 street people came to know Jesus that day, and to my utter amazement 67 of the better dressed, also came to faith in Jesus that day. They stood in line with the street people as we took pictures and personal information. The street people were invited to board buses Saturday morning. The businessmen and women were given the address of Grace Church and the welcome of an 8:30 am appointment there.

After the crowd dispersed, we gathered with the men and women, together with our crews, to pray and give God thanks for his blessings. We called Pastor David to inform him and set up the Saturday meeting. I reminded him at the same time, of the possibility of a very large crowd Sunday Morning.

Joe and I then went over to the warehouse. Framing was completed on the large bunkhouse we were building there, and decking was going on. The metal roofing was stacked and ready to go on. Joe's delivery men were unloading windows and doors. Exterior electrical panels were being set. Julio was overseeing and coordinating the work. Jesus Christ was directing Julio, and Joe, and Billy, and Jorge, and Pastor David, and Juan, and Benito, and all the rest. God's plan was happening. God's men were hearing the voice of their Maker, moving His creation toward it's completed glory.

After this, we ran by the hospital. Cleaning was being completed. The next day we would be able to start moving folks in. Cleaned sheets were in the drier. Food was ready to be delivered. Soap and toothpaste were in the restrooms. The workers were busy replacing florescent light bulbs. Old medical records were stored in boxes and Juan was downloading data off of computers. They would work into the night, but the job would get done.

Joe and I got home in time to help in the kitchen. Laura and Suzy were preparing Sabaqueras with all the stuffing, for our Mexican guests. Suzy was getting a lesson in Hermosillo cuisine, as Laura shared some of Maria's recipes. Jorge arrived with the rest, and we had dinner as a large international family. Coffee and hot chocolate capped off our evening. The stars of Arizona worshiped the God who made them.

"Goodnight, Bobby and Laura"

"Goodnight, Dad."

"Goodnight, Billy."

CHAPTER 68.

I was startled awake at two in the morning when my phone vibrated on the nightstand. "Who was that?" asked Laura.

"Don't know. Didn't answer in time," I said. "I'm looking at the number, but I don't recognize it. They left a voice mail."

"Let me listen to it, Billy," Laura said.

"Who was it?" I asked.

"A lady named Lisa," Laura said. "Her husband was at the rehab, but he left. She said he came by about midnight to their house and grabbed some jewelry. She was given one of your cards when me and the boys went by to see him at the rehab. In her message, she is pleading with you to help her."

I walked into the living room and called her back.

"Pastor Billy, I know he's going to use if he hasn't already," Lisa said on the phone.

"What should we do?" I asked.

"We need to find him," she replied. "This was our last chance. I have divorce papers, but I don't want to use them."

"What's your address?" I asked. She quickly told me her address and I looked it up on my phone. "Okay, you're only a few miles away. Do you know where he buys?"

"I know where he usually goes," Lisa said.

"Will you take me there?" I asked.

"I would but I have no one to watch my boys," she explained.

"We'll bring them to my house."

"Okay, I'll take you there," she said.

"Billy, I could hear. Can I go?" asked Laura.

"It might be dangerous," I warned.

"I don't care. The Lord will protect us," Laura said.

"Okay."

"Let me ask Suzy to take care of Bobby and Lisa's kids." With the agreement of Suzy, we hurried to get on our way. When we got to Lisa's, we picked up her and her twin three-year-old boys. We dropped them off with Suzy and made our way downtown. We asked the late-night crowd milling about, and they said to check the alley. We found Marcus there, curled up against a dumpster. He was somewhat incoherent, but we got him in the car and headed toward Tucson Medical to check him in for detox. The attending Physician checked his vitals and immediately shifted him to intensive care. His body was shutting down from an overdose.

We sat and talked to Lisa in the waiting room as a team of Doctors worked to save his life. Lisa told Marcus's story and how two years earlier he had been injured at work. He fell from scaffolding, punctured his lung, and broke both arms and four ribs. He was only 25 years old then, and healing came fast, but left him addicted to pain pills. When doctors quit prescribing them, he went to the streets and three months later was addicted to Heroin.

"Pastor Billy, the man lying in that hospital bed is not the man I married," Lisa said. "I want my husband and my boys' father back."

"Lisa, we need a miracle. Can Laura and I pray for you?" I asked. By the time we finished our prayer, the Doctor entered the waiting room.

"Lisa, your husband has made it through the first crisis," he said, "but there's another problem."

What's that, Doctor Taylor?" Lisa asked.

"The heroine Marcus injected into his arm was laced with caustic soda," Dr. Taylor said. Infection is already setting up in his arm."

"That doesn't sound too bad," Lisa said.

"Oh, but it is!" the doctor said. "I've seen people die from this kind of infection. Others have lost their arm. At the very least, he will be left with deep scars as a permanent reminder."

"Doctor Taylor, will he make it?" I asked.

"He has a 50% chance. We will know in about three days," the doctor said.

Lisa wanted to stay at the hospital, so we told her not to worry about the boys and we would call her later in the morning. "Lisa, do you have any money?" I asked.

"Two dollars."

"Here's twenty. Get yourself a cup of coffee and something to eat."

We prayed for her and Marcus and went back home. It was six o'clock in the morning when we got home, and we were soon sleeping. Around 8:00, I heard Suzy wake Bobby and take him out of the bedroom, but I was soon back to sleep.

I finally woke up at 11:00 am, and nudged Laura awake. I made coffee but the house was empty. I brought Laura a cup, and we talked about what had happened in the night.

"Billy, I was scared when we were in the streets downtown," Laura said.

"Me too, Laura. But in a sense, I was glad that all this happened," I said.

"Why's that?"

"We have to learn what that side of the world is like if we're going to reach them. We need to call Lisa," I said

"I'll call her, Billy," Laura said.

She talked to Lisa for a minute and reported, "Okay, he's awake. I could almost see the smile on her face through the phone. She loves Marcus. Billy, we have to save their marriage," Laura said.

"We can't," I stated.

"I know that, Billy. Don't get theological on me. I know it will take God. I need to call mom and check on Bobby and the twins," Laura said. She got out her phone and called. "Mom," I heard, "you took them to the park? You're on your way home?" She then called Lisa. "Lisa, your boys are fine. Billy and I will bring them to the hospital. We should be there in less than an hour."

When we arrived at the hospital, Doctor Taylor had just walked into the waiting room. "Lisa, we had to remove quite a bit of skin and muscle tissue from Marcus's left arm, but so far so good," he said. "His vitals are improving faster than expected. Right now, we are treating his arm like a burn victim. He will be here at least a couple of weeks. We will have to do skin grafts."

"Is he going to make it?" Lisa asked.

"It's up to 70% now, but I'm thinking yes," Dr. Taylor said. Lisa breathed a sigh of relief.

"I prayed for him last night," I said. "Dr. Taylor, are you a Christian?"

"Yes, I am, Billy," he said.

"Let's pray now," I said. "Oh, and this is my wife Laura."

"Pastor Billy, pray for us," Dr. Taylor said.

"Lord heal Marcus, physically and spiritually, Amen," I prayed.

"Pastor Billy? What do you mean by spiritually?" Lisa asked.

"I want Marcus to become a Christian," I explained.

"What about me, Pastor Billy?" she asked.

"You too, Lisa," I said.

"How do I do that?"

"By trusting in Jesus and asking Him to forgive your sins" I said.

"He can do that, Pastor Billy?" she asked.

"Yes, if you'll trust him!"

"Like this? Lord Jesus, forgive me of my sins, and after the miracle I saw last night, I will certainly trust you from now on. Amen," Lisa said. "Am I saved now, Pastor Billy?"

"Yes, Lisa, you are," I assured her. "Lisa, do you know our Church? Grace Church?"

"The one at I 19 and Irvington?"

"Yes, that's the one. Can you be there tomorrow morning?" I asked.

"I will," she said.

"You need to be baptized," I said.

"I do, but can I wait till Marcus gets out?' Lisa asked.

"Of course."

"Good. I am hoping he will want to see this."

"Pray Lisa."

"I will."

Doctor Taylor interrupted, "That was a blessing! One I didn't expect."

"It's all in God's plan," I said.

"Billy, I think we need to get to know each other better," he said.

"I agree. We'll make a point of it. Here's my number."

"Here's mine, Billy."

Bobby tugged at my arm. "Let's eat lunch, Daddy."

"Yes, Bobby."

"Can we go next door? They have a playground," Bobby asked.

"Not my favorite, Bobby, but I'm sure we can make that sacrifice for three boys," I said.

CHAPTER 69.

I drove home with Laura, Lisa and the boys. The two women planned to go back to the hospital and leave the boys with Suzy. Suzy took the boys to a community fair with a carnival and petting zoo. I spent the afternoon working on my first message at Grace church in nearly a year. I also made a few phone calls to make sure transportation was in place for the various groups coming to Grace Church the next morning. My message was to be the testimony of change the last year had brought.

My preparation looked more like prayer time as the review of events continually moved me toward gratefulness to God. I was no longer surprised by the visitation of angels. In addition, our past failures in Grace Church had become clear. Answers were coming. I was not the same man. For myself, the most overwhelming change was the way I looked at people. Caring was now no longer an option, and loving people meant looking them in the eyes with real hope.

I wondered what plan God had for Lisa and Marcus even while he lay in a hospital bed fighting for his life. I thought about the addicts that didn't make it, and how God's plan for them had been destroyed by sin. I wondered how many of those wanted help, but couldn't find Christians or the church, when they needed them. I repented at my past failures and I was haunted by the lives of those we didn't reach. Repentance meant promising that I would do my best to reach them from now on. As Grace Church's leader I had been responsible to lead my flock to reach these people. The church was willing to work. It was me who had failed to lead. Never again.

My thoughts were often interrupted that afternoon as

pastor friends called for an explanation of all that was happening. Pastor David had been posting pictures of the week's events on Facebook and many wanted to join our efforts. I called David to set up a simulcast of our services on Sunday morning. Ten pastors said they wanted to join us via internet on Sunday morning.

Juan came to the church and along with our media guy. They started figuring out the details of getting us on the internet. I called to make sure we could link to the many pictures and video materials I would be using in my testimony. I made sure construction photos were taken that afternoon to show how much God could do in a week of people joining together to get the job done.

Pastor David canceled Sunday school to give us more time and a lunch was planned after the service for the whole church. I thought about how at that very moment, food was being prepared, vehicles were being gassed up, media preparations were being made, construction was going on, addicts were being counseled, and all that needed to take place was happening for this whole operation to work. The Holy Spirit was giving details to those in charge, and angels were manning their stations to protect us from evil that sought to destroy God's plan. Faith was happening as men simply heard God's voice and obeyed it. Meanwhile, in Mexico, children were learning about Jesus and fields were being plowed for spring planting. God was on his throne. Worship was taking place by men on tractors, or behind computers.

I finished my slide show, with key words logged in to the computer. I planned to meet with Juan and Bart our media guy, at 7:30 am to go through my program and make sure that my presentation would go smoothly.

When Suzy returned with the boys, I used her car to go to the hospital. There, I got to speak with Marcus. Laura had been sharing the gospel with him and he had a lot of questions. I did my best to answer his questions, but finally I said, "You need to rest. I'll be back tomorrow afternoon so here's a Bible and a notepad. Write your questions down and I'll try to answer better then. You need your rest Marcus, and I need to visit with the girls."

On the way home Laura, Lisa and I, stopped at Daisy Mae's Steakhouse. The food was a little rich for my blood, but Laura talked me into it. You know how that goes when she bats her eyes and says, "Please, I love you Billy!" I'm a sucker for Laura, and if she bats her eyes it's a done deal.

By the time we got home, Suzy had the boys in bed and the rest of our crowd was asleep. Lisa joined her boys in Bobby's room and Bobby slept on a mat in the room with us. "Goodnight, Billy," Laura said.

"Goodnight, Laura. Pray for the service tomorrow."

"You know I will, Billy. Pray for Lisa and Marcus," she added.

"I will," I said.

I lay in bed listening to the feminine snore of Laura, while I thought about tomorrow. I wondered if God was going to use my testimony to explode the Gospel across Tucson. I prayed to that end but prayed also that my ego would stay in check and give God glory for whatever was next. Then I prayed for how we should take what we had learned into other churches. I thought about other denominations. We wanted them to join us, but how would we address our differences, or should we address them at all? I closed my eyes and dozed off to sleep, knowing that God already knew the answers.

CHAPTER 70.

It was 5:30 when I woke up. The house was quiet, perfect for a cup of coffee with my Lord. I prayed for the plan He had given me in the mountains of Sonora to be embraced by my hometown, and from there into other cities. I went over the scriptures that I wanted to wrap around the pictures to make the video. For me the faces were memories. I wanted others to see those faces and know that Christianity is love, and love is not words, but it is what we do.

I stopped to pick up tacquitos for my four-man media crew. They had gone there early to check the links they had set up with the other churches that would be joining us online today. We offered thanks for our breakfast and ate as I outlined the details of the plan. Finally, I tried to put everyone at ease, reminding them that it didn't have to be perfect. As a matter of fact, mistakes often make it more real as long as we work our way through them calmly. Besides, the video we would make, could be edited for any future use. We prayed together and I made my way to my old office to have a few more minutes alone with God.

There was a tap on the door and Pastor David entered. We prayed together. He told me to stay focused on the message, and that he would be handling all the other details.

As folks began to arrive, I stood at the front door welcoming them. Pastor David opened by leading us in prayer and welcoming our groups of guests that morning. I recognized several leaders from our association office, but my heart was for the homeless scattered among us.

The first picture I showed was of the for-sale sign in the

yard of what was once our home. The children and adults at the Hermosillo dump grounds came next. The school and pictures from Rancho de Eden followed. I showed the scenery and the Sierra Madre Occidental, but it was the many faces of the people of Mexico that I wanted their hearts to land on. There was a picture of the face of an angel, my friend Josiah, as I told the story that went with him. There were pictures of the cave, my meals, and the baptism of Peter in the mountain stream. I had pictures of all the grand gatherings at the ranch, including the mariachi band and the happy faces of the people dancing in the yard. I showed them my last pictures of Bryan as we had wept together. Finally, I showed them pictures of the work going on in Tucson and introduced them to our special guests from the streets and the faces of some doing addiction treatment.

I put up a list of things people could do in construction and a list of the training classes that were started. "We are not going to do signup sheets. Just be there for whatever God leads you to do," I said. An invitation was given to recommit their lives to Jesus. Pastor David and I told them that Jesus had a heart for the down and out and how the gospel was being shared. Thirty more were saved that day, ten street people and twenty members of my church. We all had lunch together, and afterward, leaders of each ministry team were given the opportunity to speak. At the end Jorge gave the short version of his testimony, and we prayed. We didn't exit the church parking lot until three o'clock.

By the time we got back to Joe's I had 84 missed calls. I made a list of the numbers, and we divided them up to return the calls. Most were folks wanting to volunteer. Joe spoke to those that were construction related, I took those that were ministry related, and Laura worked with those wanting to learn about our church programs. Before the sun set, I had a list of thirty churches wanting to join what we were doing, or to start similar concepts in their neighborhood. As the sun went down, I set my phone to forward calls to the church's answering service.

Suzy took Lisa to get her car and check on their apartment. They would be staying with us until Marcus was released from the hospital. Lisa and Laura took the boys to see their dad, and that evening Laura led Marcus to Jesus. That night we tuned into the radio station in Nogales and listened to mariachi music as we worshiped the God who made the millions of stars above us. Our brothers and sisters from south of the border danced in the yard. On this night visions of Heaven became reality, with the laughter of his children doing his will. All the people said amen, as the sweet scent of gardenias drifted in the breeze. *The Lord is in His Holy temple. Let all the Earth keep silence before him.*

POSTSCRIPT

In January of 2018, I began writing this book. I wrote in a blur as God spoke to me, and by the end of March of 2018 I completed the book. While I was waiting on the editing to be finished, a friend from church called to discuss what an old friend was being taught at a ranch in Red River County, Texas. Due to what I knew to be some out there teaching, I contacted the owner and volunteered to help with teaching. It's a two-and-a-half-hour drive, but the work there was very interesting and I thought cutting edge. The ranch is called Dominion Farms, a massive effort designed to facilitate early prison release and prevent recidivism.

I have been working intently with drug addiction and it seemed like a natural connection. I spoke with Calvin several times and on April 22, 2019 and headed up for my first meeting. Upon arrival I pulled into the main drive overlooking the hangar and Mr. Burgess's house. I had already driven past the concrete plant and the area where massive amounts of equipment and materials were stored. As I pulled into the drive on a hill, I am looking at a couple of thousand acres of prime bottom land just south of the Oklahoma border.

I stopped there to pray and only moments into my prayer God spoke. Lonnie you are looking at your book. A far better location, a man with the resources to make this come true and you are part of my plan. I began to weep…I was so overwhelmed. I dried my face, smiled and drove down the hill to what I now knew to be a divine appointment. The work there is far from being finished but before I ever wrote, God was already moving. This is what faith looks like, AND God's not done yet.

Thank you Lord, From your servant who loves you Lonnie Barnard.

Made in the USA
Middletown, DE
25 June 2021

42704585R00165